FIVE HUNDRED SIRENS

a novel by
JAY SHEARER

CAIRN
PRESS

Cairn Press LLC
www.cairnpress.com

Cover Photo by Aaron Stewart © 2014
Author Photo by Bill Kirby © 2014
Design by Jesse Blodgett
Edited by Joshua Daniel Cochran

Cairn Press LLC
4118 N. Nidito Pl.
Tucson, Arizona 85705

First Edition, May 2014.
ISBN: 9780985319748
Printed in the United States.
Library of Congress Control Number: 2014931141

*This is a work of fiction. Real places and events have been changed and
fictionalized. All characters are of the author's imagination and any
resemblance to actual persons, living or dead, is entirely coincidental.*

FOR JANE

The following chapters have been previously published as short stories:

"The Boos" first appeared in *Other Voices.*

"Unwarranted" first appeared in *Southern Indiana Review.*

"Five Hundred Sirens" first appeared in *Mayday Magazine.*

CONTENTS

I. Summertime

II. The Fall

III. After Winter Comes Spring

SUMMERTIME

THE BOOS

She was out there again, with her tall red hair, chattering a streak into her cellphone. Something vivid and fast about 'only living once.' I'm pretty sure that's what she was talking about. But my Spanish is poor—almost non-existent—and she stood a good forty feet away.

It was weird. She was acting like nothing changed.

Her son had died in the war not long before. That was my guess. I was close to certain. And knowing this gave me a sick little thrill. Made me feel somehow plugged in, beyond the newspaper, beyond TV. She used to frequent her porch all the time, but most of July had stayed out of view. And for good reason. Obviously. Yet here: a sudden appearance. Her nonstop wash of unbreakable language peppered with that radiant laugh.

He couldn't have been dead more than two, three weeks.

This was the evening we unified behind her and she looked across the street and damn near cackled. Adam called it "civic camaraderie," and maybe it was, our brief display of solidarity with this woman who may or may not have been grieving. It was nothing so special. A minor event. Had little to do with death or dying or some mother's son at war. It was fun, actually. I'll go ahead and name it.

Four of us, from four distinct second floor porches, ganging up on this skinny guy I half knew, a shy loner with Axel Rose hair trapped on the sidewalk without a bag, withering there by the steaming evidence. Pretty hard to miss. Our neighbor in the mirror with the tall red hair ripped him, as they say, a new one.

This was a Tuesday, I think, around six p.m. Tuesday or Wednesday, something like that. Plus late July and thickest humid—that I remember clearly. Shelley was inside with the baby, taking a precious moment as mommy after a long day as not. Of course I cherished the moment too. The Monarch had been difficult, needy all day, and I was beat and thirsty.

I tipped back my beer and dreamed across the street, into the wavy summer air— some dipshit fantasy, idiot dreaming, the sound of that high-speed Spanish in the background—*vive solamente una vez, no?* My idiot peace soon interrupted by the sight of an animal across the street. A vividly active animal. Laboring there.

His master, lost in thought, slouched on the sidewalk. All in all, he was pretty low impact: medium tall and monkish quiet with the dishwater blond-gray hair. Malnourished-seeming with the angular nose. Sunken posture, doubting eyes. And he walked with those small rapid nervous steps that echoed the animal—or maybe vice versa. The two confirmed the notion at a glance: that pets grow to resemble their masters—or again, it might be the other way around.

This compact, brownish-blond animal delivered its business on a patch of lawn, the swath between sidewalk and street. When the pet finished, the master started off, pulling the mutt along with.

"Hey!" said the woman, looking down from her porch, cell phone still at her ear. "You don't just leave that."

The guy turned. He looked up at his indicter, then down at the evidence, clearly at a loss for words. He stood there serenely, as if unfazed. But we could see. He was wilting. You could see his shoulders caving by the millimeter.

The guy was shy—probably always had been—in that fragile, maybe depressive way. But when drawn from his shell, I can testify, a new man unfolded who was pretty entertaining. I'd met him just once, but we'd talked for a while. He spoke with a kind of muted enthusiasm—an almost bouncy conversational style belied by the fact he was standing rock still—his favored topics being experimental jazz and indie rock and the sobering details of guitar technology.

We'd been introduced years before at a bar, where he'd come with his girlfriend to see a band. The girlfriend was the tenuous connection here. She knew this one bartender who Shelley went to college with. She was also something of a minor celebrity, a music critic for a local free weekly who let you know when she didn't like it. Seriously, she could be harsh. She killed bands, even bands no one knew, and often pretty persuasively. Thus I was a touch intimidated meeting her, having read her for years, though she turned out, in the end, to be really very cool. In his depressive shy way, so was her boyfriend.

But during this moment beneath the neighbor's porch, as he wilted ever so slightly, mute, this boyfriend was in no way cool. I hate to use the term, but from my vantage point he looked intensely 'insecure,' though saying so doesn't do the picture justice. You learn to call someone insecure in high school—a catchall for vulnerability or neediness or the slightest plummet in self-estimation. The judgment, in adulthood, loses some of its force. Likely from overuse. And I know I'm only juicing the cliché, but here was a case of super-insecure—a pained implosive physical emanation sometimes seen, in my limited experience, among functioning schizophrenics and the recently, deeply grieving.

The guy looked awkwardly off to the side, seeking words maybe.

"We don't want that lying there now," she said, leaning over.

"We walk there and the children walk there and, you know, we don't want it. Nobody wants that. You need to pick it up."

"I'm sorry..." He shrugged, wilting further. "I usually—"

"Take your responsibility. That's nasty, mister. We both see that, right? That's fucking nasty."

"I... I know. I see. I don't—"

"You want that on your lawn? In front of your house?" She looked pretty hard at him. She was pointing with her cell phone. "Do you?"

This super-insecure, dirtbaggish guitar guy seriously looked like he wanted to cry. I'm not exaggerating. Looked like he was tearing up.

"I'm really sorry." He shook his head. "I don't have a bag with me today. I usually—"

"You go get one! I don't need to step in that. I don't want to smell it."

He nodded tightly, sort of to himself, then stopped and went perfectly still. He was pondering the options. Considering— my guess—a run for it. Like simply, childishly, fleeing. Then a last blast of conscience shot through his body, a superfine but visible vibration, and he braced himself and finally spoke, still looking, for the most part, to the side.

"I'm sorry. I forgot the bag today. I... can't." And too quickly, he started off.

"Hey!"

With those quick, nervous steps, he hung his head and motored west.

I was standing at my stone-brick railing, leaning over a little, loving—I'll confess—the action, when Adam popped out from his side, from the porch just east of mine. I didn't even know he was there. Fifteen feet of brick and stone separate our porches, and we can't see the other unless over the edge, but Adam appeared then, hanging over his edge, I already over mine.

Adam lives in our building, of course, east across the hall with wife and child. I wasn't so surprised to see him there, his shiny white pate with ambitious combover popping out over the railing. Adam is always ready for action.

And he leaned out right then, in that crucial half-second, and took a breath and shouted "Boooo!" down at the guy.

Across the street, on the second floor porch just east of the woman, this other neighbor who'd been a witness—a hefty Puerto Rican in a Sox cap who I'd seen on occasion but never talked to—stood at his seat and joined in.

"Boooo!"

This all happened pretty fast. The accused halted a little when Adam started, but when this other piled on, he shipped off even faster. I grinned over at Adam and, after a half-second hesitation—I'd met the accused, liked him, was ever so slightly sorry for him, but screw it, I thought, why not? and—"Boooo!"

The sound of civic solidarity echoed off the buildings, confident and sonorous.

In the movie version, of course, a mail carrier would look up, curious, from some mailbox being filled, and instantly sensing this injustice, possibly sniffing at the air, would "boo" right along with us. Followed by a cop writing a ticket, a ComEd hardhat up on a pole, little kids on tricycles, cats, squirrels.

But really, it was just us. Three of us there. Sounded like thirty.

The skinny guy cowered, caving inward, sort of crouching to the side as he peppered off with his animal. As if our "boo" had a kind of gale force, a physical fierceness that might blow the man over. His exit, the sight of it, was pitiful. But the feel of neighborly power was inescapable and real. We surprised ourselves.

After the guy and his dog turned the corner, the woman with regal red hair looked over, first at her neighbor in the Sox cap, then across the street at Adam and I—all the participant second floors. Slowly, her shoulders hunched inward. That's when she laughed out loud.

A day later, I was pushing the Monarch in the stroller to the corner store, reading a paper as I went, a think-piece about

5

gang affiliations among American soldiers abroad, a whole new problem to guard against. I was totally immersed in this article. It struck close to home. The mother's son across the street had risen in my mind, new doubts mixed with former certainties about his not existing. For this absent son had been a gang-banger—I think—who became a soldier and now he was done.

Weeks before this, they'd come to her door. Two stiff-backed military men in uniform. Sure looked like their news was grim. The mother appeared downstairs, perplexed, then let them in. I saw it all from my second floor porch, clear as day. Sure seemed like something was up, something dark and hopeless and horribly formal. A house call from messengers of the State—the same who'd delivered the same about some mother's son, dead in a field, to some son's mother, alive at home, forever and ever amen, since there'd been wars and sons to send to them.

This was all I could think about, all I could see, as I read the paper and strolled to the store. Mortality, the blunt fact of it, was up in my brain, brimming there, about to boil, when I looked up from the paper in hot contemplation and caught a glimpse of that Axel Rose hair.

The accused—no dog—was entering the store ahead of me.

I folded the paper, placed it in the little shelf under the carriage, and quietly rolled the stroller in the store. Inside, he stood with his back to us—that familiar slouch, his signature stillness—at the end of the first grocery aisle. I pushed the Monarch, quiet for now, to the far back end with the break-fast stuffs. There were only two aisles in the store and, as it turned out, the second had what I needed, on the opposite side of the shelves from where our friend stood still. I made the hush sign—daddy's finger to daddy's lips—afraid the Monarch might give me away. His lucid green eyes were all mischief and light. I rubbed at his belly and looked across the shelves.

There, through a slim, random gap in the boxes where the Sugar Pops ended and the Quaker Oats began, I could see the guy's face. And it was truly grave. No longer super-insecure. More like super-fading. Super-lost. Like, barely even there.

He was emptily staring at a blue and white phalanx of Wonderbread. Then someone—a woman, the voice revealed—approached from the front of the store and said to him gently, "Hey you."

He turned and sort of wince-smiled, though barely. This friend remained out of my frame. Her caring voice, face unseen, asked, "So how you holding up?"

The guy waited a moment. "I'm... well, it's hard."

"I'm sure."

"I'm passing."

"Passing?"

He nodded quickly, repeatedly, barely containing himself. A gentle hand touched at his arm.

"Oh, Kevin. I'm sorry. I'm so, so sorry."

And right there, the guy—this Kevin—broke down. He buried himself in her shoulder. I lost sight of his face, saw only the neck and that dirtbaggish hair. And after he'd had a good little cry—muted, eerie, twenty long seconds—his friend spoke up again.

"You know, you were..." Her halt was strange and he noticed it.

He rose again, sniffling, red-eyed. "What?"

"Oh I... I shouldn't say."

"No. No. Say."

"It's..." She waited a long beat. "You were beautiful together."

He looked off to the side, back toward the Wonderbread. I dropped down a little for cover.

"Maybe so." He bit his lower lip. "At this point, it's impossible... well, we could only..."

He couldn't see it to the end of a sentence. He was shot. Her disembodied hand consoled at his shoulder. They were silent together like that for a while.

"You know," she said eventually. "I don't want to focus on this—and I'm sure you don't either—but I just hate it had to happen that way."

His brow tightened. He shook his head.

"The worst way," he said, and again he was in at the shoulder. "She had to go and *do* it."

"I know. I know."

And he wept. Right there in the store. Wept and wept and wept.

A voice next to me whispered, "Hey. Yo." I looked at the front end of our aisle to one of the stockboy-cashiers, a burly Mexican kid who I vaguely knew from having shopped there. He had a can of peas in his hand and motioned with it toward the weeping, as if to say, "What's up with that?"

I shrugged—honestly, what did I know?—grabbed a box of Quaker Oats and wheeled the carriage to cashier, the sound of Kevin's awful, half-muted weeping rising up through the store.

When we got outside, the Monarch started babbling. As if the baby had waited—and tactfully—to broach the subject until we were alone. It was like he knew. I had this sensation all the time now. He spoke to me, "da da bo bo," etcetera, as if to say, "That poor guy's going through a real hard time, why'd you have to go and boo him?"

Well, my thoughts exactly. Spot on, Monarch. We'd been mean. Meaner than we could have known. The guy was having a serious crisis, and whatever it might be, I bet he blamed himself for it. You could see it in his eyes. Inescapable self-disdain. I bet he heard the boos in his head already. He didn't need bullies on second floor porches making the nightmare real.

Just like that, I was off taking guesses. Soon enough, I was sure I knew.

This guy's girlfriend, the music critic for the free weekly—I was suddenly convinced—had killed herself. She'd gone and done it.

She'd been warm and funny and superintelligent—you could tell just by listening to her talk—but she also had a morbid streak, a semi-romantic one. And she'd once written about suicide, though I forget why. The commemoration of some rock star's death? Some Curtis or Cobain? I couldn't recall. Still can't. All I really remember was the effect produced by this one lucid passage concerning the *death draw*.

She italicized it—the *death draw*—as if the letters themselves were *drawn*, pulled east on the paper by some unnamed force. Don't remember much else from that piece, but I think I got the spirit of it. She was saying that everyone was pulled this way, somewhere back in the green rooms of consciousness, buried or not, all of us drawn. There was nothing wrong with this *death draw*, she was saying, natural as an ocean tide, as the change of seasons.

Or whatever, okay? My point is she possibly grew to thinking it a bit *too* natural. Too right. And maybe—most likely, what else could it mean?—she "had to go and *do* it."

Now I couldn't stop thinking about her. I kept seeing the night we met years before, which helped to educate my guess. Maybe even more than the *death draw* article.

This was two plus years earlier, pre-Monarch. Shelley's friend from college, Hugo, invited us out to a bush league show, some band at the tavern where he tended bar, telling us Melanie Trident would be there, that we had to meet her, she was "fabulous talk." How I fretted, intimidated—would she think we were lame?—then warmed to her, instantly drawn to her, in fact, as she glided, calm and keen-eyed through the bar with her gloomy partner shuffling behind.

I hate to say it because it sounds a little lame, but I clearly remember thinking that she looked a little, or even a lot, like Morticia from The Addam's Family—Morticia from the original sitcom in the sixties, though not as wan or undernourished. This Melanie Trident was vital. Her complexion was pale, sure, but only by genetic default. Pale like robust ivory. Like Morticia on a multivitamin plan. With the long super-straight petrol black hair and the lean alluring body in thrift store clothes.

We met by way of the bartender Hugo—she and her boyfriend and Shelley and I—standing at the far end of the bar proper. And we got along well fairly quickly too. This Melanie Trident first immersing her charms in, of all people, Shelley. Not a match I expected to flourish. I didn't know her at all, only read her, but I'd known Shelley for six, seven years. I lived with her, loved her, knew her better than anyone, but she was no artsy-polemical hipster obsessed with sound and word. Shelley was a bright-eyed nutritionist from Ontario, a luminous blonde with a ready smile. She was positive vibes and full of light and not scared to admit it—that's the face, at any rate, she showed the world—while I knew deep down she considered hipsterdom a tired, adolescent charade. Not someone you'd guess this Trident would take to. But there they were, chatting it up.

I ended up talking to her boyfriend Kevin, who chatted *me* up regarding his collection of vintage guitars and guitar amps and the genius obscurities he revered. We sort of half-watched the band, talked, drank. It was pretty fun for a while, though I noted—how couldn't I?—that this Melanie Trident had quite the thirst. She tipped back beer after beer after beer, then shifted to whiskey, and barely seemed altered. Shelley, in turn, had a few more than usual. As did I. As did Kevin. And the being altered was starting to show.

An hour or two later, the dynamic had shifted. Shelley yakked it up with Hugo and some other guy they knew. I sat solo at the bar. And Melanie and Kevin had taken a table in the far corner near the window, quietly arguing over god knows what. About fifteen feet off, I watched them from my barstool. And together, in this case, they were not so beautiful. Kevin would shake his head weirdly, flipping that heavy metal dirtbag hair, then wince and say something intense, or he seemed to. The entire time, Melanie Trident stayed deadpan, staring, and darkly so—a Morticia now closer to the mortuary. She said whatever she needed to say. Never lost it or gave herself away.

She did though, a little, to me, after her Kevin rose from the table and left the tavern in what seemed a huff. Through the bar window, she plaintively watched him go. I waited a minute or two and then—on an odd, uncharacteristic whim—slowly walked over and joined her.

After I arrived at her table, we didn't exchange a word for some time. I remember that much clearly. She half-smiled when I sat there but neither of us spoke. She would stare out the window, then take long despairing looks at the band playing down at the other end. Unclear if she liked them, though my guess was not. Wasn't the kind of thing she'd endorse—a middling, predictable funky folk set only serving as background noise.

Seven, eight drinks in, the vitality was starting to drain from her. With those long looks into nowhere and the inward-seeking silence. She was serene enough, together enough, but I guess also clearly troubled. You could see it. At least I could. Because I am too. Sometimes I am. I too have been drawn by the *draw*, okay? It's a built-in fixation, a family thing. I have discussed it many times with my sister.

At last Melanie spoke. Staring down at the band, she sighed, just slightly, then said, "Why do they play nothing new?"

"I uh... I think they're playing originals."

She waited. "Exactly."

She took another slow drink from her glass, then turned again to stare out the window. She touched at her super-straight hair.

"Phil ..." She was like that, the kind who remembered you, who made you her familiar. "I don't know, man... It's... sometimes it's just so *wrong*."

I waited.

"What is?" I said, and gestured toward the band. "You mean—"

"Everything," she said, interrupting, still looking off in the distance. "Every damn thing."

She stared off a while more, then seemed to catch herself, as if suddenly conscious of what she was showing. She turned to me and touched my forearm, inches from where I held my beer. She looked down at the end of the bar proper, where Shelley was making Hugo laugh. She watched them in action a while.

"Shelley's a peach," she said.

Together, we looked over at her.

"Yeah," I said.

Her hand crept up toward the nook of my elbow. She leaned in a bit. And now the effect of drink was showing. Openly exhibiting itself.

"You'd die for her, wouldn't you?" she said, and swiveled toward me, letting the buzz take over.

I turned to her then and she looked inside me, way into the back of my brain.

"Yes you would, sir," she said, with a slight knowing pat on my arm. "You'd kill."

Now my neighbor Adam says sir like that. Exactly like that. "Yes you would, sir. You'd kill." And I don't mean to shift gears too abruptly here but this is what I'm talking about. Mirrors everywhere. I get this sensation. All the time now. All the time.

I got it the night Adam and I had a drink at the very same bar two plus years after the night with Melanie. Adam and my old friend Victor—my local remaining friend from college—came to this same bar the week after the incident with Kevin and his dog, all three of us out, all three of us daddies. It was maybe around the first day of August, if not exactly that day. On a weeknight, for no apparent reason, we elected to go get a drink.

I'd done this here and there with Victor for years, but lately I invited Adam along, who I never would have expected to become a friend. He's self-involved and a bit of a prick, but he's always got something to say.

And we were sitting at a table in that same bar, two or more years later, and Adam was telling Victor the story of the boos. Victor thought it was pretty funny, but he didn't seem to find it as momentous as us.

"That's wild," said Victor, not so enthused. "So you guys booed him."

"He's not impressed," said Adam, looking at me, showing slight surprise. "Come on, guy. Back me up here. That was an act of civic solidarity."

I agreed—of course it was—though I somehow neglected to mention the other less "civic" incident: that day the accused wept in the store. I was keeping that one to myself. I remarked instead about the woman, the mother, across the street. How it was great to see her so vibrant so soon—though also, let's admit, a little creepy.

"That again?" said Adam, and he looked to Victor. "He's convinced himself of this." Then he turned back to me. "You have no evidence that kid is dead."

"I have evidence."

"Let's be direct, sir. You do *not*."

But I told the story anyway, the story of the messengers of State: the stiff-backed men in uniform who came to her door in early July. That story passed quickly. Both Victor and Adam heard it before. And this, in turn, led to a detailed explication and full-bore discussion of the War.

Now, drinking as a daddy with a brutal wake-up call is a different game. At least for me it is. What used to take four beers now only takes two, and if you go beyond three, you might be in trouble. And that night I reached, I believe, five.

We talked and drank and half-argued over exit plan strategies and the hatred of Bush and our *New York Times* knowledge of Shiites and Sunnis, Green Zones and body counts, Islamofascist-blah-yada-ya. I was conscious of my escalating anger, how it felt more like true anger now, less distance there. The war had made an appearance across the street. And I was holding court, impressed with my eloquence. I was saying it was up to us, something about how we as a people had to take responsibility, how we should gather by the millions outside government buildings and *boo* them in unison. Until something changed.

Victor thought that one was pretty good but Adam only rubbed at his failed combover and actually sort of hissed.

"Oh, you don't give a shit," he said. "Not really."

I stared back at him, frowning.

"None of us do, sir," he said. "We do not give a shit."

I started defending myself, but he held up a finger to silence me.

"The only thing that will ever get us involved." Adam paused and sipped at his whiskey. "Like, actually involved, is a *draft*. It's too obvious to even point out. That's the only thing that would ever make you or me or anyone here give an actual, genuine fuck. If they forced us to go. Us or our children. That's been our agreement with the powers-that-be for decades now, right? 'Us' meaning white middle class America. Do what you want, and we'll complain, but politely. Just don't send anyone we know off to die."

I stared back at him. Victor was nodding. Adam was giving me the sneaky grin.

"So hang on to your anger, brother," he said. "You won't really use it until they take something away from you. Or threaten to. Something you love or prize or whatever. Be glad no one has yet. You know? Shit, sir. Be overjoyed."

I tell you this because of what came after. Because Victor left, and then Adam and I stood outside the bar in the warm, drunken August evening. Because Adam got in a cab, despite the fact I'd driven us there. He said he had "business to attend to." And he grinned sort of evil as the cab pulled away. Well, I knew what that meant. He'd told me all about her—his "little machine," his "partner in excess libido." He'd been seeing someone beyond his wife for years now, a young girl fresh out of college who worked at the Copy Boss he managed and owned. And until then, I hadn't really judged him for it.

Now I wasn't so sure.

Because, in a way, I knew he'd been right. Because no one had threatened to take anything away from me. Or him. Nothing we "loved or prized." And this all blended—in my five beer mind—with memories of that kid across the street, the soldier, who I'd met a few times while strolling with the Monarch, who'd been cute with the baby while keeping his cool, that possibly gangbanger distance.

Because Melanie Trident had been right too. I would die for Shelley. Even more for the Monarch. And I know I should really stop calling him that. His name is Henry—who I hope is called Hank. I'd kill whoever threatened him or Shelley. I swear it, sir. I'd murder.

All this swirled through my over-beered head as I drove the Civic home, as I coasted down the alley behind our building and found that our parking lot was full. This will happen some-times when a friend or relative visits someone in our building and happens to park in the extra space. I shrugged it off and parked out in front.

The problem was I only had the back door key to our building. I'd lost the front key weeks before, which was annoying but not such a horrible loss. I almost always come in the back from the parking lot. But this means when I do park out in front, I have to walk down a long dark scary gangway to get to the back door.

And I was doing just that, walking down the long, dark gangway in a beery haze, thinking of all I meant to protect, how glad I was I had what I had, even though I'm a bit of a fuck-up. Just a fuck-up stay-at-home dad, okay? But you only live once, right? Only once. Had to stop pretending I was only half living.

Then I thought I saw this *trace* of a figure entering the gangway from the alley. I wasn't sure—it was a passing wisp, a motion, I'd been too involved in my head to see. Despite the cold rush of fear that swept up through me, I soldiered on without losing a step. It was dark. Perhaps I'd be mugged. Perhaps they'd come to take something away from me.

I heard the footsteps approach—light, swift steps, unhesitant, fearless—and up through the darkness she came into view.

I gasped, tensed. The cold shot through me. My heart skipped a stone and my hands jerked up. For a second or two, I swear to you, I really thought I'd seen a ghost. The robust ivory indie Morticia, the suicide writer with the petrol-black hair, was feet from me and gliding forth. With that super-white vitality that seemed to glow. A phantom for all I knew. As if she'd floated up through the darkness and said to me, stereotypically, "boo!"

She didn't though. She only turned to me with her keen-eyed calm and said "sorry," then kept on moving. Sorry I guess for having scared me. But sorry also—I couldn't help but think—for not having been dead.

The next day, when Shelley got home from work at the

clinic, her never-ending ECHELON Study with its stress-inducing rules and funding requests, I caught a dark vibe off her almost immediately and left soon after to get some air. I went for a walk to think things through. I ended up back in front of our building, looking up at the second floor porch across the street. But tall red hair wasn't there.

I had no idea about her son. Not really. I should just walk over and ask her.

The night before had filled me with doubt, spooked me to the core, right after that rare moment of certainty. And I won't get too detailed about it here, but it's only fair you know this. Melanie Trident, apparently, was now the official girlfriend of Hugo. Hugo the bartender. They'd been secretly together for a while, I guess. I scolded Shelley for not telling me this, but she claimed she only recently heard. Hugo's purple Jetta was the extra car parked in our space. I should have noticed, but didn't. Too buzzed, I suppose. And Melanie had driven separately. She parked on the street. Like me.

I had zero idea. I should stop taking guesses. I hadn't the slightest clue.

I glanced down at the end of the block and noticed Adam out jogging. In his cut-off shorts and ratty t-shirt. The lean and dedicated runner. He sprinted the last thirty feet to the building, then hunched over, breathing hard. He grinned up at me, sweat rolling down his pate, then fished from his pocket a rumpled pack of Winstons.

"I've got to stop this," he said, lighting a smoke.

"Yeah," I agreed. "You should."

He winced up at me, still bent over. He exhaled. "I meant the running."

I chuckled at that, and we exchanged how-ya-beens, then discussed a little the night before at the bar with Victor. A few minutes later, we couldn't help but see. Guess who was coming up the sidewalk? Across the street, just like last week? With those small rapid steps that echoed the animal, or perhaps vice versa.

"Look," said Adam. "It's old No-Bag-On-Me-Today."

"Right."

"The Turd Santa," he said, and took another drag.

I chuckled, repeating this. "Turd Santa?"

"M-hm," he said. "That's him. It's off-season now, so naturally he leaves 'em on the sidewalks and lawns, but come Christmas time?" Adam turned to me, brow up. "He flies his trusty mutt to your chimney and lets it drop one down the hole."

"Christ, Adam."

"A sleigh pulled by thirteen rein-dogs. All prepared to squat for Santa."

"God."

He snickered to himself. "He's a gift-giver, sir. He's selfless."

We stood there together in the gray August heat and watched him passing that woman's building. He kept his head down and motored west, making sure this time the mutt didn't stop.

Unwarranted

You could hear them pretty often now, going at it in the mid-afternoon. Nearly every day, around three or three-thirty—unfailingly then, as the Monarch napped—and there I'd be, a slave to it. Standing rock still under the vent, often on a chair or stepstool, listening intently, my heart gone tight, as Adam and his face-free partner in excess pounded it out across the way.

You could hear them, I swear, like the two were in the room, which never failed to amaze me. They lived across the hall, not above or below us, but off to the side, a good twenty feet of hall-space dividing us—oak, plaster, beams, air—and the effect, due to the odd proximity, was less like innocent overhearing and more like we'd bugged their apartment.

All of this due to the vent in our living room, the wide shiny slatted one up in the corner, newly installed that August. It was snugly attached to this odd metal thing, an industrial grade tube-like box disappearing at a curve through our inmost side-wall. Had an odd bulk, this hard metal thing, like the ductwork from a failed spaceship, failing circa 1935. Ran through our drywall, just as theirs did on their side, to the internal organs of the greater building, then shot straight down to the hellish orange throb of the furnace in the basement no one had the key to.

I'd stand there on a stool and listen.

Made me think spaceship also because of her. Well, him too. Their dual performance like a countdown toward space. This slowly escalating heartfelt moan—ten, nine, eight, seven—rising over Adam's raw groan, that steady, unwavering guttural sound, one note repeated continuously, automatically, until one or the other of them came.

If hers was headquarters, his was machine: a snooze alarm malfunction, a truck backing up. *Runh, runh, runh, runh.* Wasn't clear if he was having all that much fun.

Weird to think of it that way—him as machine—for that's what Adam called her. Or used to. The confidential moniker, his "little machine." Rarely uttered, cold and possessive. Came to surface somewhere or other only after the third or so whiskey. And only ever man to man, and maybe even only to me.

This is not his wife I'm hearing. This is Adam's secret sneaking through the vent. In part why it bummed me out, I suppose. And it did. Both excited and depressed me. Though finally, frankly, let me confess: I really looked forward to it. They were so consistent and the show was so available, and the Monarch, in his Radikul SafeZone Crib, was always so thankfully down.

Understand that the mid-afternoon for the homebound is already a quiet killer, what with its hazy, dotted sunlight slicing through the half-up blinds. And that vibrant silence when you turn off the radio? The kind that creeps through your brain's back door to whisper insults and cruel advice? I guess you could say they erased all that. At least for a little while, anyway. Five, ten minutes. Sometimes far longer. It was my secret too, let's not forget that, both sweet relief and sick forgetting, where no one needed to know—or could know, really—but me. That I cherished. That I craved. I guess it's what I've always wanted. To listen in. Invisible.

Until that one day in late September when Shelley came

home early from the spinal cord clinic—early and unannounced—to unveil me a couple times over. A week later, even stranger days came, but this first one was key. I was found out.

Just up there on the stepstool, inches from the vent, ear nearly pressed to the steel meshing, and almost soundlessly, in she walks. Without a word.

They had been devotedly at it across the hall for ten solid minutes or more. I should tell you, they were in rare form that day. Slight variations in their performance styles rose or burst in tantalizing ripples that, I must confess, were fast persuading me. I was, in fact, a touch "alive" down there, though the sound of Shelley's approaching footsteps nearly deflated us all.

But then again, didn't. Let's be honest. And there she was from nowhere, a practical ghost, Shelley, my lifelong partner, standing beside me—beside and a little beneath, to my left—staring up at the astonishing vent.

Not astonished by me—I was turned to the side on the stool, she couldn't see a thing, not yet—but rather by the intimate, lurid detail floating from the silvery slats above. Chin up, her eyes sparkled. Her lemony hair hung lush behind her.

"Listen to that," she said, mouth downcurling, eyes blooming. "They are getting it *on*."

I only nodded in agreement. Yes, honey. That is accurate.

We listened in some more.

"My god," she half-whispered, then waited, gaze fixed to the vent. "Maribel is a tiger."

Shelley assumed this was Adam's wife. Why wouldn't she? She heard sounds from the vent before. Never these sounds, of course, but she knows the score. When we've previously listened in together, it's mostly been mid-volume conversations, most of which we can't quite decipher, or arguments, loud ones, too easily heard. And two voices rising with ecstatic and machine-like vigor from our silvery, addictive vent can only mean Adam and Maribel, the neighbors we've known for years. But this is not Maribel—what Shelley couldn't know—and it is only Maribel, among the four of us, who isn't present in our living room that giveaway afternoon.

This absence will in some sense be corrected, or filled, but in that moment, that afternoon, as Shelley—beneath me, to the left—stood in awe of Maribel's imposter, I had other concerns pressing. To recap, I had been standing on a stepstool, ear to the vent, my old school Bermudas giving me away, when my life partner soundlessly appeared. She hadn't noticed yet. Then soon enough did.

When she saw, she went rigid at the neck and leaned in forward to confirm her guess. She lifted her chin, not ready for eye contact. Even grinned, bemused-like, though also, I knew, a touch creeped out.

"Oh my..." she said. "Look at you."

She crinkled her brow and grinned-frowned weirdly. The gesture was mixed—part cheeky, part appalled. Neither of us knew what to do.

I chose awkwardly then—or 'chose' is wrong, this was bodily impulse—my body decided to step from the stool. But 'step' is wrong too, this was more like falling, and tripping, sort of crumbling down there into her arms. Not as slapstick clunky as it sounds, actually. There was something almost smooth about it. And Shelley held me at a vague remove, just for an instant, then smoothed into it even more and there we embraced. We gelled, pressed. A famished kiss. Our hands advanced. Glided, gripped, felt, faltered, over curves and indents and outposts.

And for an instant or two, it looked like we both might get there, the airborne infection transferred joyous through the vent, what hadn't happened for a while, believe me, but—like in a sitcom, and sitcoms sometimes have that pang of truth because this sort of thing will happen—the next instant, the baby cried.

He wailed. The Great Discharge. Instantaneous raw complaint. As if cued by the cheesy director. We unkissed, half-unembraced, and looked back over our respective shoulders. He was up. The Monarch.

Shelley hates it when I call him that. I guess I'm starting to hate it too. But harmless habits are hard to kill, and well, it's not like he understands what I mean. He's an infant, right? Hasn't been out here a year yet.

Shelley claims he understands just fine, that a snarky or part-condescending tone will communicate meaning galore. It penetrates, she says, like a secret code. A signal decoded in large part by the child, a secret kept mostly from the sender, who maybe didn't even know he was sending.

But now our Monarch was returning the favor in escalating grades of anger and need, really tearing it up. And the combined output was chaos. Insane. The SafeZone Crib versus the Vent.

The Monarch wailed. She moaned. Adam did his odd disturbing grunting thing. With me and Shelley in a crumbling embrace, though crumbling is wrong, this was more like wilting, like papery curling back into ourselves.

We stood there staring at each other, listening to all three voices as they rose in volume and intensity. All together now. No end seemed near.

And I was just about to dare a half smirk or grin, to see if she'd take the bait, but instead came the other, first, from her. Pity crossed the brow. I don't think Shelley even knew she was doing it. Just a wrinkle, a *ripple* of pity like a flat sharp stone skipped across water. This said in pity code, Poor Phil. Poor, poor Phil. My lifelong partner forced to play nanny, assigned to play maid, because I have to finish my dissertation and hold down the high-paying job. He's slaving, trapped, bored to the bone, and now here he can't even get some.

Gradually, gently, I pushed her away. That look of pity sort of pissed me off.

And then—right then—from outside, a gun was fired. Crack! Crack! Two sharp explosions, dominant and pointed, the first we'd heard since living there—by then, three years in the neighborhood. And this harsher sound stilled us all. Across the hall, they'd paused operations. Even the Monarch was mum.

Shelley gripped at the meat of my forearm.

"Go check on him," she whispered. "Please."

I nodded twice and stepped tightly away, moving north

toward the baby's room, the SafeZone where all sound had ceased. It was extra still as I went, the air so silent. The vibe began to creep me out. Why *had* he stopped crying?

Worried, I looked over my shoulder. Shelley held her palm to her chest. She gave me a weird little nod. And then—right then—he started up again. Just wailed.

Looking back, I lifted out my hands, palms showing, and nodded—there we go. But I didn't think twice about it. I walked without pause past the baby's room, shooting instead for the door to the porch.

"Hey!" But I did not reply. I could feel her standing behind me, arms crossed.

The big wooden door creaked. I opened the screen.

"Phil—"

And closed both doors behind me.

Outside on the porch it was still, extremely so, far more than it had been inside. A gelatin silence. Aftermath silence. A quiet that grips and draws you in or down. Quiet like quicksand.

I froze in this pudding for five, ten seconds, then stepped slowly toward the lip of the porch. I propped my hands on the stone slab railing and looked down at the quiet street.

No one. Not a soul. No breeze. Nothing.

Just the old brick buildings staring back at me, their stone porches very much like mine, set gangway to gangway in a red-mustard row. Just the flags and steeples and malnourished trees. Not a little league gangbanger in sight. No bullies, no babies, no kids, no dogs. Not a peep.

The neighborhood was like this here and there. In some moments wildly alive, in others motionless. A vibrant hive of life, here gone undercover as a ghost town, which could swarm back to living at the slightest trigger. But then why use this word 'trigger'? That seemed misguided. The shot had been near, unacceptably close, perhaps in the gangway that ran along the apartment below us. Had it been a gun? Might have been a firecracker. But no. That was a firearm. Can't say how I knew, but I was certain. The precise timing between explosions? The sharp force of the discharge? A gun. It had to be faced.

Early the next morning, before Shelley went to work, I walked to our corner store and saw Adam, who I hoped I might engage in discussion of the gun. Yesterday's anonymous gunshot—just the sort of situation Adam loved to unfold. The threat or threats in our local midst. Our response to or denial of them. We talked about these things all the time.

He was sitting on the broad metal step to the store, reading the paper and smoking a Winston. A Rorschach blotch of sweat spread across the breast of his motheaten t-shirt like a scorpion or a rodent—a random stain from his morning jog. He was having, as always, his after-jog smoke, hairy legs crossed, one stylish Nike bobbing as he read. He sipped at a bottle of neon blue Gatorade and rubbed at his failed combover, leaving a localized patch of hair raised unintentionally skyward—a furry patch on the left, as if one side of the brain were startled and sending a nonstop signal to the scalp.

He was fiddle-fit, marine corps fit, yet a dedicated smoker all the same. As long as I'd known him, he'd been like that. Chiseled and contradictory. As I've said to Shelley many times before, our Adam was a bit of an asshole, if not a complete and comprehensive asshole, yet I liked him. He was my favorite asshole by far.

As I approached, he gave me a furtive-seeming glance, then returned to reading his paper. I wanted to talk about yesterday's gunshot. He'd been jarred by it—must have been. The sounds from the vent had never resumed after those sharp explosions. He must have something to say.

I stood before him as he read intensely on the broad metal stoop to the store. He lowered his paper and met my eyes. He had a way of staring up with furrowed brow and letting you know it was time to listen. This was reflex for Adam, his need to hold forth, especially regarding politics, as if big Tim Russert had turned to him intently and asked him to *Meet the Press*. The press in this case, as in most cases, being his neighbor Phil.

24

He lowered his paper and pointed to the cover, where some government official was answering questions in committee.

"I have no idea, no one does, sir, how history will treat this one," he said, pointing. "No one treats it like, say, how we treat Watergate. Not yet anyway. It's nowhere near Watergate. It's more like... Whatever-Gate." A long, tight draw on his Winston, and he exhaled. "The nation seeming to concur as one, like... warrantless wiretapping? Brutal torture of prisoners? Raping the barely developing world with arrogance and sanctimony? Whatever. What*ever*."

I chuckled. Then he got that look. Where he's in my eyes. Way back in there. He waited, then said, "But does it not make a basic kind of sense?"

"Doesn't what?"

"Wiretapping the enemy."

I looked back, half-nodding, not quite agreeing.

"I mean, without bothering to ask a judge," he said. "You know, like... deciding who the threat is, then selling this threat to your people, then following it up, as any good worker will, with devoted, committed action. If necessary, beyond the law. Beyond the prescribed limits of *law*."

He took another drag on his Winston.

"Because what's the law?" he said. "What's justice? Who decides? When? We're all lucky enough, secure enough, safe enough, stuffed enough—on turkey and mashed potatoes and pie—to know that... it just doesn't take that much to stay within the limits of the law."

He waited, thinking, then said, "Doesn't even take that much to stray a little outside of them... No. We're safe." He looked up at me here, little dagger in his eye. "Even with the random gunshot or two. You and I—we're safe."

I nodded softly. Okay. So somehow we'd come to it. And I was just about to reply, to get the ball rolling, when Adam pointed across the street.

"Look," he said.

I turned to look over my shoulder. It was one of those sleek, skinny cameras that hang at every intersection as you go west toward oblivion after Western Ave. The tiny blue light blinked on, then off.

"See?" said Adam. "Everybody's listening in."

Of course this was true, or true enough—but also too true—and in other ways than Adam had in mind. He had no idea, at least not then, how his voice came grunting through the vent, that surveillance-like delivery system built into our building's anatomy. Cameras and microphones, in multiple respects, were showing up everywhere unannounced. Little ears and eyes dotting the landscape.

The following week—four or five days later, a Tuesday I believe—I was strolling the Monarch back home from the park and encountered another little eye. Little ears came after, also unannounced, but that part's awful.

This was early to mid afternoon, and as we approached our quiet mustard-brick building, about ten feet away from the front door, I noticed the heels of a silver ladder peeking out from the gangway just west of us. There was a grunting sound too—a different sort of grunting—mixed with a muttered, muted swearing, under-the-breath and in a different language, jagged and harried and hot.

I gently pushed the stroller toward the gangway—the Monarch now nearly asleep—and stopped just parallel to those slanted silver heels. I followed the rungs of laddered aluminum up to the source of the swearing. Turns out it was that big guy, Yuri, the Ukrainian handyman for our place and many places nearby. He had a bolt gun tucked under an arm and was trying to twist a camera back in place—a sleek, skinny camera he'd bolted to the wall, direct against the bright red bricks of our somewhat creepy neighboring building. He sensed me and looked down, annoyed and sweaty, with a crooked and forced grin.

"Look at this," he said, meaning the camera. "It don't move. This is shit, this thing."

He had deepset brooding eyes and a hint of suspicion set faintly at the corners of his mouth. Quite an imposing presence, this Yuri. He was well over six feet—early forties, gruffly demeanored—and built like a linebacker gone to seed. I watched him go, this giant, our Yuri, perched on a tall lightweight ladder, weirdly angled and perilously placed, wrestling with this thing in the wall.

"Why do they want that there?" I asked.

"Landlord," said Yuri and shrugged, then wiped the sweat from his broad forehead. "He want more safety here."

"Safety," I said, deadpan, not buying it. Again, he shrugged.

"From these gangbangs," he answered and up-nodded with his chin toward the building across the street. "These guns, you know? These kids."

At the mention of "guns" as coupled with "kids," I half-popped my eyes. Yuri noted this and waved a hand before his face, like *aah whatever,* letting me know he thought the threat was overblown—when the bolt gun slid from under his arm. It shot straight down to the gangway concrete, bouncing violently, likely dying. Yuri cursed intensely in several languages. He shook his head and started coming down, then stopped himself and pointed up at the camera, which was swiveled not down at the gangway but inexplicably across the way—straight toward our side of the building.

"I fix this later," said Yuri, and nodded. "This piece of shit." He smiled as he descended, grunting a little, happy, I gathered, to be done with it.

The results of Yuri's labor, I knew from experience, tended to land a little shy of what you'd hoped for. He was overworked, likely underpaid, and too busy, it seemed, to answer every call from all the buildings he maintained. The wide set of blinds in our living room, in fact, had been broken for about a week at that point, bunched up near the top of the window case, refusing to unfold, thus leaving our extra tall living room windows exposed to the side of the building next door. I called him twice about helping us fix it but hadn't heard back.

"Yuri?" I said. On the sidewalk now, he raised his formidable head and looked over with raised brow. He looked tired. Truly pooped. "When, uh... when do you think you'll get around to fixing our blinds?"

His tired face bunched up in confusion. He waited a beat, glancing to the side. "Blinds?"

He stared down the gangway, distracted now. He noticed the bolt gun's broken body, the black plastic shell cracked and half-gutted, its wires poking out like exposed intestine. He turned, forgetting my question, and walked slowly, plaintively, toward the dying tool. It was actually kind of moving.

I gave up on enlisting Yuri in the healing of our blinds, and gently brought the stroller with sleeping child into our building's front lobby area. I lifted it up the first set of steps, then rolled the stroller with sleeping child into its assigned corner. I undid the complicated seatbelt harness thing and very softly, with insane caution, lifted him up from his SafeZone seat.

Well, the rest, in its way, came pretty fast. And right after, I sort of half-guessed it was coming. That is, I should say, my body guessed. A toxic premonition. A feeling like an internal gust, a chill from the flu, goose bumps rising to crown the scalp. Nearly to the door as I hiked the stairs, Monarch on my shoulder, I could swear, out in the hallway, I heard Adam going at it, he and his "little machine." A vague distant throb, that *runh runh runh*. Which surprised me, even disturbed me.

It just seemed all wrong. Right from the start. When they went, they went at three-fifteen, three-thirty in the afternoon. Always. Consistently, devotedly right around then. That fifteen minute window. I looked at my watch, a sleek black SportKing digital. 2:23. Strange. I turned the key gently in our lock.

Inside, they were a little louder, but not by much. You could hear her now too—just ripples. Little enticing teals and tingles, the beginnings of some serious congress.

My first thought, again, was what are they *up* to? They never start this early. *Never.* But my second thought was sharper, stranger, for I stepped into our living room, attempting to turn the corner toward the baby room, and then noticed through our wide set of extra-tall blind-free windows, the sleek black camera staring back at me. A skinny uni-eyed robot insect, fixing its crosshairs directly *at* us. Inside our home.

I had to tell Yuri this was not acceptable. No way. Outside, I hadn't realized the camera's flawed placement was so personal, so bluntly invasive. And we will not have a sleek, black surveillance camera trained upon our lives. Either fix the way the camera's swiveled or fix the goddamn blinds. Yuri!

Faster now, I moved toward the baby room and lay the loosely splayed Monarch along the blanketed padding of his Radikul SafeZone Crib, complete with posturepedic balancing system and secretly enmeshed massage vibration.

He was down hard. I stepped fast to the porch, hoping I could still catch Yuri.

And I tell you it was physical, for I got another signal, that prickly rush, the nervous system's premonition shooting flares across the skin. I stepped onto the porch and leaned over its lip, that durable slab of gray concrete, looking for Yuri, west then east, where I saw—about thirty, forty feet off, right near the end of our particular block—his beaten blue Dodge pickup, huffing and puffing, heading east and away from us.

But I had no time to curse Yuri. For as I watched him chug off, I felt another, sharper chill. Not a premonition. Raw recognition. I saw on the sidewalk, down at that corner where my eyes had lazily strayed, Adam's wife Maribel approaching, holding the hand of their child Jorge—their remarkably composed four-year-old with the deadpan Buddha eyes, wearing a suit and tie for some reason.

My immediate response was panic for Adam. This could be bad. Had to think fast. Had to think uniquely. And when I stepped back inside, the sounds from the vent were louder, more enthused, that slowly escalating spaceship rising—and in this case, certain to crash.

I stood paralyzed in the living room, staring up at the vent, not thinking fast or uniquely, thinking mostly oh no. Oh no, oh no. And I felt the eye of the camera. I could sense its intrusion. I turned to see it staring, this uni-eyed robot insect mistakenly aimed through our living room windows. A little green light was blinking in the sleek black casing next to the lens. My god, was it actually *on*?

I stared back at the camera—it had me, I was stone—as the sounds from the vent grew in volume and intensity. I let out a little giggle, a kind of nervous dribble, and stood there a few frozen moments too long. Then I turned, remembering, and moved swiftly toward the porch, gently past the baby's room, didn't want to wake him, and out again into the open air.

I looked down over the lip of the porch to see Maribel and Jorge standing at the building's front door. She had her key in the lock. Oh no. Oh no. She turned the knob and they entered.

I stood helpless on the porch and contemplated options. With slight hesitation, I decided. I would pound my fist on Adam's door and deal with whatever followed. But when I got back inside and opened our front door—so prepared to take action—Maribel and Jorge were already there, making the turn up the staircase. Oh no!

"Hey!" I said, a warped tight smile stretched to my ears like a mask.

"Hello, Phil," said Maribel, in her soothing voice.

"Beautiful day out there, huh?"

"Yes, yes. So beautiful."

"Not going to the park?"

Maribel grinned crookedly. She looked down at Jorge, then back at me. A truly beautiful woman here—what in Christ's name was Adam giving up?—with her petro-black hair and wide-set eyes, so luminous and knowing, in her form-fitting Levis and breezy lime blouse, whose demeanor was vibrant, whose attitude light, with a patient tolerance that was antithesis to Adam and his stormy contempt, who also, if pushed, could explode like brushfire into righteous inconsolable rage. We'd heard as much through the vent more than once. And now she was puzzled twice over, for her gaze was fixed on our slightly open door. She could hear them pretty well here—faintly, but clear enough. We all could.

"I think we save the park for later," she said, staring at the door. She dropped Jorge's hand and moved slowly toward me.

"They say maybe rain coming."

"I didn't hear anything about rain," I said. "Nothing about rain. Really, Maribel. I... think you've been misinformed."

As she moved toward the door, I slid down, sort of *sleazed* over with my hand, and gently drew it closed. I felt her soft palm on my knuckles. Together like that, we listened—the *runh runh runh* beneath a rising "oh yes." Icky escalations and telltale grunts. Clear as day. Just horrible. She stared hard in my panicky eyes and helped my hand turn the knob.

"I am not misinformed," she whispered, and then tipped open our creaky front door. She stepped inside my apartment— did she think she'd find them inside? Her lips went tight and she glanced back at little Jorge. "Quedate aqui," she said. "Ya vengo. You... talk to mister Phil."

She gave me a sidelong glance, not at all amused, and then moved, sort of hovered, toward the horrible vent. There, she stood beneath it, staring up with her arms tightly crossed. I looked down at Jorge in his black suit and tie, a funeral home director, a mob boss in miniature. Did he hear what we were hearing? Was that possible?

"You sure look nice today," I said.

"Picture day," he said. "They take my picture at the school."

"I see."

He was a good kid, a great kid even, soft-voiced and super-composed. Had a quick way with the language—both languages, I'd guess—and lucid green eyes that seemed wise and confident, strangely capable of sizing you up.

"Mister Phil?" he said. "Where's mama?"

I leaned in and looked at Maribel, her back, her neck rigid beneath the vent. She nodded tightly, mockingly, as Adam and his partner came to a rousing close.

"She's on her way," I told him. "Real soon."

Adam revealed the whole story later. Much later, in fact. He'd started early with his other because it was picture day, because he knew Maribel would be leaving her intensive composition course at Harold Washington far earlier than usual, leaving to pick up Jorge from the preschool where his picture would be taken that day, where the kids first in line got out super-early. But not, Adam thought, this early. Not nearly. They arrived a solid hour ahead of expectation.

Maribel moved slowly back from the vent toward me. Her eyes were red-rimmed and watery, her bearing defiant, yet also, you could see, pretty damn depleted. She looked into me, through me.

"You hear that pretty good over here."

"I... Yeah, it's—"

"Good reception."

"Look, Maribel. It's not like—"

"How long you've known this?"

I tightened at the neck and my mouth dropped slightly.

"Just... I didn't know. I was—"

Maribel touched my arm. A generous touch. Firm enough but still forgiving.

"It's okay, Phil," she said. "Don't lie now... It's okay." She looked the other way, at the other apartment, hers, and eyed it as if staring through the wall. Stood there like that a good long while, then reached out gently for her child's hand. She said, without looking at me or anyone, "Everything is fine." Her gaze was dreamy now. Distant, defeated. "Everything is perfect and clear."

I watched them cautiously descend the steps. In thickest silence, descending at an angle, the mother and her baffled child. I wanted to say something, just didn't have it in me. Jorge even looked up and caught my eye. You could see he knew. Something had happened. Something strange, ineffable, that lived in a language he didn't yet speak.

I listened as their feet stepped softly through the hallway and they took the last of the first floor stairs. The front door swung open and then they were gone. I stood in the hallway and listened to the quiet, absently staring at their door.

Then Adam's doorknob swiveled, and from nowhere he appeared—the disheveled combover, the eyes, the stubble, his torso exposed through a furry red robe.

"Hey," he whispered, then waited, eyes scanning the

hallway. "Maribel here?"

I took a moment to mull that over, then said, "No. Why?"

"Jesus," he wooed, visibly relieved. "I thought I heard her voice."

"Not that I know of."

"Thank god," he said, then grinned at me, a wink without winking. "You know, a mere minute ago, my uh friend and I, we—"

"I know."

That set him back a second. He waited, then said, "Oh yeah?"

I hated him right then. The look in his eyes disgusted me. He nodded, grinning.

"She's a wildfire, brother," he said. "She's a four alarm fire."

"I bet," I replied and turned to our door. "Good for you."

My back to him, I could feel his confusion. He heard the weirdness at the edge of my voice.

"Everything alright, buddy?"

My back to him still, I gripped our doorknob.

"Everything is fine, Adam," I said, staring at our door. "Everything's just peachy."

As I sat on the sofa in the living room, I heard the first of the thunder cracks. So Maribel was right. Looked like a storm coming. Jesus. Wonder where they strayed? The rain came quick then, flaying our window at a violent slant with that slashing noise that can get a bit scary. I sat and stared at the camera, that one-eyed insect and its blinking green light. On, then off, relentless, indifferent, filming me there as best it could through the angry sheets of rain.

Never Been Pinned

Adam suddenly dashed for the john and I was alone in the living room. I stood there half-drunk on the giant orange carpet and tried to take in what I could. I'd seen his apartment before, a couple times over, but each time only briefly. And what I noticed first, what really got me, was that photo.

Framed in glass on the corner mantelshelf, angled slightly inward toward another—his wedding photo, also framed—stood a stunning image of my neighbor Adam in maroon polyester singlet and flat-soled Dan Gable wrestling shoes. Seventeen, maybe eighteen years old. Fresh-faced Adam hunched in his stance, fierce-eyed and rippled with muscle, a gold medallion hanging from his neck like the mark of a knighting by some unseen king.

This instantly brought us closer together, in a serious way, an inside way. I'd been a wrestler in high school too, and knew pretty well how the sport did you in. Its harsh demands and severity of discipline. I'd been through that shit too. Though I never really won anything. Nothing important anyway. What Adam accomplished in high school seemed momentous, of lifelong note.

The toilet flushed and Adam emerged, out from the bathroom and back toward me. He was lean as ever, ultrafit and overattentive, not the slightest ounce of fat on the guy. Not really all that different-looking from this other Adam on the shelf, save for a wrinkle or crease or two and that leathery lived-in texture of skin. Plus the hair, especially right then—his unwashed combover a staticky mess.

"Another?" he asked.

I nodded. "Certainly."

I had no idea how many we put down. Didn't care to do the math. Our wives and respective sons—Adam's a four-year-old, mine an infant—were both out of town. His to Mexico, mine to Ontario, leaving us here in America, set free to roam in the glorious middle, where, if we wished, we could drink until the birds chirped and the sun peeked over the malnourished trees. We were even going to see a band! Due on stage at midnight. I was brimming over with beer-fed joy.

But this rosy feeling faded fast and hard when I noticed the second revelation—a pair of worn pink panties on the armchair in the corner. I knew it straight off. These were not Maribel's. Not the panties of Adam's spouse, but rather the panties of his secret other. That was my semi-educated guess.

A dingy pink, slightly torn at the waistband. The tattered elastic about to peel. With a possibly motheaten pinhole or two peeking out from the ass's edge. These were not Maribel's. No chance. Maribel was too together, too organized and attentive to the detail of hygiene, to be caught dead in such an underthing.

And these panties also told of my betrayal of Adam. A fading pink flag for the emerging turncoat. Though at that point, I was hard-pressed. Was it really Adam I betrayed? I had hidden something far worse from Maribel. Still, I felt cheap. Standing there, waiting on a beer in his living room. Knowing what I knew, what he didn't.

He returned with two more and stood by my side, handing me an Old Style. He cracked his own and sort of half-froze like that, his finger still curled in the tab.

"Oh Christ." A wicked, slightly embarrassed smile. "That's nasty... sorry."

He stepped over, extended a finger, and levered the panties up from the chair. He shook his head, half-grinning. I up-nodded at them.

"They're hers, right?"

He crinkled his brow, a bit vulnerable here. "Hers?"

I turned to the mantelshelf, to their wedding photo, where a knockout Maribel in wedding cake white held a bouquet to her breast and smiled sweetly, her black-tied and capable groom to her side, looking pretty fierce too, actually. Fierce, I suppose, at having won her.

I pointed. "Well... not *hers*."

Adam lowered his eyes and went a bit sheepish. The room thickened with his silence. For the first time that night—most of it spent in local bars, a roving two-man bacchanal—there was genuine weirdness in the air between us.

"You and I were having such a nice time together," he said, gazing at the bristled weave of the carpet. He gently squeezed the panties in his fist. "Let's forget all that for now."

You could see he was unsettled, that rarest of states for my neighbor.

"Okay," I said. "Agreed."

I looked back to the mantelshelf and pointed again.

"But this is new."

He saw what I meant, then grinned.

"You like that?" he said, warming some. "I found that last week. Just like... chanced on it in some box in the closet."

"No no, I find this very interesting. I wrestled too, you know."

His eyes sparked. "No shit?"

"Yeah."

"What weight?"

"Senior year? Um, one forty five."

Adam pointed to his chest, delighted. Partners in crime, he and I. He said, "Guess what, brother," and tapped at his heart with a finger. "Senior year? One forty five."

"Really?"

"I shit you not," he said, and nodded toward the photo. "State champion of the state of Maryland. One hundred and forty-five pounds. Senior year, Claiborne High."

"That's astonishing, Adam."

He took a swig from his can and shrugged.

I shook my head. Couldn't quite believe it.

"You were state champion?"

"I'm afraid so."

Where I come from, a state championship in any weight class is tantamount to tenure earned among the gods. A place in history. A forever location. But it must be that way everywhere, right? Adam was a *state champion*. This must—I thought through my buzz-fed brain—explain the guy somehow.

"That's a big deal, right?" I said, and looked him square in the eye, tried to get way back in there. "I mean... don't you think that had influence over your—oh, I don't know—your entire *life*?"

Adam sniffed. Part laugh, part acknowledgement. Again, he shrugged.

"Seriously," I said. "Don't you think that *marked* you somehow?"

"You're speaking too intensely."

"Am I?"

Adam took another swig, then pointed to the photo of his high school self.

"It's no golden ticket, sir," he said. "It leads nowhere. Or whatever... maybe a college scholarship. Maybe some podunk dipshit 'fame' in a highly provincial and cultish environment. But ultimately, no—nothing. Just the hard-on of it. Of having accomplished it."

I nodded. "Say what you will. I'm still impressed." I took a long swallow and raised a toast to him. "Cheers, my friend."

He half-heartedly lifted his beer, amused enough, you could see, yet also with the slightest hint of pride mixed in there.

"And you?" he said, brow raised. "Think it marked you?"

"Everything marks you," I said, letting the buzz take over. "Anything you do for any true length of time. Absolutely it marked me."

He nodded. "True enough, sir. True enough." He turned toward the armchair in the corner. He stuffed the wadded panties in his back pocket and sat. Took another swig from his beer and said, "So were you, uh... you any good?"

I let the silence hang a little on that one, then told him how I hadn't been great, never champion or anything, more of a dark-horse contender, the type without notable talent or finesse who nonetheless never gave up. Average ability. Exceptional pluck.

He nodded, liking my frankness.

"Never been pinned," I said, inflection rising, as if this were a mark of distinction.

Adam laughed, an abrupt discharge.

"Nice," he said. "Well... that counts for something." He nodded to himself, then added, "Sure it does."

This was an old joke between Shelley and me. Years prior, we'd been out with friends at a most favored bar and got to talking about wrestling, specifically high school wrestling, about how strange the sport seemed to them. How brutal and intimate and ritual-hazing-like. These kids—just kids—half-naked at the center of a giant mat, *mano-a-mano*, where the ultimate aim was to force your opponent's shoulder blades flat to the mat for three solid seconds. Didn't happen all that often, but when it did, the sight was harsh, absolute, a pathetically straining crimson-faced kid squirming under some other kid's body—under or next to, depending on the hold—like a suffocating fish or insect getting squished. When I won, it was usually by points, not a pin, but I watched plenty others go down that way. I never liked to look at them after they'd been pinned. It was shameful. So diminishing.

Never happened to me though, and when I told as much to Shelley and company, they laughed—much like Adam—and couldn't stop razzing me. Shelley in particular kept mocking me, spreading the ludicrous news. "Have you heard?" she'd say when someone new came to our table. "Phil's never been pinned. Not once!"

Never been pinned. Never been pinned. Back before the Monarch arrived and nights like the former simply evaporated.

Well, Adam was pretty entertained by this and suggested we go out on his porch for a smoke. But as I followed him to the front porch door, placed in his apartment exactly as was mine—like every other unit in the building, in fact—I noticed again the wadded up panties peeking out from his back pocket. Reminding me, mocking me, my silent pink judge.

Oh, hell. I wished it hadn't happened. Even wished I was drunk enough not to care. But it had, and I did, and I knew I ought to tell him.

He had asked me point blank, but I lied and said no. I hadn't seen Maribel in the hallway, not at all. She hadn't heard the sounds of being cheated on. But now she knew. And she knew I knew. And Adam hadn't the slightest clue anyone knew anything.

I looked over at him now, out on his porch, a week or so after that awful afternoon. He cupped his Winston with a curled hand and lit it in the easy breeze. He had such a look of lazy contentment, with the wild hair, lounging in his ratty cutoffs, having a summer smoke. I decided I'd tell him later. At the show or just after. Give him the dirty news off-site. He looked too content here, he really did. In his ratty lawn chair in the soft evening air? Let's forget all that for now.

Adam leaned back and took a long look across the street, where ten or eleven preteens, mostly Puerto Rican, hung on the first floor stoop of the building that directly mirrored ours. These same kids hung there every summer, and often quite loudly. Par for the course in summers here, though as these kids got older and the gunshots got closer, I really had to wonder if we shouldn't just move.

Adam flicked his remaining smoke over the lip of the porch. He sat up a little, dug a hand down his pocket—deep down, really digging for treasure—then leaned back again in his chair. He held a lighter's flame to a rumpled half-joint. Took a hit and passed it my way.

"Look at them there," he said. "Those kids. Christ. They might not even get here."

I turned to him. "Here?"

"You know," he said. "Where we are, tonight. Fondly discussing our glory day careers as we drink and smoke and get old. They might not even make it."

"I wouldn't know."

Adam shook his head as I handed back the joint.

"You ought to."

I nodded. "All I know," keeping my voice low here, "is that lately they make me uncomfortable."

Adam waved this away.

"Oh, they're harmless. For the most part they are." He gestured with the joint between his fingers. "Sure, they deal a little dope, maybe crack, in the alley. They flash their signs and pose their poses, but they haven't taken the full plunge yet. Not completely. What are they—twelve, thirteen? Maybe fourteen? The uh... what do you call 'em?"

"Little league gangbangers. It's Shelley's term."

"Well, it's accurate. For now it is. Little league, thankfully, is not yet pro."

I nodded, thinking.

"Maybe not," I said. "But 'pro' in this case is far easier to get to. Much easier."

Adam nodded back, took a hurried sip. He thought about that one a while. We looked down at the kids across the street.

One of them, a wiry little guy in a Raiders cap who I hadn't seen before, was taunting the beefy one in a Bulls jersey, the ringleader of sorts who'd been present on the stoop for years. Then this latter kid, the big one, stepped swiftly from the stoop and grabbed the other, tackling him down with an audible thud. The stoop hooted and shouted. Action had arrived!

"Here we go," said Adam. "Takedown."

The big one was riding on top of the Raiders cap, taking brisk little jabs at his too-present ribs. The skinny one hollered out.

"Not fair," said Adam from his lawn chair on the porch. "No punching."

And right then, seconds later, a cop cruiser—smooth blue and white with inactive siren—rolled by the scene real slow.

That stopped them pretty fast. The big one in the Bulls jersey stood humbly on the sidewalk and spoke with the officer, who stayed in his car. Adam leaned in toward me and whispered discretely, "Thank God for the Law."

I laughed and whispered back, "Well, I don't know about thank God."

Adam leaned over even closer.

"Don't give me that elitist hippy *shit*," he said. "I know you thank whatever lord is yours the cops drive by on evenings and weekends."

"Yeah, well..."

Adam grabbed my wrist and held it tightly. His eyes were indignant.

"Don't deny it, motherfucker," he said, holding up my wrist in stiff reprimand. "That's dishonest. Do not deny your gratitude for the presence of the *Law*."

"Oh my god!" I said, suddenly staring at my SportKing digital. "It's 12:20!"

He dropped my wrist. "12:20?"

"Yeah! We should go."

Adam looked away and took a sip from his beer.

"Seriously. They went on at midnight or probably right after. I don't want—"

"I'm not going."

This stunned me. He sounded so certain.

"You're not going?" He shook his head no. "But Adam, that's... impossible."

This was crushing on multiple levels. Worst was this cold fact: our car, the Civic, was in the shop. I'd noticed something wrong with the steering alignment when I returned from the airport that morning. They said it might take a couple days.

"I'm carless, Adam. You forget?"

"Oh right," he said, and winced. "Shit."

He looked off for a while in the distance, really chewing on it, then sighed and dug deep in his other front pocket.

"Here," he said, dangling a key before me. "Take mine."

I stared at the battered black plastic, the old school key-holder thing, absent of auto-locks or gadgetry, just an old piece of plastic like an industrial arrowhead, home to the long jagged key to the Dart. I grin-frowned, then looked him in the eye.

"Seriously?"

We sat in the parking lot behind our building, together in his Dodge Dart, the windows rolled down, as he showed me how to properly apply the club. He gripped at the red rubber casing and stretched the metal bar across the wheel.

"You absorbing this?"

I nodded.

That Adam used a club surprised me a bit. It both subverted and confirmed my theory of club use, or any manually applied anti-theft device. That is, you only see the club on the cars of the poor, on dirtbag used cars or much-loved new ones, likely bought with little money down. Now, Adam's car was as dirtbag as it gets, but Adam himself was not so poor. At least, I didn't think he was. What with his reasonably successful two-store chain of The Copy Boss shops? Made pretty good money—that was my guess. He kept the Dart, clubbed the Dart because he treasured and loved the Dart. No reason other.

He handed me back the keys. "Be careful now," he said. "Exercise caution and discretion in your travels." He dug in his pocket for the remaining roach but couldn't get the proper leverage. Arching his spine, annoyed, he switched to the pocket in back.

"Damn these," he said, tossing the tattered pink panties on the dash. "There." His leverage improved. "That's better."

The panties had landed on the far side of the dashboard, where I noticed, wedged in the corner beyond them, a set of CDs that sincerely surprised me.

"No way," I said, sliding them in to hold and examine. "You listen to these?"

He looked over. "Sure. They're alright."

I stared at the covers. Public Enemy and A Tribe Called Quest, not the sort of bands or music I'd guess my neighbor would like. Even know about.

"Adam, these are two of the best hip-hop bands ever. Absolute giants."

He grimaced, amused. "I wouldn't have taken you for a hip-hop fan."

"Me? Are you serious? I can barely believe you *own* these."

"Oh no, no," he said. "I don't. Those are hers."

"Hers?" I asked, puzzled at first, then glanced at the panties on the dash. I nodded. "Aah... I see."

This was part of the charm, I suppose. She opened up worlds to him—spheres of influence, culture, taste—where Maribel couldn't possibly compete. And she, this other, was also the reason Adam wasn't going. This dawned only right then. I'd chalked it up to mere middle-aged lameness, but no—her.

She was also why, after Adam exited the Dart and moved toward the building's back door, taking pinpoint tokes on the last of the roach, he smiled to himself and flipped open his phone. I saw it all through the rearview.

Whatever. Let them have their fun. I forgot all that pretty fast. Just sat out back in the soft summer air, the breeze easing in and out between the windows. I turned on the Dart's internal combustion, then pawed around for a treasured CD. I picked up *Midnight Marauders* and slid it in the slot. I bobbed my head, instantly taken, and kept the Dart in park.

Well, I was damn near elated at that point. And it wasn't only the chemicals I'd ingested. They were part of it, obviously, but there were other factors too. The independence, for one. The recklessness, frivolousness, the summer of it all. I was set free, on fire, the untethered bachelor, just kicking out some tunes in an idling parked car! No wife, no child, no time expected home. Not a care in the world!

I sat for a while in the lot like that, skipping past the random song or two, landing eventually on "Sucka Nigga," which I remembered as a somewhat guilty favorite. It always made me queasy back in the day: an active dance floor of mostly white post-college kids singing along as if they'd earned the word. *Sucka Nigga. Nigga Nigga.* But there, that night, I did not give a damn. I bobbed my head joyfully and sang out loud.

"Sucka Nigga... Nigga Nigga."

I grinned to myself. Who cared if I missed that show? I'd do what I wanted when I wanted.

As if to answer this thought, its pride and its smugness, the guy in the hoodie appeared right then. That's when I sensed him at any rate. Who knew how long he'd been standing there?

"Hey," he said, with a deadpan chuckle, then looked around the lot to see if anyone was near. He looked back to me. "Hey nigga nigga."

I nearly shot through the roof at the sight of him, so shocking was the sudden figure. From nowhere this light-skinned Latino, pallid and lean, with a sharp hungry cast to the cut of his features. He was standing by my window in the dark. My god. Must have seen me there as he passed in the alley and decided to pay us a visit. With that wiry, tense body next to the car? His hood inexplicably up in the heat? He was staring at me, only feet away, really, with eyes like dull blades.

I turned off the music. "Hey... What's up?"

"We're going for a ride is what's up." He canted his gaze to the pocket of his hoodie. He had it like they did it in the movies, or rather, old movies—didn't see it much anymore—that is, a perpetrator with an assumed gun, possibly a fake or decoy, poking out from under their clothes. No mystery here, though. He let me see it soon enough. He wedged himself up against the corner of the window and brought her out in the open air, a pug little pistol, silver-plated, with that fearsome black mouth that contained your death. He was poking it in, just slightly, through the window.

"You be a good nigga," he said in a taut whisper. "Let's make this easy."

I took a faint little dump in my pants right there. Just the tiniest escape of waste matter. My first, my only, communion with gunpoint. I'd never had the privilege to look one in the mouth.

Before I could think—should have honked the horn!—the guy was in the seat next to mine. He said, "Let's take that ride."

I asked where and he told me don't worry. Just go. And my first thought was yes, sir. Whatever you say, sir. Just don't shoot me. Just please don't kill me. My next thought, however, after turning east down the alley, as instructed, was that my friend here wasn't very prepared. What—no ski mask? No disguise of any kind? I could easily pick him out of a line-up. His ash-gray hoodie hid nothing.

We drove down the alley in darkest silence, as if our destination were the waiting grave. I glanced over at him a couple times, taking snapshots for the memory's archives, that dome of a skull, perhaps shaved—couldn't tell with the hood up—his distinctly angular desperation, the pale lips and seen-too-much eyes. Some flavor of junky, I was guessing. Who knew? I could pick him out from a line-up though, easy. Even next to a look-alike.

I had the fleeting thought as we drove through the silence that this was the same guy from years before, the suspected purse-snatcher who Shelley, along with a few other witnesses, had picked out of a line-up I considered a sham. That summer we had seen this guy steal someone's purse at the outdoor patio of bar. That the suspect in the lineup was the same we'd witnessed at the bar became abundantly clear. The cops didn't even try. In his early twenties with a shaved head, light-skinned, dagger thin, likely Puerto Rican—he stuck out like a fluorescent siren. Next to him stood three dumpy-looking others in their late thirties, early forties, all dark skinned with full heads of blackest hair. All Mexican-seeming, a good deal older, thirty to forty pounds heavier! The line-up, I'd thought, was insulting. I mean, while you're at it, why not a *black woman*?

Yet standing behind the one-way glass, I knew it was the guy. Recognized him right off. Still, I would not give him up. Just on principle. I told the cops I couldn't tell. Later, Shelley said my choice was irresponsible. "You contrarian asshole," I believe were the words.

Now here, years later, in Adam's Dodge Dart, I took furtive glances to my right, wondering if it might be him. Upgrading operations? Beyond the purse?

"I'm still here," he said, sensing my eyes. "Don't worry about me. You drive."

He had just then chosen our destination, the closest ATM at the bank on Western. And I'd grown more relaxed—though that's not the right word—with the knowledge of where we were heading. He wanted my money. No problem. My pleasure! Just don't shoot me. Just please don't end me.

We landed in the parking lot of the bank innocently enough, as anyone might, and I moved toward the cash machine, keeping it natural. He stood in the corner of the ATM lobby space, up against the glass, where anyone could see—including, I was hoping, the camera. He kept the gun secured old movie robber style, underneath the ash gray cloth of his pocket.

I took out five hundred, placed the bills in my wallet. Thank god for the daily limit on withdrawals! He wasn't all that satisfied but seemed to understand. As a joke I even asked him—sort of bravely, I thought—if he needed a receipt. Then his eyes got mean.

"I will fuck you up if you push me," he said. I decided not to speak again.

We were back in the car when I forked it over and made my little misguided joke. The guy counted out the bills, then held a hand out for my wallet.

"That too," he said.

He hadn't taken much, considering. When I got home, I would immediately cancel my cards. God knew I needed a new wallet anyway. Plus it didn't look like he intended to kill me, and for that, he had my eternal gratitude.

Then, much against expectation, he said, "Give me the keys."

"The keys?" I was stunned. I'd thought the money and credit cards more than sufficed.

"Give me the fucking keys!"

I nodded nervously, forked them over, and watched as he opened his door. He got out to circle the Dart toward the driver's side. I noticed the club in the corner of my eye. The red rubber casing over stainless steel sitting on the seat in back. I reached over, grabbed it, held it tightly across my waist. Might just have to surprise him.

To my left, the door opened.

"Hey!" he said, stepping back quick. "Put that shit down. *Now!*"

"Okay okay okay okay." I slipped out, tumbled out, sort of hunched from the seat, still clutching the useless club. He shoved me to the asphalt and jumped in the Dart. As a final insult, the rumpled pink panties came hurling from the window, landing on the pavement before me.

He pulled out, then peeled away with a getaway screech, also cliché-seeming—more footage from the movies. I sat there in the parking lot with the club in my fists and watched the Dart zoom south. I stared at my pink little partners.

We couldn't seem to part, these panties and me. We were trailing each other like abandoned strays.

Hours later, I stood before Adam's back door, which he'd left a little bit open. Just a sliver. I gently pushed at the painted wood.

"Adam?" But nothing.

He hadn't picked up once when I called from the station, and I noted his cell phone, likely asleep on the kitchen table, next to a gaggle of empty cans. I picked it up and confirmed what I knew. It was off. Had been for hours. I turned the phone on and the text hit the screen. Thirteen messages, likely all from me. None of which—let's be frank—had delivered the actual meat of the news.

"Adam. Phil here. Call me when you get this."

"Adam. I'm at the police station on Wood. Call my cell!"

"Adam! Call this number!"

And on and on.

I didn't know the number for his land line. We only knew each other's cells. We were neighbors, after all. Mere feet from a knock on the door.

I walked gingerly through his kitchen, then the living room. I looked up at the old school ductwork of his vent—those sounds! Strewn on the floor next to the sofa was a rumpled pair of knit black boxers. Next to these a lime green bra and lime green panties—this latter pair in slightly better shape than the tattered pinks in my back pocket.

So the sofa was where it started. Where they likely always started, the get-together place by mutual reflex.

I stepped quietly through the sort of second living room before the porch, just like in our place, noting the empty child's bed in the corner with the steel safety guardrail thing. The air conditioner in the window was chugging hard, clearly overworked. I curled my head around the doorjamb of the bedroom and saw them there, dead asleep on the king size. Soft streetlight streamed through the blinds, stark white stripes across their bodies.

Well, she was terribly beautiful. I'll cop to noticing as much. Soft, vulnerable, so very youthful. I'll confess I felt a small pang of basic lust.

I stuck my head a little further in the room.

"Adam?" I whispered. I gripped at the smooth walnut doorjamb. No one stirred. I whispered more intensely. "Adam?"

So at peace, lying there together. I just knew I didn't have it in me. I couldn't shake them or touch or disturb them. Couldn't speak out loud with actual volume. I was paralyzed at the doorjamb.

"Adam?" I whispered again, though softer, even softer than the first. A futile, almost soundless sound. "Hey, you guys."

But no one moved. I tried to speak again but my throat was dry.

I stood back a few feet from the mattress and watched them there, serenely breathing.

SHARPEN THE AX

When I finally told him the morning after, Adam coolly absorbed the news without the slightest flash of anger. Surprisingly generous about the loss of the Dart, he chose all the same to avoid me. We would have no further contact that week, in fact. Not until his family returned from Mexico. And this only increased my sense of being cursed. I called Shelley at her sister's place in Montreal, seeking consolation, but all I got was voicemail. I tried calling my sister Beth, who knew how to lift a sibling spirit, but again: voicemail. I tried Victor. No answer. I waited.

Around noon, Shelley called back.

"Hey hon," she said. "You're okay?"

When I told her the tale—how I'd been carjacked and clubbed to the pavement, how paranoid and permanently dazed I felt—she suggested I "write it out."

I wasn't sure what she meant. Therapy writing? Jotting down my feelings in a journal?

"Oh no," she said, up there in Canadian Paris. "Actual writing with an end in sight. Like you used to. You know... your plays."

"Well, that's not exactly writing it *out*."

"It can be. Why not?" The Monarch moaned in the background, thankfully hundreds of miles away. "I guess what I'm saying," said Shelley, "is... use it as a kind of therapy, sure, but also really *do* it. Get back in there. You know, kill two birds."

I hadn't written in ages, years. Over half a decade. Not a scene or monologue or sketch of ideas. Certainly no plays. The going, I knew, would be rough.

All the same, I got right to it. I rolled up sleeves and went to town, sharpened the ax, et cetera. I stayed in the game for two solid days. And for a while there, I was enthused about it. The results, however, would deflate this feeling.

First, I tried realism, mere recall, the mugging/carjacking as it flatly occurred. From the start, I knew it wouldn't satisfy. I didn't care for the ending. So I changed it to where I, or rather my dramatic double—Murray—bravely and heroically defeats his mugger. He beats the guy down with the club—artfully, never striking the face. But this ended up sounding like vigilante revenge fantasy from a closet racist who watched too many movies.

I tried one where Murray had to pick out his perpetrator from a police line-up but in crucial ways, cannot. The lighting is dim and they all look despairingly, generically the same. The perp he fingers lowers his hoodie to reveal none other than... Murray! He has chosen *himself.* But that seemed blunt and close to stupid so I drew an X across its face with my blackest, sharpest pen.

I went more absurdist, if not outright cosmic. A one-act on a giant wrestling mat where Job wrestles God and it goes into overtime. And this time maybe Job wins! I tried a long scene with a talking ATM with HAL-like consciousness who dispensed Marxist theories about income stratification and scolded whoever drained it of funds.

It all seemed forced and sophomoric. I stopped. Enough.

This was at the tail end of two solid days. I went out on the porch with a freshly cracked beer. I felt ragged, unwashed, toxic, farty. Didn't know if I had it in me. The going was not going well. I sat in my chair and stared across the street.

There she was, watering her plants in the early evening, she of the tall red hair formation. With the taut proud bearing and bean pole leanness. The mother. Hadn't seen her in a *while*. And this gave me pause. The mother. Mother of the dead kid. Not looking glum exactly, but something there. Some mood.

She gently poured water on her plants, face neutral to maybe not pleased.

The Mother of the Dead Kid. There we go.

I had my subject. Had it all along. Train the camera away from yourself. Write the neighbor's pain, not yours. I shelved it for the evening and had another drink. I liked this idea, writing *that* out. I fell asleep in a beery stupor alone on the living room sofa.

Then, of all things, the dead kid came back. Her son. Appeared from the wild blue while I was working for Shelley at the clinic. Suddenly, all bets were off. It led to no writing, even stopped what I'd started, but it gave me a project where I went slightly mad. And in a good way, I think. A strong way.

Days later, at the spinal cord clinic, directly before me in the harsh fluorescent light, my summer's obsession returned.

Return of the Dead Kid

I was staring at the x-ray of the bullet in his spine when he rolled his chair up to Shelley's office. I'd seen many like it in the years of the ECHELON Study—black blobs in shock ivory vertebrae you wished you could whiteout or airbrush away. But the invasion is permanent nearly every time, and this guy's, clearly, was lodged in the money spot. An MRI risk, code red. No way he'd be allowed in. I'm a rank amateur but I knew that much. One glance from the doctor and the kid would be dismissed.

And it's hard to believe in retrospect, but I had no idea it was him. Something had changed, some small reduction—vitality, lifeforce, just the slightest loss—as if a small stream of air had been let from the balloon. He'd put on weight too, a good twenty, thirty pounds, and stopped wearing those signature glasses, the artsy Clark Kent-ish kind that seemed somehow intimidating. I believe it was the glasses, or rather their absence, that camouflaged him most.

He was silent at first—expressionless, gaze downcast, curled-up fingers wrapped in biker gloves, crookedly pressing pen to clipboard. He checked both Latino and African American. Age twenty-three. High school diploma. Wants, like nearly every ECHELON subject, to one day go to college.

And I was warming up to tell him he would likely be denied, that his bullet had landed in a no-MRI zone. But I glanced at the clipboard and saw the notes from his interview, in the familiar black box under "Cause of Injury," where it read *Shot in combat.* Next to this, in the margins, Shelley's loopy scrawl, *Any guesses, Phil?*

It was not unlike Shelley to leave a note on the paperwork, cute little forewarnings like *You'll love this guy* or *This one's trouble!* but never *Any guesses, Phil?* That was new. It had a kind of flirtatious cruelty I wasn't sure I approved of.

"So," I dared, for we'd passed all formalities and it looked like he might half-trust me. "This was your first tour of duty or...?"

"First," he said. "First and last." He let that hang a second, then said, "I'm officially underused."

"Oh, that's not true I'm sure."

"One tour and out. This is what you get." He tapped at his wheelchair. "But fuck it. I was lucky."

"Lucky?" I sat at Shelley's desk, swiveled in her seat slightly toward him. I looked him in the eye, or tried to. "You mean because... cause you didn't..."

"Die. Yes." He nodded and neared a smile. He used to be lean and sharp as a knife, not unlike his mother. Now he was puffy and trapped in a chair. But nowhere near defeated, I should add. Nowhere near despair.

I nodded back, then said, half-surprising myself, "I suppose not dying is always best."

He chuckled. "Against the other, it stacks pretty high."

I chuckled back. "Nice. Yes it does."

He rapped the knuckles of a biker-gloved hand on the armrest of his wheelchair.

"Knock on wood," he said. We both saw where he knocked, which contained no wood. He shrugged. "Or whatever. Knock on aluminum. Knock on whatever's near."

"Agreed."

He nodded at me, waiting. "You know why we do that, right?" he said.

"No, actually," I replied, curious. "Why *do* we do that?"

He wheeled up an inch or so and leaned over with a biker-gloved fist. He knocked on Shelley's heavy, oak desk.

"We're waking up God," he said. "Or the saints or whatever. Whoever it is that's watching over us. Because whoever's watching over us—" He waited. "Hasn't been fucking paying attention!" He knocked at the desk. "Like... hey! Wake up!" He knocked again. "Wake the fuck *up!*"

I shook my head and grinned. "Where'd you get that one?"

He shrugged. "Right here. That's mine."

"Nice."

I leaned back in Shelley's chair, nodding in approval.

At this point, I still had no idea who he was, or rather, who he had once been to me. What I saw instead was a worthy diversion, someone who could pull me from my sick preoccupation, from the toxic pudding of cynical suspicion that had engulfed me for nearly a week. Ever since I was carjacked in the Dart, I'd been sulking around, listless and paranoid, certain I was marked by forces abroad as a low-rent Job they were just getting started with.

But clearly this kid had it far, far worse and seemed to be taking the hit chin-up. I liked his style and hoped some might rub off, like a vapor or fume of courageous perspective, a contact high of hope-for-the-best.

I looked up from the clipboard and saw, held before me like a summons being served, the bright orange informational tract from his ECHELON Study package.

"What's this?"

"Oh. That's..." I squinted, trying to see it. "That's just a form explaining the study. What we're looking for in subjects. What's allowed, what not."

"No no. Right *here*," he said, pointing. "What's Syndrome X?"

I paused a moment, pawing through the backshelves and closets of memory. Syndrome X. Shelley had described this in detail some time ago. What was it now? I plunged on.

"Syndrome X is uh... it's when your metabolic rate and your insulin—or no, no maybe it's your... insulin resistance, yes, I think insulin resistance. It's when that's out of sync with, out of profound balance with... something else that's... vital."

He lowered his chin. "Come again with that."

I lightly tossed his x-ray on the desk, caving perhaps too soon.

"To be frank, I don't understand it myself. I uh... I don't really work here."

"You don't work here?"

"I'm covering for my wife. It's her study, not mine."

"Wait. You're not *employed* here?"

I felt the sheepishness rise in my veins. I nodded tiny nods.

"I'm afraid not." He looked me in the eye, somehow both indignant and amused. I held my own for a moment, then looked away to the hallway for help.

"Really sorry. Let me find someone who can explain this."

"Forget all that," he said, unzipping, then reaching in his bag. "I don't need to hear it. I mean, it's fucked up you don't work here, but... Here. Look."

He held up a CD, showed it a second, then slid the little booklet from beneath the plastic cover. He opened it up to the page in question and handed it toward me.

"That's Syndrome X," he said. "To me, it is. That's how I know it. How many know it." Stone serious, he held the booklet toward me. "Go on," he said. "Right there."

His fingernail hovered under the title. "Syndrome X." Track five, in starkest bold.

I took the little booklet and silently read. And I got through half a verse or so, liking it, sort of, though also a bit repelled. A touch overdone—perhaps, perhaps—but still it caught me in a personal way. And I was just about to ask him who this was, where this curse had come from, when he spoke.

"Alright now... out loud."

"You want me—is that necessary?"

"Sounds better that way."

I didn't have to but thought I should, perhaps to compensate for my recent incompetence.

"Okay then," I said. "Out loud." I looked over his shoulder for passersby in the hall, worried this might seem weird to the staff, then cleared my throat and started in the middle. Solemnly, I read aloud:

"Can't be stopped and I won't be stifled
crossin' the scope of the sniper's rifle
I been hunted, I been blunted, I been ass-cocked and cunted
but my mind is steady and my soul's never stunted—"

I looked up. He nodded. Again, I cleared my throat.

"First, call the nurse! They stacked all the decks!
This paranoid curse is a living hex
I know what I feel—that shit is hot on my neck!
Sniper in the sky gave me Syndrome X!
But all I ever catch are the side effects."

I closed the booklet and set it on the desk, unnerved in a whole new way. A vision had appeared to me, as if summoned by the ceremony—the mouth of a gun peeking out from the hoodie of the mugger who'd chosen me the week before. That pug little pistol with the silent mouth that spoke to me more than whoever held the trigger. Only a second—just a flash of the guy—but enough to set me back pretty good. I rubbed at my mouth and bobbed my brow.

"That's a strange one," I said. "Who's that?"

"Mutilation."

"Mutilation—" I searched. "Huh. Never heard of him."

"Not many have." He waited. "That speaks to you?"

I nodded, half-hedging. "I suppose it does."

"Speaks to me," he said.

"Yeah, well... I'd guess it would."

"Okay but..." He held up a finger. "It's not only because I got *shot*. It's deeper than that, okay? Weirder than that. When he talks about crossing the scope? And he, like, feels the snipers?" He picked up the clipboard and pen, flipped over his MRI release form and drew a stark black X across the white of the paper. He held it up to me.

"That's it. The sniper's scope. On the rifles of the snipers all around us. The ones we can't see. Including, though obviously not only, the rifles from above." He looked up a second, then canted his gaze back to me. "That," he said, deadpan, eyes smiling. "That you must give your respect."

I nodded again. "Heaven keeps the powder dry, huh?"

"Real dry."

At first, this tickled me. The image was stark. Militant angels. Sociopathic angels. Angels aiming rifles from the cornertops of buildings, from inside clouds, ready to take you out if necessary, if you crossed their code or just clearly deserved it. At first, this lightened my heart. You get your own personal book depository in the sky! Insurgent angels. Lee Harvey angels. Trained commandos with wings and halos and overdeveloped senses of vengeance, their scopes set hot on your neck.

I nodded, agreeing, chuckling along, when the force of the contradiction dawned.

"Wait," I said, going rigid. "I thought God wasn't paying attention."

He thought about that a moment, recalling the reference, then grinned. "He's not. Never has been. God or the saints. Whoever."

"But it would then follow," I said. "That *no* one's paying attention... including what you've just described. These, uh, angels with their rifles."

"Oh, I didn't say they were angels. No one said angels."

"You said heaven. Didn't someone say heaven?"

He lowered his chin, perhaps disappointed.

"You think it's only angels up there?"

The fluorescent lighting hummed above us. My cell phone vibrated in my pocket. I looked. It was Shelley calling from her sister's in Montreal. I stood at my chair.

"Just give me a moment," I said, and stepped for the hallway.

"Be back soon." I flipped open the phone and left the room. "Hey there."

"Hey," she said. "Where are you? You at the office?"

"I am. I'm with a subject, in fact. Well, I doubt he'll be a subject. His bullet's stuck where it matters. I wouldn't even need a doctor to confirm it. But... he's a trip, Shelley. You met him. You know. Remember your note? Any guesses—"

"Trip or no trip, tell him no. We can't dither around with lawsuits-to-be. Don't even take the measures. And sorry to be curt, but listen. I'm on the run here so... did you pay the credit card?"

"Was I supposed to?"

"Please do. I'm fairly certain my checkbook is in my desk somewhere. I'm praying it is. If you find it, could you call in a check by phone?"

"I think it's on the desk, actually. I saw it when I came in."

"Good, great. Thank god."

"But listen, Shelley..."

"Hold on."

The Monarch was crying now, way up there in Canada, a fierce wailing from across the border, thankfully hundreds of miles away. I looked back at Shelley's office, her open door.

"Shelley, you have to tell me." I paced further down the hall, away from the door. "What's up with this 'any guesses, Phil?'"

"Excuse me?"

"Any guesses, Phil? Your note. That's the guy I'm with now."

"I can't hear you, Phil. He's inconsolable. Let's talk later."

"Okay but—wait! Shelley!" I was nearly shouting. "Remind me. What's Syndrome X?"

"Syndrome X?!" she said, nearly shouting back. "You know that. Come *on*. Are you—"

A muted click and shutter sound told me we'd lost the connection. In the quiet hallway, I stared at the cellphone, at the dead black oval eye. I looked up and over my shoulder, toward heaven, for signs of my guardian sniper. You there?

Only the harsh fluorescent lighting, beaming back its clinical cheer.

I meant to ask the guy more about this syndrome, its statutes and laws and allowances, but when I returned to the office he was gone. I stared at the space where his wheelchair had been. I looked in the hallway and both bathrooms, then asked the receptionist who pointed toward the elevators.

"Just now gone," she said.

My first worry was I had inadvertently scheduled him for an MRI, which would be unethical of me, if not murderous. My second concern, after returning to the office, involved Shelley's checkbook, which was not where I'd noticed it—far corner of the desk, next to the tower of post-its.

I reached for the clipboard and looked for his name, which I hadn't caught. There. Dominick. Dominick Lafuse. My eyes slid down to his emergency contact—I believe I was drawn to the word *emergency*—and that's the moment all guesses were off. When I knew. Shelley, goddamn you.

I stopped in the hallway and stared at the clipboard, at the address that was almost ours—same street, same numbers—differing only in the ending digit, an even digit, meaning this kid's emergency contact lived directly across from us, directly in sight of us. My mind went to ticker tape, alarmed recognition recurring in a loop, like, Holy shit. It's him. The dead kid!

I grabbed my stuff from the office and dashed for the elevator, and hurriedly race-walked down the hall.

We had a relationship, me and the dead kid, though it only ran one way. Years before, in fact, I used to spy on him. Though "spying" isn't right. I never hid. This was more like witnessing. Mere spectating. Nothing too creepy, but the windows were generous. I hardly had a choice at first.

I'd be out on our second floor porch in the evening air, relaxing or reading, having a beer, and look across the street and see him there, inside the apartment that mirrored ours, where the gauzy curtains would billow and curl and give me little glimpses of a half-lit life. Didn't see much, but I saw enough. Plenty. More than I cared for. And then the kid was gone forever. I penciled in the motive as college tuition, but really had no clue. Just knew he enlisted and left town. Months later, as wars will do, the guy got done completely. Dusted, blown up, crashed, burned. That's what I thought—sincerely believed—for the longest time. All summer.

Holy shit was all I could say. *Holy shit, it's him.*

I stood at the elevator, tapping a foot. What was the name now? Oh, yes. Dominick, which struck me as strange. I'd thought of him as more of a Luis or Roberto or even, say, a Barry. I wasn't sure Dominick fit.

He used to wear smart black Clark Kent glasses, which would sometimes slide to the bridge of his nose at a stylish remove from their purpose. His presence was a settled-in cool, relaxed and attentive, whip-smart and at the ready. My knowledge of him felt real and full, but of course this was all illusion, an aggregate of uninformed notes from afar. Added up, it seemed like knowing him, though the dead kid never knew me back.

I used to watch him, sometimes in the evenings, often late at night, at times in his apartment, sometimes out, while he hung on the stoop with the little league gangbangers, watching over them, keeping tabs. Unsure if he gangbanged, it was hard to tell.

They'd have late night pow-wows on occasion over there, in the dead kid's room, discussing heatedly what I couldn't hear. Shelley had a name for this sick curiosity, "Underworld slumming once removed." She claimed I wanted to see something "shady" or "criminal," that I desired a glimpse of a dark secret world I could talk about later as if I were there. Perhaps she's right, but I knew what I saw or what I thought I saw. And once I thought I saw him roll a gun in his hands, someone else's, examining it closely, seeming to admire it.

I stood at the elevator, tapping a foot. The sole of my sneaker on the sound-absorbent carpet, tapping a one-two rhythm to the tickertape phrase. *Ho-ly shit, it's-him. Ho-ly shit, it's-him.*

Tapping, waiting, hoping, doubting. Come on, elevator. Come *on*.

The dead kid had girlfriends too, a couple, but only one who mattered, the one who came over when his mother was out or fast asleep. She was the one who sent him, I think. Really *sent* him, like Shelley does—or has—for me. Sweet-seeming, fresh-faced, lively, lovely, but tough and keen-eyed when she needed to be. Her complexion was coffee with cream. Her hair, an immaculate inky black.

I saw them slow dance once, half naked before the windows of his room at two or three on a warm wistful morning in June. Sounds corny, maybe, but he was the graceful one, the one who could spin and gently twirl her, whose balance of line and limb was the prize.

The elevator opened. I was in, going down.

And what would I say if I did catch up with him? I couldn't tell him everything. Or really, nearly anything. I mean, for months, I'd thought he was dead. Assumed he'd been ash for a *while*. How could I tell him that? Like, "Hey! Sorry to intrude, but I thought you should know that I used to spy on you from my second floor porch, but then I thought you'd been killed! I would watch you like a creep, a full-fledged voyeur, up until I thought you'd been body-bagged! How about that? Is that not *wild*?"

Okay. The checkbook. Stick with that. Or no. The MRI business. And why not just call him? No. I wanted to see him, to confirm this guess, to finally, gratefully, get plugged in.

The doors opened at the first floor, and I shot for the building's front door. Out in front: a multitude of men in wheelchairs Or not "multitude," no—more like a gaggle. All similar-seeming silver and black wheelchairs, the high-end kind with a million little levers. Every other hand biker gloved, every other ear set to cellphone. My eyes flitted, floated, seeking him, from the cluster of wheelchairs to the honking traffic to the tight-walking passersby—med students, lunch-breakers—then finally to the backend of a city bus, this giant lumbering slug. It was beeping loudly—beep beep beep beep—a grave calibration I thought I recognized. I moved toward it.

I crossed to the opposite corner and watched. There he was, the dead kid, speaking intensely into his cellphone. He rose in increments on the wheelchair platform, inch by inch leaving view.

The bus pulled off and he was gone. Once again, he evaporated.

There's one last part that seems to fit, though the dead kid was not so involved. Not present in body, at any rate. And not for lack of my trying to find him. I did, that evening, try to locate him. In retrospect, I can't quite believe I went. I suppose I wasn't fully in control. I saw this, after all, as resurrection, and my life at that point craved the charge. Plus, as you know, I'd been mugged. This somehow felt like a chance at redemption. A momentary pass. Though I'm not sure why.

That afternoon, when I got home, I found Shelley's checkbook on the kitchen table—that's where I'd seen it, on the corner next to a tower of post-its. That much was solved, a big relief, actually. I ignored Shelley's voicemail and went seeking this Syndrome on my own. It was waiting for me, right there in the living room, a familiar black X across the book's cover, this lucid gem on Shelley's top shelf, entitled, of course, *Syndrome X*. More specifically, *Overcoming the Silent Killer that Can Give You a Heart Attack*. I read it closely and tried to understand.

I hadn't been so far off the mark. It *was* about insulin resistance. And Shelley's explanation came back to me slowly. Clearly she'd cribbed from this guy. People with Syndrome X resist their own insulin, fight off what's meant as a kind of protection, forcing the body to make more than necessary.

I took notes, made charts, attempted to paraphrase. With Syndrome X, the body's system of protection, its keepers of peace, its government, sent out one too many cops, an excess of peacekeepers, who got in the way by trying to save you. Syndrome X was an aversion to your own inner cop. In essence, you *rebelled against your body's own government*, which worked in turn toward killing you by making up the difference with a surge of troops.

But it all left me deeply unsatisfied. I closed the book and googled the website of Mutilation, under-recognized recording artist, where "Syndrome X" was a free song sample. Again, a bit much, but I saw the appeal. In style as much as content. A kind of aggressive rap-singing crossed with a militant growl.

Can't be stopped and I won't be stifled...

Later, that's how I went hunting for the dead kid, that martial roar running through my mind.

The primary address of Dominick Lafuse was a good ten, twelve blocks southwest of us. Apparently, after serving abroad, he decided to live on his own. I'd called him multiple times by then, but an automated voice with a British accent told me the number was "unreachable."

I even tried his emergency contact and watched through the blinds across the street, to the apartment directly mirroring ours, where he'd once lived and I'd often watched him. But when his mother came to the phone, which was sitting on the ledge of her porch, I hung up. She stood there, staring at the receiver, then looked up, it seemed, at me. I stepped back from the window, again the creep.

You can be watched as much as watching. That's the part I tend to forget.

That evening, I went jogging. Or rather, pretended to. This was my ruse. I'd jog a couple blocks, stop, walk. Jog a few, stop, walk. It was brutal. And when I got there—a pretty rough hood to be sure, with abandoned buildings and poverty in the air—I unfolded his personal info form and looked for the address, which I knew was near. I ran, huffing, nearly ruined, to the T-square dead end where the numbers on his street simply stopped. Just a trashed-out field with a charred abandoned building fifty yards off from where his address should be. The numbers just stopped. It was crushing.

I walk-jogged around those streets a bit, seeking signs of his wheelchair, his signature biker gloves, his depleted yet steady cheer, but nothing. Don't ask me what I meant to do if I found him. Feign surprise, I suppose. Dominick? That you? What coincidence I should chance on you while out on my evening trot!

Instead, nothing.

Exhausted, no more jogging in me—why would anyone choose such punishment?—I walked down the long street that led to the thoroughfare where I hoped I could catch a bus.

Two figures walked toward me then, stepping slow through the gathering dusk. Young guys, Latinos, just cruising along. As we passed, one of them caught my eye.

It chilled me to the bone, this eye of his. I thought I might know it. The eye, the face, the wiry tense body wearing the same hoodie as last week, ash gray and unseasonable for August, the hood up for some reason. But I couldn't be certain. A hundred kids around here look vaguely like that. Still, that tickertape raced through my mind. Same phrase, new subject. *Holy shit, it's him.*

Or maybe more like, *Is that him?*

I picked up the pace, looked over my shoulder, only to find him glancing over his shoulder. Our eyes locked a second. Alleged mugger to the clearly mugged—*Is that you? Seriously?*

I didn't hesitate much or choose to play hero or spend time fact-checking if it was him. I glanced back again, as did he the moment after, sensing perhaps the heat of my eyes. We moved opposite directions at a newly slow clip with thirty or so feet between us. Then I looked one last time, as did he, but this time the hoodie kid stopped. Looked like he might come after.

I reached over to a withered tree and knocked a few times—*Wake up! Wake the fuck up!* Then ran—no, sprinted—at a vigorous clip for the thoroughfare I hoped would bus me home.

Five Hundred Sirens

That night the moon was the thing, maybe even more than the sirens. It was laughing. That's what I saw anyway. The same basic premise of the man in the moon, only here he looked like he was cracking up. A vague effect—at least at first—that leapt out at you like a corny cartoon the moment you realized it was hiding there.

But Adam didn't notice. Not until later. And Adam was the kind of guy you'd expect to notice, who'd want to be known for noticing, who'd use the occasion as a metaphor to condemn those less aware. Like, missing or avoiding the unavoidable moon as a glaring sign of denial, close cousin to the Elephant in the Room, only here the room was half the planet and the elephant was hanging in the sky. Laughing at us, and really pretty hard.

I stood at the window behind our back door, hoping my neighbor would come out for a smoke. I badly needed confirmation someone else saw this too.

Minutes later—which had been happening a lot around

then, thoughts of Adam summoning Adam, as if mere thinking could function as a pager—he emerged from the back door to his place and stepped toward his own back window. He gave a silent nod-up, tense and rabbity, hardly looking my way. In weathered Sox cap and merlot-colored robe, a furry monstrosity he called his "third skin"—no explanation as to the second—he cupped a Winston and lit it. He looked up and cocked his chin to the side, but must have missed it entirely, for he looked down to the parking lot and asked me, blandly enough, "Shelley and the baby make it back okay?"

I waited a moment, surprised he hadn't seen, then nodded and pointed to my door. "Dead asleep at the moment. Both of them."

"Beautiful."

"Maribel asleep?" I asked, returning the favor. "Her and the boy?"

He turned slowly to stare at his door. He took a long drag, then exhaled.

"Dead and buried," he said, a bit woodenly, depleted-seeming, then caught my eye and sort of came to. "Just like yours. Precisely as yours." The slightest grin rose in his gaze, or began to. "Look at this," he said. "Look at us. All our attachments off in la la land. You and me all over again."

"Two peas in a pod?"

"Two peas who want out of the pod."

"Yeah, well... I'm not so sure that's true."

"No?" He stared at me a second, then faintly *pshawed* and turned to look through his window. "Oh you know it's true."

With all attachments back from abroad—his from Mexico days before, mine from Ontario only that evening—we were husbands and fathers yet again, a bit stunned by the bluntness of that fact, as if caught in the headlights of a grave responsibility we'd forgotten could run us over. A week off. Now it was done.

I looked up at the moon, still laughing.

"Look at that thing," said Adam. "It's such a... bully."

"A bully?" I said. "You see it that way?"

"Absolutely. Don't you?"

I turned to see the confusion. I'd looked up where he'd looked down. My gaze gone to the laughing sky, his down to the sober asphalt, to the sleek black rental supplied by his insurance people, a potent new model of high-end SUV known as the Chrysler Mercenary.

"Let's take out the gift." He turned to me. "Let's get out there in the big black boat. I need it, sir. I require it. I'd bet my deductible you do too."

"Aw man... I can't tonight."

"Come, now." You could see he'd had a few drinks, probably some pot. "Do your part for the war on terror."

I snorted. "I've done plenty already."

"Hardly!"

"Adam. Please." I hunched in disbelief, jerked a thumb at my door. "They *just* got back."

"Mine didn't?"

Big difference, of course. His had returned days before. Mine, only hours ago. Yet still you could see nothing would stop him. That ornery sparkle had lit in his eye, the contrary damn-it-all air. And I liked this sometimes. I'll cop to that. I had real appreciation for the push in him. Other times—and this was one of them—I considered it a childish imposition.

"I didn't want to bring this up, sir, or use such brutal language, but really now." He nodded, egging me on. "Don't you kind of owe me?"

I looked down at the rickety floor. It buckled here, caved there, vague commercials of future collapse.

"Am I wrong?"

For the most part, he had been quite generous about it. It hadn't entirely been my fault, and Adam acknowledged as much. For borrowing your neighbor's cherished Dodge Dart is not a crime—not at all. But letting the engine idle in a dark unsecured lot as you sing along to the raucous stereo? Practically advertising you're easy pickings to any passing thug who hoped to steal a car? I let my guard down. Exposed myself. I got cherry picked, plucked and pitted, when I might have had a fine night out. Instead, a gun to my head, and then the Dart was gone.

When he'd heard the news, Adam wasn't angry or even mean. I'd expected a raging explosion. Instead, a meditative pat on the back. It's alright, buddy. Happens to the best of us. You're an oblivious dumbass but that can happen. Who knows? Maybe the cops'll find it.

Didn't once raise his voice. The downside, of course, was I owed him one.

I nodded along, agreeing. "Adam, I just... can't."

"Nonsense. Of course you can!"

His grin was up and running now. Full effect.

"Damn you." And he pointed a finger. "Philip Palliard. Do your *part*."

Again, he meant for the "war on terror," but several leagues beneath the standard understanding. Which terror? I think he was asking. Which war? Is this anything new or uniquely true?

An abrupt crashing came from my kitchen. A heavy thud and clatter sound. Startled, we stared at each other. I turned my knob and hurried inside, closing the door behind me.

When I flipped on the light, I found there, on the swirled mosaic linoleum floor, a mess of curved white plastic and shiny sharp metal implements. Clear plastic tube things. Screws, lids. As if the ceiling had rained symbolic rubbish, leaving us the diorama of a landfill. I remembered. Oh. Right. The ice cream maker from on top of the fridge. A mouse must have knocked it over.

I listened to the air in there. Nothing stirred. So the mouse had saved me. I laughed at that. The mouse had saved me from the war on terror. I looked down at the mess it made.

We had four, actually. Four fucking ice cream makers, all gifts. Wedding, birthday, one probably Christmas. And I was thinking, a shout out to my neighbor, how about that for the war on terror? The weapons of excess and frivolous comfort, of a world that showers ice cream makers on people who do *not make ice cream*.

I wasted no time and stepped over the landfill, moving

through the chaos of the bright mustard kitchen, then the darkened living room, its lonely air, and finally to the sort of second living room, where I stopped for a visit to the crib.

The boy was out cold on his back, a breezy lime blanket spread across his body. I gently touched him, his downy head, the unguarded face, that rare flesh, smoother than smooth. I hunched down and watched for his breathing. You and me, I was thinking. Like it or not, you and me. Tomorrow it's back to Daddyland.

His little chest rose, then dipped.

I patted softly at his belly and stood again, then moved to the doorway of our bedroom. There was Shelley, splayed lengthwise across the bed, belly-down, a still-socked toe, nursery red, hanging off the bed like a slain fish. Half blanket, half alabaster body, fully dead asleep. Just buried. Snoring pretty hard too.

Adam says Maribel can snore hard as well. A sound we agree that was downright profound back when they were pregnant. Adam used to say that's how we'd get Al Queda—put microphones on our spouses snoring-with-child in hidden beds next to Tora Bora. That would root 'em out of the cave.

I was grinning there in the dark bedroom doorway, thinking this, seeing it—America's long most wanted smoked from their hole by the uvulas and adenoids of non-native spouses, sleeping beauties under bulletproof glass—when I first heard the bleat and whine of the sirens. Fainter there, back deep in the apartment, but pretty stunning all the same. Not an ambulance or fleet of cop cars. Something louder, stranger. Air-raidish or tornado-related.

I moved swiftly now toward the back door, smoked from, blown from my cave. I stepped past the crib, then the living room proper, the siren sounds seeming to lift before me like increments of oncoming waves.

When I opened the door, they doubled in volume.

Adam stood rigid-backed at his window. He turned to me, wide-eyed.

"That's madness!"

"I know!"

"Pure!"

"I agree!"

The aim or source was pretty elusive. A tornado, we knew, was unlikely. The skies were crystal clear. Forecast said clear and sunny for *days*. We stared out our respective windows, in relative silence save for the sirens, looking neither up nor down, but out, into the wild night air, hoping to see it, to catch a glimpse of that sound, this wailing alien death knell you had to guess was a call to the basement. Or your bunker or whatever. Like under attack. Take cover!

Yet somehow we knew that wasn't it. Too World War II. A bit corny even. Like, five hundred sirens screaming as one, in cacophonous off-key harmony. You. Are. In Trouble! But we didn't believe them. Not in the way they meant to be heard. We were still—and still are—immune to apocalypse, certain as infants it could never happen here.

Adam felt the draw right off.

"We have to go find this," he said, enthused. "We must drive into this."

I shook my head. "Not me, man."

"Yes, you. Us."

The sirens wailed, relentless and cheesy. I shrugged. "Sorry buddy."

"Sorry buddy?" he said. "That's all you got? Sorry buddy?"

Again, I shrugged. Adam shook his head, then thought about it, muttering. He swung open his back door and stepped inside, sort of pitching forward as he went. Half a minute later, he re-emerged, slamming his door behind him. He marched toward me with steely purpose, his fierce eyes locked to mine. I stepped back as he neared, but he stopped before me and grabbed my wrist with militant precision. Cold steel gripped to my skin there. A click. Then I looked down.

He had cuffed us. Our wrists. My left to his right. Just like that, we were one.

He smiled bitterly. "Sorry buddy. I cannot endure it alone. Not tonight."

The sirens wailed in the distance. He pulled at our door and it shut behind me. And I started to say something but stopped before saying. Pulled along, I followed. I was certain any protest would be useless. Though I must have flushed, for I felt a bit woozy, the blood seeming to flee my head. I stumbled a little as we descended the stairs. Why fight it? I was his. Neither of us spoke until we reached the Mercenary. Adam clicked it open with the autolock device.

"You first."

Both of us grunting, I got in, climbing over the driver's seat, then the gear shift. The fragile mathematics of handcuffs—hostage first, then hostage taker. Adam followed, closing the door, and our auto-seatbelts settled across us with a soothing Mercenary whir. He turned the key in the ignition, drawing me forward, then we settled back and he lowered the windows.

"Listen to that," he said. We listened to the sirens. "What *is* that? It's like... God must be sleeping through the snooze alarm."

I chuckled. "Right." Then I looked down at the cuffs. "You don't have to keep these on. I'm in the car. You got me."

He looked down at our wrists, resting together on the complicated beverage holder—heating, cooling, spill control.

"I understand that," he said. "But I like it. Heightens the sense of intimacy, you know? I mean... this doesn't bother you, does it?"

I shot him a withering look. He snickered as he guided the soundless Mercenary into the back alley. "You need to develop a more mature sense of trust. You know the prayer, right? Accept what you cannot change?"

Staring ahead, I snorted, then glanced again at our cuffs. Why did he even own a pair? "So are these like... a sex toy?" I looked up at him.

He waited. "They are, actually."

I waited. "But not a toy you use with Maribel?"

He lifted his chin, struck by that. "Right again, sir, but... let's leave that matter to the side for now."

I smiled. "So whats-her-name wears these? Or... you do?"

"Shelve it, Phil. Practice sensitivity."

Out in the night, the sirens wailed.

It repulsed me, I suppose, to wear an aid to sexual domination, and perhaps one used quite recently, yet also—and this surprised me—it sort of half turned me on. They brought me closer to her, his invisible other, his longtime secret thing or fling. So many times I'd heard them through the vent in the living room while the Monarch napped in the afternoons. Handcuffs were involved? What else?

It amazed me how much Adam got away with, how he lived his contradictions with open abandon and hid his transgressions with relative ease. The guy was nearly forty. How far would he dare to take it?

"There's a road cocktail in there," he said, pointing to the glove compartment. "Start us up, will ya?"

I took out the curved silver flask, had a swig and passed it over. We drove in silence, save for the sirens, passing the flask back and forth. We went south to southwest, where of course we shouldn't. The sirens, it soon became clear, were not our true target or aim. A mere curiosity, background music. We weren't driving toward them but rather through them, off to the places he'd sought before.

Adam had multiple names for this practice, depending on the mood. Playing Chicken with a Drive-by was one, but that had fallen from favor. Drive-bys were shot *from* cars, not into them. Ghettospotting, I'm afraid, was another, but we both agreed that was lame. I was partial to more lighthearted fare. The Counterintuitive Tourist Bus, say, or Let's Play Demographic Hopscotch! But those were just names.

What he did—and I'd only gone twice before—was drive on purpose into iffy neighborhoods, into stretches of poverty, perceived ganglands, to the dealers and bangers and blown-out lights, the abandoned buildings and mostly black people. He'd blast aggressive music and see what he could see. It was passive slumming is what it was. Spectating from the safety of a locked car and calling it an act of engagement.

He pressed play on the CD drive, taking my wrist along

with. The sounds of a genius aggression rose from the speakers, the opening friz of honeybee guitars, then the bass, the drums, the riff had dropped. He bobbed his head, driving one-handed. We coasted under the ghost town tracks and passed the somber public housing.

Here it was in its furtive glory—doing our part for the war on terror. In Adam's way, a different way, starting with a basic premise: that the adversary to the war on terror could not be seen, could barely be named, was *ipso facto* invisible. Adam argued for a different kind of witness. Go seek the so-called "invisible" as revealed in your actual world. Go local, toward the visible terror that's been made invisible, or at the very least, swept to the side. The threat or threats in your very midst. Go to where they're visible, to where they've been *pushed*.

Well, I considered it a stretch. Vague, simplistic, conflating, self-serving. Yet something in it made perfect sense. Could it be the terror was closer to home? A steadily escalating humdrum life as manager-owner of The Copy Boss shops? Nominal monogamist, father of one?

We drove along into destitution, into a neighborhood I couldn't name. We swerved and slalomed through alien streets, Adam seeming to know the way, then landed on some gloomy corner where half the lights had blown. He shifted to park, then turned off the music. The sirens wailed away.

We sat there a while, not speaking, just listening. And then, just like that, the sirens stopped.

"Wait," he said, stunned by their absence. "That's it?"

I listened. "I guess it is."

"Damn... that's abrupt."

We were both a bit crestfallen. The sirens had grown sort of comforting.

Adam nodded to himself, accepting the loss, then pressed the lever in the armrest and our noiseless windows rose. All of a sudden hermetic in there. Safe and sound. He spoke to the control panel. "Air conditioning." And on it came. He said, "Mercenary, massage us." And our seats began to vibrate gently, a soft soothing whir that pressed at our backs. For a while then, it was lulling and peaceful. We passed the flask back and forth.

Just sitting immersed in massage vibration at the dreary corner of a vacant street. Only one guy smoking across the way. And another loafing on the sidewalk here.

The latter guy approached. Stepped calmly toward the car. A short, stocky black dude in a Marlins cap, with ass-low jeans that turned out to be shorts. Adam pressed the button and the window unrolled.

The guy leaned down, gripped the lip of the window. He was all business.

"What you need?"

Adam fake smiled. "Nothing for us tonight, my friend. We're just taking a rest."

"A rest," he echoed, deadpan, then noticed our cuffed wrists. Adam touched at the guy's hand.

"Tell me," Adam said and pointed. "What's up with that building there? Used to be a club or a loft that had parties. What is it now? Anyone live there?"

He meant the big red brick building on the opposite corner, darkened throughout, with boarded-up windows and a shadowy someone smoking on its crumbling front stoop.

The guy half-laughed. "Looks pretty fucking dead to me."

"It does, doesn't it?" said Adam, nodding. "Well thank you for your insight. Best of luck, friend." And they both moved their hands as the window rose with its silent hermetic affront. You could see the guy was baffled. The questions, the cuffs, Adam's robe. The subtle sound of tiny rotors whirring through the posture-friendly leather. Were we cops to him? Creeps?

He moved down the street and out of view, only once looking back.

We sat there in siren-free silence, cuffed across the beige beverage island. Adam stared at the boarded-up building. "Massage off," he said, and it ceased. He gestured limply with his cuffed hand.

"Jesus this hurts," he said. "Honestly. More than I ever would've guessed."

I looked down at the beverage holder. "The handcuff?"

Adam stared ahead. He drew in a breath through his nose and sighed.

"Adam, what are—"

"Maribel left me."

"Left you?"

He nodded, staring ahead. "Evacuated."

My head cocked back. Didn't make sense.

"Just... up and left?"

"Up and *stayed*. Never came back from Mexico. She's setting up shop in Michoacan as we speak."

"Shit, Adam, that's... she's been gone this whole *time*?"

"Never came back."

I took a moment to let that sink in. Since Thursday, I thought they'd been home. Adam had implied as much. This was Saturday, three days later.

"Where's Jorge?"

Adam looked over, furrowed his brow.

"With her," he said. "You insane? He's down there with mommy. Christ. Don't be foolish." He shook his head, resigned to the facts. "We both know better than that."

I hardly had time to absorb it. His phantom family. The ghosts across the hall. The weird sense of betrayal at having been halfway lied to. Adam nodded toward the red brick building and started to look a bit wistful.

"That's where we met," he said. "That's where I won her."

He took off his cap with his free hand and rubbed through the underfed combover.

"Ten, eleven years ago. Third floor, I think. Huge artsy loft space where they had these parties. Art parties, performance parties, that sort of crap. Not precisely my scene but... back then? I had no scene." He shook his head, grinning. "Just an aimless grad student, a fuck up with a head of full of vacant opinions looking for some arty action. A thrill. Some tribal adventure. But that night—" He nodded to himself, dead serious. "That night Maribel was there. Maribel Jimenez of Michoacan, there with her cousin Placo, the painter. And just... the finest, most exquisite thing. Luminous. A vision of vulnerable grace. She was hot too. Obviously. Smoking hot, but... her *way*, that's what drew the eye. The way she looked across an aimless room? A room full of fuckups and toothless poets and over-talkative grad student types?" He *sssssed* through his teeth. "A song, brother. A siren song in a sea of chatter. I'd never been drawn like that."

He nodded to himself, smiling. Then the smile faded.

"I knew the bassist in the band that night. Friend of mine. Decent friend at the time, actually, not too close but, well..." Waiting a beat, hunching over, really starting to tell it. "I was especially loaded. Not out of control, but feeling fine. Some advanced feeling. On a plane, as it were. And I don't recall why. They'd been playing disco classics or something, ironically perhaps, but who could say? And at some point, I just stepped up to the mike and started into—of all things, I shit you not—'Don't Stop 'Til You Get Enough.'"

I wince-smiled. "You mean... Michael—"

"Jackson. Yes. His disco era masterpiece. And not falsetto or anything, not an impression, just me. Me and my little voice. Oh I didn't expect it to go anywhere, but the band surprised me—they followed like that. And once I knew they were behind me, well... I sold it, brother. Danced like a jackass. Gave it my untethered *all*. And do allow me to say, I don't think it inaccurate to say—in that moment, I *owned* them. I possessed them. That room was enslaved. And... I never do that. I'm not a performer in the obvious sense. I suck, in fact. My singing voice is horrendous. Not at all pleasing to the ear. And in terms of the stage, if you can believe it, I'm actually a little bit shy. But that night I wasn't. Not in the least. I sang that song with unconditional enthusiasm, like recklessly. I gave it *up*, Phil. Every inch."

He shook his head, remembering. His voice softened.

"She was charmed by it, sir. She was drawn." He reached over with his cuffed hand and lightly grabbed my shirt. "She came up to me. I had no idea that was feasible, that such a moment was achievable. You understand? *She* approached *me*."

He let go of my shirt and looked up at that building.

"Among the single most gratifying moments of my life."

"I bet."

"And one of the most surprising."

"Ha."

Again, his smile faded. I tossed in two cents.

"So that's when you guys hooked up?"

He nodded, sort of grin-frowning.

"The bassist hung himself two days later."

"Excuse me?"

"Hung himself. My friend the bassist killed himself. He'd always been the self-loathing inward type, and then he went ahead and did it. Two days after that party."

He shook his head, then grinned a little, if not a little guiltily.

"You see, that was the joke. That my singing had sent him over the edge. Like 'Don't Stop 'Til You Get Enough' was just too much to bear." He mimed pulling a noose at his neck and made a *crrrking* sound. "He'd had enough, you know? Like, Stop! Enough!" Again, the gesture of noose and neck.

I chuckled uncomfortably. "Jesus, Adam."

"But wait—that sounds cruel, but this is important. That's the joke at the birth of our union. The grim bit that melded us together. Like, I killed a friend but scored a lover, the same who'd one day become my wife. She still brings it up sometimes." He rubbed at an eye. "Oh we weren't cold about it. I grieved, she supported. We talked it to death, had lots of life-affirming sex. I mean, we'd *just* got together, but... in a very real way, it's what glued us. That hanging as much as anything."

He shook his head in remembered disbelief.

"A morbid sort of dirty joke," he said, "that remained entirely our own. Told mostly in bed, never shared with outsiders. I mean, you're seriously the first I've told."

"I find that hard to believe."

"It's true."

Adam leaned up and nodded at the building.

"Right there," he said. "Right up there."

And just then he noticed. Finally. I witnessed the act of his noticing. His gaze rose, brow crinkled. He was seeing it quite clearly now. For just above that desolate building, you-know-who was hanging in the sky.

"Great Christ," he said. "That's insane."

"I know."

"The moon... you seeing this?"

"It's laughing. Yeah."

He froze like that, staring up at the sky. He waited, then said, "Whatever he sees down here, it's awfully funny."

"Hilarious, apparently."

Adam stared up at it, not laughing back, then looked down abruptly and started the car, his face gone mostly serious.

"I don't like that," he said, averting his eyes. "Don't like that at all."

"Come on—it's lovely!"

"Don't like it."

He cranked the music and U-turned swiftly, fleeing both memory and moon. Didn't speak once until we were home, only stole a glance or two at the sky whenever we stopped in traffic. I suppose he thought it was laughing at him. He'd had, after all, some atrocious luck. Cherished car stolen on a fool's watch. Wife and child flee the nest. Still, I think he'd say he deserved it. You could see he was resigned to the damage he'd done. Multiple years of consistent cheating? Of problem drinking and an absent heart? That'll swing back to haunt you, sir. That'll come back to cuff you on the wrist.

But he never gave up. I'll grant him that. On the way home, he found new hope. He thought he spotted his stolen Dodge Dart racing by in the passing lane. We gave chase for a couple terrifying minutes, but then it turned and disappeared from view. Adam smiled broadly, sweating at the brow.

"That was her," he said. "She's alive!"

I wasn't convinced—we'd barely seen it—but Adam read it as a blessing.

He sought hope again later—again, perhaps desperately—after landing in the lot and setting me free, keeping his half of the handcuffs on. They dangled as he waved and entered his apartment. I rubbed at my wrist and entered mine.

That's the last I saw Adam for quite a while. He disappeared days later, leaving a ghost town across the hall. Left a serious hole in my life as well. The diapers and feedings and strolls through the park took on a different pall. I craved Adam's push. His drama, his war. I wasn't so sure I could declare my own.

That night, in his way, he kept on fighting. Fending off terror, avoiding the moon. Made the afterhours call to his available other, the little secret his wife had uncovered and likely left the marriage over.

Despite being outed, they got right to it. Those two went to town. They woke me up around three, three-thirty, the moaning and grunts and icky escalations seeping through the vent in our living room. And when I turned on the lamp, I was shocked to find her. Shelley, already there. In panties and tanktop, arms crossed, standing under the vent. I hadn't noticed she left the bed. It really sort of spooked me. She glanced my way then looked back up.

"Quite the performance here," she whispered. "Maribel is simply on *fire*. Adam—I don't know. Adam sorta sounds like the guy from Slingblade but Maribel's just so... expressive."

I nodded. "She can be."

"Poor Jorge," she said, with a sympathetic pout. "No child could sleep through *that*. He must be terrified."

I slid my arms around her waist, nestled my chin in the nook of her shoulder. I didn't correct her. I let it go. Give the ghosts one last haunt, I thought. Let them be there in Shelley's eye. Somehow that seemed hopeful. We stood under the vent in the lamp-lit night, swaying a little, listening in, seeing what we chose to see.

THE FALL

THE WOAHS

When Adam Swivchek fled the building, and indeed our lives, he duct-taped a brown paper package to the central panel of our back door, scrawling *At Last!* across its face in urgent magic marker. I like to imagine him writing this and cackling—maniacally sleep-deprived in his underwear or robe—then dashing cinematically down the stairs, and out to the alley, clearly insane.

He wasn't necessarily the raving mad type, but ever since Maribel and Jorge left him, I'd really had to wonder. He'd cheated for years in more than one way and the chickens had finally come home. Is that what he meant? *At Last!*

I stared at the thing on our door there, then unstuck the package from the half-warped wood—at that point had no clue what it was nor the slightest what was unfolding—and moved the fifteen feet or so toward Adam's back door, just slightly ajar. I pressed gently and it opened with a creak.

"Adam?"

Silence, barrenness, both absolute. I stepped in, amazed, and floated through the place. No furniture, appliances, no shelves, no pictures. Nothing at all. Stripped spotless. Must have brought movers in at night or something.

All I could muster was, "Whoa."

"They gone, no?" said a voice behind me. "Disappear?"

This was Yuri, the building's linebacker handyman, standing behind me in Adam's kitchen. Our Ukrainian Colossus with the deepset brooding eyes, bearing spackling tools and a bucket of caulk.

"Poof," he said, grinning widely. "No more."

"Did he call you guys or... "

He showed me the envelopes he'd found that morning duct-taped to Adam's front door. Two of them, one for the landlord—likely the last of the rent—and the other for Yuri, with a crass drawing of an upraised fist, *By Any Means!* markered beneath it. Fifty dollars he'd left him, explained Yuri, then shrugged, like, 'nice but eh! whatever.' The money and this thing, this little guy here. He took from the envelope a tiny clay bust of Malcolm X.

"Weird, no?" said Yuri, chuckling. "What this mean?"

"I have no idea."

He noticed the package in my hand. "What you get?" he asked, as if we shared a secret Santa.

"Let's see."

Shelley called from the back hallway just as I cracked the seal.

"Phil?"

Yuri grinned with knowing eye as I moved back toward Adam's open door.

Shelley stood impatiently behind our back door, wearing summery stay-at-homes—wispy lime blouse, salmon skirt, white canvas sneakers, no socks. She held the Monarch in his SafeZone Portaseat. She lifted her watch for a look. "It's time."

Shaking my head, still stunned, I approached.

"What you got there?" she said, raising her chin.

"This?" I said. "A gift. From Adam."

"Adam, eh?" Some mockery rising, a glance at Adam's door. "What'd he get you? Drugs? Explosives?"

"Be fair, now."

"Perhaps some sort of yellow pages for the available whores in our area code?"

I stopped in my tracks. "That's not fair."

"It most certainly is."

"I said be fair and that is not the practice of fairness."

"Why so defensive? I don't mean *you*."

"Adam left."

She grimaced. "Left?"

"He's gone now too. Go look." I gestured over my shoulder. "It's stripped of the slightest trace."

She handed me the Monarch in his overpriced Portaseat and swiftly stepped toward the neighbors' apartment, glancing back just once. I could hear her speaking briefly with Yuri, then all went silent as—stunned as me—she took the barren tour. Minutes later, she re-emerged, arms crossed, mouth open.

"Holy fucking shit."

"I know."

The Monarch nattered on beneath us.

We rode in the Civic in a heavy silence, the Monarch babbling occasional phrases over the whoosh of the air conditioning.

"Da da me no."

Clear syllables, dribs and drabs of future language. Shelley drove with deft precision, accelerating often, not at all shy about passing a car.

I reached in the envelope and slid out the contents of the Adam package, which at that point sincerely surprised me. A pristine copy of issue four, volume twenty-three, of the fabled *Midwest Contrarian*, the obscure and since-defunct quarterly review containing Adam's one published essay. I turned to the table of contents to confirm it.

The Ravings of Safety—A. Swivchek—46.

He'd mentioned this essay multiple times but never got around to showing me. For years, he'd insisted I read it, and enough times, with enough insistence, that I'd come to doubt it existed. It was famous and elusive, this "Ravings of Safety," and I think I preferred it that way.

Shelley leaned up into the wheel, accelerating, then shot us abruptly into the passing lane.

"He said nothing to you?"

"Haven't seen him in days."

She shook her head in wonder and briskly slalomed on. Soon enough, we pulled up to the clinic. The tires screeched. She waited, meditating.

"I can't tell if I find this disturbing or cathartic. I mean—" She turned to me. "I'm not done being angry with you. Over the other thing."

"I understand that," I said, nodding. "And again... I'm sorry. I should have told you earlier."

"I can't imagine why it took so *long*." She stared through the windshield. "Five days, Philip. Maribel and Jorge had been gone five days before you told me."

"Actually, they never came back from Mexico. Technically, they'd been gone two weeks."

She looked at me, not so amused. "I'm more disturbed by your silence on the matter." She winced just slightly, her crinkle of worry. "I can't believe you'd leave me in the dark like that."

"I know. I guess I was protecting Adam."

"Protecting him?" She shook her head tightly. Sort of lightly *harrumphed*.

We sat in silence a while, then I reached in back for both clipboards and the big bag of ECHELON materials. I got out, patted and kissed the Monarch goodbye, then leaned down through the window.

"I should have told you earlier. I'll cop to that. I mean, I *did* tell you, but—"

"Not soon enough."

"I know."

She took in a deliberately even breath, a relaxation process she'd read about in a magazine that nearly always increased the tension. She stared ahead.

"See, Philip. I don't think you understand this but... it was almost like *you* had something to hide."

I shook my head and tried to gesture, but my hands were full of ECHELON materials.

"Just Adam," I said. "I was hiding *him*. I mean, come on..." I held out my arms, baring all that stuff. "I have nothing to hide."

"No?" she said, turning to see me.

"Well... nothing of consequence."

She waited, struck by that. "I see. 'Consequence' enters the picture."

"No no. It's not like—which picture?"

"We should stop," she said, and looked at her watch. "You're late for my job."

I nodded, agreeing. We gave silent goodbyes as I stepped back to the curb. Shelley jumped hungrily back in traffic. I watched the Civic zoom to the corner, where it turned and soon left view.

I had nothing actually. Not a thing to hide. For that matter, very little to show. And the fact of that whistled through the air of my life like a white flag trailing a softly shot arrow.

But as I waited for the elevator to the twentieth floor, a bright red memory flew in, answering that arrow with another, this one flaming and shot with force. Only the summer before, in fact—Adam and I with two anonymous women we'd met on a lark at some indie bookstore reading. Drinking whiskey with them later by the lake.

We'd laughed, flirted, paired off, frolicked. She had brushed up against me, touched my thigh when we sat. Nothing happened—not for me, not really. It was softball flirtation, junior high stuff. I barely touched her, more like refused her, unless it was her refusing me. This subtle advance from, or toward, this younger someone in a fetching black knit skirt—the frivolous air, cannabis eyes, that steamy way of saying goodbye. I fantasized about her after—that's as far as it went. Felt a lot like cheating, though, its warm-up or rehearsal. A practice run in having secrets not to tell.

Adam, however, was advanced in this department. That night by the lake was child's play for him. There, he'd betrayed both wife and lover with someone whose name he'd barely caught.

"Detach yourself from the institutions," he once told me, a few drinks in and holding forth. "Snap those so-called loyalties in two, like the dried-out branches they *are*." He grinned at this. "At least in your mind. Or, you know, in the way your mind sees things." Then, only half-joking, he half-whispered, "You can reattach the branch with some glue or tape. It'll come off easier next time." Detach, Reattach, Detach, Reattach. Seek moments of transcendence in forbidden connection, individual pleasure. Then wake up and take responsibility! That too. Give back, as it were, after taking.

Always bugged me when he talked like this. A bit cake-and-eat-it-too, I thought. He wanted it both spartan and sybaritic, like a Walden Pond with a nightclub attached. A full-service Walden with a daycare center staffed by promiscuous art chicks. Here and there go into town passing undercover as bourgeois. Now and then condemn the evils of money while making serious gobs of it yourself.

The doors slid open to Spinal Rehab. The institutional glare and sea foam carpeting saved me from being swallowed up. The Thursdays we swapped lives were as much a relief to me as they were to Shelley, who got her time with the baby. I, on the other hand, loved the out-of-house sense of utility—the hum of the lighting and smell of antiseptic, the antibacterial wash. It had curative value and took your eyes off yourself.

I looked beyond the front desk, where the TVs hung in corners of waiting rooms, beaming their studio audience cheer. I was hoping no one showed today, however. The ECHELON measure for SCIs was not the cure I craved.

I sat down and opened "The Ravings of Safety," to page forty-six, which I'd read a little in the car. Adam had advertised his academic writing as a kind of "bombastic critical theory." Yet I found the prose surprisingly formal, if not a touch wooden. Abstract, dense, sometimes hard to follow, but I think I got it all the same. And halfway down the next page, a paragraph leapt out at me, starker than the others.

The intoxicated Social Body—blind drunk with comfort and amusement—roots out its freakish appendages, its extra limbs and unsightly protrusions, and never pausing to debate or ponder, severs them, pitches them into the darkness, where the Severed and Separated chance on survival, in retro-generative iterations of crassly discarded disease. This is the Obvious. Denial of the Obvious is Madness.

I wasn't sure what he meant while reading in the car, but here in the clinic I thought I saw evidence of what he called the Obvious. Also, the Severed and Separated. A host of black and latino men in wheelchairs for life, nearly all of them exceptionally poor.

Yet this Madness itself is rarely obvious. This is especially true when manifest collectively, when the Social Body and Common Brain smilingly succumb as one, unable to smell their own synapses burning. Most of what makes Madness Mad is the quiet fact of its denial.

I read the last sentence again, then underlined it, not at all sure I agreed.

A moment later, I was abruptly interrupted—if not saved from myself. Black rubber treads rolled up to my sneaker.

"Hey boss."

I looked up, smiled, set the journal aside. Walter. Nice. Here's the cure. Extra-large full-of-life Walter, chugging along in his manual ride. He had a long lived-in stretch of a face, dour when passive, that bloomed into smiling at the slightest tickle. Standing, he'd be well over six feet. We'd only met once but recalled each other well. He had done another study Shelley co-authored, and I once helped lift him to the DEXA table. I knew too well his bone density, the brunt of his body mass index. That single lift assist—five to six seconds—strained my back for weeks.

I weighed Walter in his chair on the giant scale and had

him sign some paperwork. Then I interviewed him as I had before, and with nearly identical questions. This was the ickiest aspect of the job. I was dreading the black box to come. *Cause of Injury*. I recalled that well enough. Who could forget? Years before, Walter's wife had shot him. I don't know why—still don't—though apparently they'd stayed together. And when we got there, he told me so matter-of-factly—no shame, no embarrassment, no big deal—that I went ahead and probed off-interview. He confirmed they were still a couple, yes. Yet something in the numbers seemed off. The year they'd married? His Date of Injury?

That bloom of a smile gently rose.

"Oh no," he said. "She shot me before we were married."

"Before you were... "

He nodded, long since resigned to it.

Under my breath, I went "whoa." I glanced over at Adam's journal. *Most of what makes Madness Mad is the quiet fact of its denial.*

I knew I was pushing it, but continued to probe. Third question in, Walter went dour. He answered concisely, brief frosty phrases meant to shut me up. I did as asked, faintly blushing. I couldn't wait to run this by Shelley.

I never got the chance to, though. I forgot big Walter entirely—which would come back to hurt me later. When I arrived home, our apartment was empty. I was just about to dial Shelley's cell, then heard familiar voices next door. I went via the back hallway, as I had that morning, not at all expecting what I found. It was a serious surprise in a day of surprises, and made me question once more if we were cursed.

A stranger stood in Adam's empty kitchen in a form-fitting chocolate skirt. She was staring at a watermark above the cupboards, her petrol black hair in a pristine ponytail that hovered at the curve of her back. I watched her through the half-open doorway.

It took a second, then I saw who it was.

Lean, alluring, poised as ever, with that strangely robust ivory skin. Her posture implying engaged thought, her blouse suggesting revelations—though not quite following through. She was just as I remembered her. Melanie Trident, the music writer I'd once thought killed herself. Clearly alive, she glanced my way.

"Tell me," she said, and pointed. "Does that or does that not look like a snake eating its tail?"

I stepped toward it. You had to look a few seconds for the image to gel—an oblong circle, scaly-seeming from the wall's damaged texture, with a stark demarcation, a swish of grime where the tail seemed to enter the mouth.

"It does." I knew that I knew it, and strangely, it came. "Like whatsitcalled... Ouroboros."

"Exactly." She was amused. "Bravo. Ourobouros. Archetype of the cycle of renewal." She grinned, catching herself. "But sorry. Enough with the lectures on tape." She held out a hand. "Nice to see you, Phil."

"And you too... I'm sorry—" I pretended I'd forgotten, then nearly said it with her. Melanie. Melanie Trident. My robust ivory indie Morticia who wrote about music and suicide, girlfriend to Shelley's friend Hugo—a recent coupling by way of an affair. I found her sort of fascinating, had for a while. As did many others, I'm sure.

Shelley entered the kitchen then, beaming in her salmons and limes, the Monarch in a snuglee against her chest. Hugo followed close behind, taut-muscled and superpoised in his ragged Polo, cutoffs and sandals.

"It's settled then," said Shelley. "We'll be neighbors!"

Hugo shrugged indifferently, smiling—why not?

Shelley was exuberant.

Melanie, pleased.

Apparently it was settled—and that fast. We had our replacement neighbors. The Swivcheks were yesterday's news. Literally. Hadn't even been twenty-four hours since I'd found the *At Last!* package taped to our door.

Shelley knew Hugo from college, one from her entourage

back in the day, a "best friend" among several who she had fooled around with, she says, just once—then they'd "gone Platonic". Colombian guy. Born there at least. Exceedingly, ruggedly handsome, if not too much so. He'd been a med student at Loyola, then quit. Was a bartender now, had been for years, with aspirations to write. Of course I'd been a writer once as well—a playwright, but no longer—and their friendship bugged me in that regard only. My wife, it seemed, collected fools like us, and I wanted no reminders.

Among the lot of us, including A. Swivchek, only one wrote for actual money. Still, Adam would be entertained, I'm sure, by the accident of his replacement. He'd read the work of Melanie Trident, this music writer for a free weekly who destroyed bands in single sentences, who also digressed into fascinating passages that examined what hovered at the fringes of music, or—no—the forces beneath it, italicizing often for urgency's sake. The *death draw*, as you know, was one of her favorites. *Sexual hysteria* another. *Crew ship complacency. Theme park adolescence.* Most of it was pretty persuasive.

With Shelley's recommendation to our landlord, they'd take over the Swivcheks' within the week. They'd been looking to shack up, she and Hugo, and Adam's place had landed in their lap. It all seemed too fast, even disrespectful. Traces of the Swivcheks still haunted the room. For a second—an aural flash—I thought I heard the sirens blare, air-raidish or tornado-related.

I searched for Adam all week as best I could—tried his cell countless times, but the number remained "unreachable." With Monarch in stroller, I went to The Copy Boss—the original Boss, on Division—and asked around, hoping I'd finally meet his grad student, the extracurricular thing or fling that so recently tore up his marriage. But she wasn't there. No one knew anything. He hadn't been in much that summer, they said. A call to his other shop—the Boss on Halsted—quickly confirmed the same.

I read and reread the "The Ravings of Safety," as if I'd find some signal or clue. Erratic in tone, vague in its thesis, but still, something there held me. Probably the familiar ring. It was stocked with Adamisms I'd heard before, such as: living in comfort and safety meant others must live in poverty and terror. Adam argued—as he had before—that the right thing to do, the only *moral* thing, was to "sever and separate" from Safety ourselves. Cut away all institutional pressures—career, marriage, family, religion—as a statement of solidarity with those who'd been tossed aside.

Well, that "solidarity" seemed pretty suspect but I couldn't argue with the one-way page. I wanted my neighbor back, to spar with, be verbally abused by. It seemed he'd clutched his Ravings a bit too close to heart.

The week they moved in was uneventful. I hardly noticed. All was fine until the second week, that Friday afternoon, when a voluptuous guitar riff shot through the vent—our shiny slatted delivery system that hung near the doorway to the living room. This came around three-fifteen or so, well into the Monarch's naptime, the very slot Adam and his other used to fill, his grad student from the Copy Boss—wife at class, son at preschool, secret other on the afternoon sofa. Well, the shift in content was jarring. Where there'd been sex, subtly tantalizing, now there was music, overly loud. I stared up. The vent rattled faintly. Good god, that's loud. That could wake the baby.

I went swiftly via front doors, pounding on theirs. Not angrily, just to be heard. She answered in a thin-threaded Meat Puppets t-shirt—it hung to loose-fitting cutoff jeans. Smooth white marble thighs and calves. Unwashed jet black hair to her shoulders. That calm and keen-eyed carnal aplomb crossed with a faint scent of afternoon booze.

She tilted her head. "Too loud?"

"Could you?" I made the universal gesture for turn it down.

She apologized sincerely and hovered off to do so, then returned to invite me in.

"Oh I can't—" I gestured back over my shoulder. "The kid.

He's sleeping."

"No no no. You must. Hugo's out and I've finished for the day. Come on." And level-eyed, she took my hand. "Just one."

"That's um... that's not exactly responsible."

She shushed me, then came in close. "We'll hear the baby crying through the vent."

"The vent?"

"Yeah." She looked over toward it. "It's dependable. Besides..." She glanced at me coyly. "A breach of decorum firms the soul."

I had by then—against my will—something of a halfway hard-on, or a quarter's way, if that's possible. I followed fast to the nearest chair.

"Whiskey okay?"

"Yeah uh... whiskey." I waited. "You know, water will do."

"Whiskey and water," she said. "Done." She glided off toward the kitchen.

I let it go. The fractional swelling was dying down and I figured a few minutes couldn't hurt. Their place—clearly theirs now, no longer the Swivcheks'—drew you in with its dark cozy feel. Amazing how quickly they'd set up shop. The lighting was low, the lamps Turkish-seeming, candles aflame to each side of the laptop. There were oil paintings of opaque abstraction. Dark blues everywhere, greens, blacks. Concert posters encased in glass. Zeppelin, Mingus, Sleater-Kinney. A stylized bohemian wombness in there. Slight scent of incense. Trace of weed.

She returned with my unwanted beverage.

"Would have taken you for a straight up man."

I shook my head no. "So... what else have you heard through the vent?"

She smiled coyly and sat in the soft blue chair next to mine. "Oh, not much. Only been two weeks. Sometimes voices we can't really make out. An argument once." She tilted back her head, remembering. "And yesterday, wow—in the morning? You two really sank your fangs in. You're explosive, huh? Both of you."

"I guess we... I forgot that. Boy."

I turned to see it. The old school vent in the corner of the living room, where it ran through the drywall, just like ours, to the internal guts of the greater building. A secret twin. But how obvious—not so secret. For all the three o'clocks I'd listened in on Adam, I'd spent little to no time considering he might be listening to me.

I took a long bracing gulp of water and whiskey. Melanie, meanwhile, was staring at, sort of examining me, her head tilted slightly to the side.

"Philip," she said, as if stating the fact of me. "Philip Palliard. Full time father. Tell me..." Holding her glass at a thoughtful remove, she made circles in the air, clinking the ice. "Do you feel at all emasculated by your role?"

The word hung before me as if scratched in the air.

"No. I... No."

"No?"

I stared into my glass, tilting it slightly. The ice cubes softly rolled. "Well, a little, I guess. But I wouldn't use that word."

She shook her head tightly. "Philip," she said. "Don't. Do *not*. It takes balls to do what you do."

"Balls?" I said. "That's debatable."

"Don't be foolish." She took a long slow swig of her beverage, maintaining eye contact. "Don't buy the eons of bad thought before you. You, my friend—" She pointed with her glass. "Take part in an irreversible shift. In our evolution. It's just true. There'll be adaptations that respond to what you do."

I laughed, maybe snorted. "Adaptations?"

She shook her head, annoyed. "Oh I don't mean you'll grow tits and *nurse*." She touched at her hair. "Social transformations. *Coup de' tats* of the presumed contract. And not merely the swapping of roles. More like... the elimination of them." Her voice grew softer. She seemed touched or perhaps just quite high. "It's a beautiful thing. Now if only people would stop having babies."

"Ha! Yeah, well... don't expect—"

"And start sharing bodies."

I stared at her. Wasn't sure I'd heard right. But something

in her eyes seemed to confirm it. A serene sort of mischief or muted suggestion. I took another bracing swallow. She looked off toward the window, half-smiling.

"Oh don't mind me. Seriously. Do not." She took another sip, then said, almost soothingly, "You can clearly see I'm a self-absorbed diva." Something occurred to her. She looked at me defiantly. "I rarely go to the bottle this early. Honestly. *Rarely.* But today's special." She pointed toward the laptop garnished with candles. "I've just now finished a book."

An impressive tower of pages sat on the table, rising over the random kitsch.

"Oh! Well, congratulations."

"Thank you."

"What's the uh... What's the book—"

"I'm no breeder, Philip."

I nodded. "No. I wouldn't have guessed you were."

"Think I could write with a yowler on my teat? Too much to care for in excess of career. Really. You people amaze me."

I took another swallow. "Think Hugo wants kids?"

"Hugo wants nothing," she said and polished off her glass. "Nothing he knows I won't give."

She stood and started back toward the kitchen. I stood as well, meaning to go. She stopped in her tracks, then turned.

"You're not leaving?"

"I'm playing with fire here." I gestured across the hall. "DCFS would have my ass."

"Oh please. DCFS would yawn and have another donut. They don't care about *you.* But... I understand. Listen." She smiled serenely with inviting eyes. "Stop by again."

I nodded, thanked her and left swiftly for our place, my heart pounding as I moved toward the crib. There the Monarch was on his back, down hard. His little belly rose and fell, so slightly. Still alive. Thank god.

I sat in the bathroom and—nicely buzzed on water and whiskey—masturbated more intensely than I had in years. When I finished, I saw, in the corner of my eye, open on its face by the sink, our well-thumbed copy of *The Midwest Contrar-*

ian, set to its favorite place. I cleaned up, then took it and read randomly.

What Madness sees is what Sanity abandons. This too is a false distinction. When should we call Madness Mad or in accepting it, say that Acceptance is Sane? Which are we when we recognize or accept our denial but continue the behavior once denied?

I turned it on its face, then washed up again, avoiding the mirror as best I could.

All the same, it was a good September. Above average.

Melanie was home most days, writing, listening to music. I was home most days, caring for and feeding the Monarch. Shelley was immersed at her ECHELON Study, and Hugo was out more often than not, either bartending at his day job downtown or writing on his laptop at our local cafe.

Melanie would stop by here and there. Knock lightly on our door just to say what's up? She was sweet with the Monarch, sweeter than you'd guess. Held him, played with him, made funny faces. And then, of course, there was the talk. Long conversations on the state of the culture. Politics, music, film, theater. Turned out she'd once seen a play I'd written—co-wrote actually—in which I had also acted. My finest, most recognized hour. *Perpetual Union*, a full-length play. She had her criticisms, but claimed she half liked it. She even encouraged me to write again. A friendship was forming, but by no means a safe one. Sometimes we sat a bit too close.

Shelley in turn spent more time with Hugo, went out with him on random weeknights, returning home with a boozy levity I really think she needed. We both did.

Well over a month into having new neighbors—our new-found domestic balance or bliss—Shelley came home from the Study one evening looking tight-eyed and bitterly flushed.

Towel on shoulder, I burped the Monarch.

She crossed her arms and started in.

She could not believe me. What was I thinking? Grilling subjects about private histories? About sensitive material, ethically suspect?

Walter Jorgenson had happened by that afternoon as she and Dr. Meng discussed the Study. Dr. Meng, the internationally revered spinal specialist, was asking Walter about his injury, the nature and placement of the bullet. But Walter, strangely irritable, misread the question and told them instead the story of its origins—his wife shooting him before they were married. And he wondered why everyone was so damn curious. Mr. Phil had "already grilled him on that one." Could he have his check please? He wanted no more of this. He wasn't some freak on Jerry Springer.

"He said that, Phil. He compared our interview process to Jerry fucking Springer in front of Dr. Allen Meng. Do you have any idea how crushing it would be to lose Dr. Meng's endorsement?"

No time to answer that one. She whipped out a signed copy of an MRI request form with a stark black X across its back. My signature was at bottom, just beneath Dominick Lafuse. Evidently I'd scheduled the kid for an MRI he wasn't fit for. I had neglected the okay on bullet placement. Ouch.

"Jesus, Phil. Seriously... I could lose everything. Everything."

Again, no time to answer or apologize. Livid, she dug into her big black bag and pulled out a solitary Polaroid. She straight-armed it toward me.

"And who's this?"

I took the Polaroid and knew at once. I winced. Now how the—? This was Adam's mistress, his graduate fling, done up in a powder blue bonnet and dress as Little Bo Peep with cane. A pointedly sexy Little Bo Peep. Her dress billowed out like a soft explosion just above the thigh. The jacketed bodice, cleavage revealing, egg white stockings stretched to the knee, buckled black shoes, Bo Peep hat. That she was Asian—not the Peep expected—made the image all the more alluring.

"A fetish of yours?" she asked.

"Where'd you get this?"

"Floor of the car. I picked up this thing and it slid out." She dug in her big black ECHELON bag and pulled out the package Adam taped to our door the day he left. Shelley swiveled it to read the face. "At Last? Why at last?"

"Honey—no—that's Adam. Adam wrote that." I turned the Polaroid and lifted it toward her. "That's her."

Shelley stared hard, drained of moral force. She squinted.

"No way." She caught my eye. "That's her?"

I nodded. Shelley took the Polaroid. She examined it for some time.

"Well, she's hot enough."

I nodded, looking. "That she is."

Shelley looked up. "You like that, eh?"

I shrug-winced, De Niro-style. Then she remembered her anger. She flipped the Polaroid back my way. I took it. She stepped for the porch. The Monarch leaked or puked on my shoulder as I looked down again at that fetching image. So this picture was a party to Adam's *At Last!* He knew I never met her and had always been curious. He was finally showing me by showing her off. What? Had it been Halloween? A dress-up game to get things going? Her gaze was hypnotic, so gently suggestive, that timeless expression of tender mischief I'd seen so recently across the hall.

Days later, on a bright Friday morning, Melanie Trident knocked on our door. The air outside was lush as mid-summer. A generous blast for late September. I opened up and she was all in blue. Steel blue vest. Sky blue skirt. Rare cowboy boots dyed Play-Doh blue. And the day was so beautiful, she began. High of seventy-five! Would I care to come down to the lake with her? She was meeting friends for a lakeside brunch. Come, bring the baby. Why not?

I thanked her, but just couldn't do it. Too much stuff to prepare. Blankets, bottles, the stroller—all that. She hiked down the stairs, mock-disappointed. She waved. I waved back.

But when I returned with the Monarch that afternoon—our routine two-thirty stroll through the park—Melanie was there again, fresh from her picnic, turning the key at her front door. I *sshhed* with a finger to my lips. The baby was out cold in the snuglee. She cooed at him, then raised a brow. Whispered, care to come in?

There were particles of magnet in the air, I'd swear it. Half the feeling was a curse of the weather. We moved through the kitchen, and she pointed to the watermark. Their tail-eater, our mythic snake, had grown a bit larger in the month since. A little more tail down the throat, I suppose. I felt it in my own throat, really quite dry.

In silence—deference to the Monarch—we entered the dark, cozy living room. I took the baby from his snuglee and, at her suggestion, carefully lay him on a futon in the corner. Without asking, she handed me a water and whiskey, which I downed rapidly. She lit a joint and passed it over, then put on some Miles. *Big Fun*, volume low. We sat on the charcoal sofa and quietly discussed, if memory serves, baseball. Who knows why.

After the first of the lulls, there were several, she touched softly at my arm and whispered, I really must tell you something.

And launched into a sincere if bracing defense of the conceptual scaffolding of her newfound lifestyle. Pursuits of happiness, individual liberties, constitutional props on flesh foundations. She'd been meaning to tell me. She felt I was a friend. And she knew I was devoted to Shelley—bound to her, no doubt would kill for her—and thus had no intention of harming that union. That said, she'd discussed the prospect with Hugo, and they both agreed that if we—by some remarkable stretch of fancy—somehow also agreed, well... oh don't mind me, she said, so that's out there. It's nothing. Nothing. Absolute air.

A lull dropped, lengthy and charged. Silence gushed forth as if from a hydrant.

All of a sudden, we were at it. I couldn't even tell you who led. A kiss, then groping, disrobing, unlatching. We made out a while, etcetera, etcetera. Soon enough down on the cobalt carpet, the Monarch asleep only feet away. She prepared herself for the final step and mounted gently, still in her skirt. She let out an *mmmm*. Like that, we were one.

Well, it didn't last. Just a few faint strokes. I saw my son in the corner of my eye—his fragile body in a baby blue onesy, little chest rising, then sinking. My god. Pretty small dollars to call it honor, but something—my body—revolted. Some ancient loyalty buried in the nerves. Were he sleeping out of eyeshot? Well... no telling.

I gripped at her hips and rolled out from under. She whispered, what? I moved toward the front window area, naked from the waist down. I looked down at the empty street, the unoccupied sidewalks and porches. Aging steeples, ghost town trees. Spent a good minute there, half engorged, knowing she was waiting behind me.

Then, like insurance, they came. Rolling ahead, other side of the street. He in his high-end wheelchair—our Dominick, who'd once lived across the way. Shelley right behind him—my life-betrothed—stepping intently, with professional purpose, flipping her chain of keys in a circle. Flipping them, catching them. Flipping, catching.

Again up my throat, whoa. A hundred *whoas*. Lottery balls massing under the chute. I slid on boxers, harnessed the snuglee, put the baby back in—still asleep—and muttered my weak farewell. Smoking now, her back on the carpet, Melanie waved a silent goodbye. Her eyes looked if anything amused.

"I guess that was a bad idea," she whispered.

I nodded. "Shelley's here."

"Oh!"

I used back doors again, just to be safe, but Yuri, our handyman, was out there on a ladder, fixing a camera to the building's back wall. He glimpsed me through the window—I saw his eyes pop—as I motored home, sneakers in one hand, shorts in the other, still half-engorged in flimsy boxers, drooling baby against my chest.

His camera caught a crime before he had turned the other on. Yuri'd memorize that one for sure. He knew where I lived, who'd moved in. Any defense would be denied.

Inside our place, with rapid heart, I watched from the window as Shelley dialed her cell. Mine rang from the pocket of my shorts. And, Hey hon. Could you help us out?

She'd given Dominick a ride home. Felt guilty, she said. We'd denied him for the Study, if not nearly killed him—though I still say that's a grand exaggeration. So the biggest surprise might be Dominick. I talked to him some, filled a few things in, but that's another story entirely. Shelley went up to our place to watch the baby as I lift-assisted Dominick up the stairs with another neighbor's help. He'd come to visit his mother. And thankfully leaner than big Walter Jorgenson. By comparison, light as ash.

Later that night, Shelley surprised me. I'd taken a midnight shower, and walked into our bedroom in a furry towel. I found her kneeling—no, posing—on our bed.

"Wow," I said. "That's... great."

"You like?"

My mouth hung open. It wasn't the sort of get-up she wore or game she played. She had gotten the idea—was competing even—with the image of Adam's Bo Peep. And I sensed a slight awkwardness at the fringe of her daring, but the charged anomaly of it, even that whisper of insecurity beneath the pose of confidence—would her husband like or laugh at it?—set my pulse through the roof.

We even went a second time later that night, as if I'd harnessed the energy from the Melanie transgression and converted it, flipped it, coal to solar. Though that, I'd argue, was wishful thinking.

Sometime later, Shelley snored at my side, still wearing her fetching hood and cape—the remains of her Little Red Riding gear strewn across the bedroom floor. I was propped by a pillow, the reading lamp on. Having another go at The Ravings.

I'd found one more clue from Adam that evening and hoped I could string it together. That surprise slid from the package when I'd finally thrown it in the trash. But no—more! A *second* Polaroid, Peep's companion, which slowly altered my take on the first.

I flipped ahead to the essay's conclusion. It read:

Safety binds us to the language of psychology. It inures us to the Obvious, to the damaged and discarded, the doll parts in the dumping ground. Safety cannot see the crushed skull in its path nor hear the sound of the child being beaten, the neighbor's wife raped.

I glanced down at my wife in her hood and cape, naked under the covers. We had our troubles but I could not lose her. That seemed abundantly clear.

Craven Safety craves more of itself. Excess Comfort feeds like a tapeworm on the belly of its own boredom. Both demand earplugs and blackened windows. Both say don't worry, I am the answer. Both say death is nowhere near.

I slid the newfound Polaroid from the back of the pristine journal. It was a rare picture of the four of us—Shelley and me, Adam, Maribel—out on their front porch. I could barely remember it. Some barbecue or party a few years back. We each had our arms around our spouses, everyone laughing at a joke just made. A nice photo, actually. That day at least, we'd enjoyed ourselves supremely. A moment's comfort captured forever. Safe, you could say. Death nowhere near.

I took out the Polaroid of Adam's Bo Peep and held the two pictures side by side. What is this? What's he trying to *say*? I examined the two together for a while, then slid them both within the sharp white pages and tossed the journal on the floor.

I clicked off the lamp, turned on my side, and festered there in the darkness.

Body Mass Index

It's Dr. Joe I'm indebted to, ultimately. Dr. Joe and Walter. I'm writing plays again. Or trying to. Several Thursdays ago, the urge returned. And it feels so good. Spectacular, actually. Though I have my doubts. I do have my concerns.

We hovered that morning above Walter's body, at rest on the MRI platform. The formidable mass of Walter Jorgenson lying on a padded table, lift-assisted there only seconds before. The terrain of Walter on the ingoing bed, rising at an incline from throat to chest to the obvious mound in the middle, the adipose tissue that has serviced many studies—Epidemiology, Nutrition, etcetera. Walter has done some time.

Fingers laced across this mass, Walter yawned broadly.

"Tired?" I asked.

"Long night," he replied, then smiled, his signature blossom. "Might have to take a little nap in here."

I looked over and across Walter to the radiologist I'd assisted, also quite hefty. Latino, early thirties, goatee and glasses. Dr. Garcia, I believe. But, as he says, "call me Joe."

"I've had it happen," he said, across Walter. "Couple of

times."

"They fall asleep in there?"

"A few have," he said, and shrugged. "Can't help it."

Their bodies are quite similar, actually. Big, solid, hefty, broad. Defensive linemen. Formidable. If Walter hadn't been wounded at T4, where his wife shot him with his own handgun twelve to thirteen years before, these two could almost be twins. Of the body.

The story of this shooting is a sore point, actually, between Walter and me. At Shelley's bidding, I'd apologized. Had to call him on the phone and do it. I think he's exaggerating but that's his business. Everything seems back to normal now. I simply have to stop fucking up.

We left Walter there and returned to the control room, where we sat behind the dense protective glass. Joe manned the board like a sound engineer. Or no—more like an editor of film, reproducing the guy in slices, the brief magnetism that radiates from tissue, lifted from the body like a shadow's stain.

And there went Walter, sliding into that supersmooth MRI tunnel—leather, beige, a perfect oval—drawn inward by the mouth of the magnet into the eye that sees inside.

At the corners of Dr. Joe's mouth, a slight grin rose.

"Let's hope this guy nods off," he said.

"Oh?" The tone surprised me. Seemed cruel somehow. "Why?"

Against expectation, Dr. Joe winked at me. "I ordered a scan of his dreams."

Now... as manifest in my play, or rather, my notes for a play—haven't yet started the true composing—an ambitious if troubled night shift doctor, Dr. Verde, heftily framed, hypothesizes that our dreams have molecular composition. They are measurable and capable of being contained, like, as he claims, all brain activity.

Could it be that a dream, Dr. Verde asks the audience, has actual physical density? A thing we could bottle like a vapor or mist?

Of course the doctor discovers how. Twisting the principles of magnetic resonance, he captures and bottles the brainwaves of dreams from the sleeping minds of his patients. He redirects said vapor or mental mist into a complicated mammoth machine, then reconstructs and reconfigures until he's got an image on a screen.

At first, they're too fuzzy, hard to make out. He still has to work on the audio. Finally, he scores. Clarity! Complications quickly ensue.

This is where the action in the play picks up. Where Dr. Verde's patients' dreams begin to change form in stunning ways. Stunning and somehow lurid.

They are altered by having been measured, recorded, though the patients have no clue they're being recorded before or after dreaming. "Like the Heisenberg principle with a blindfold on," says Verde in Act One, Scene Three-ish. And then, strangely, his patients start to dream of Dr. Verde himself, often in compromising or embarrassing ways, the found footage of which places our Verde in some very complicated waters.

Shelley touched softly at my shoulder. I stared at the screen and stopped typing.

"You're writing?"

I nodded, grinned sort of sheepishly.

She cooed. "Is he back then?" she asked. "The real Philip Palliard?"

I shrugged. "We'll see," I said. "He's a little rusty. Cross your fingers." I looked up at her a second, then returned to work. I stared at the screen. "It depends."

She leaned over and plopped a kiss on my temple. I watched her move back to the kitchen, where she fed our Hank his carrots and peas.

At thirty-four, my wife's body is pleasing to the eye, perhaps all the more so for the additional tissue singing at her curves, a newly lit fullness it's nice to see nearly a year after the fact. And more than that of course. The straight hygienic blondness, the bright Canadian energy, the subtle wit and secret worry—it all feeds a resonance I've again found magnetic in new and exciting ways.

But I was telling you about my play. My notes for a play. *Magnetic Resonance*. Working title only. And that's the thing. How it keeps shifting. Focus, I'm afraid, will prove difficult. For I was watching Shelley feed my son Hank, his little body just a dumpling with limbs, his face, his eyes all mischief and light—and admiring how she cares for him, the visible shift that occurs in her, a warmth and vibrancy that surrounds her like an aura every time he's near—when she lifted her chin and said, "This should be me. All the time."

"I'd like that," I said, watching them there. "Is that... the real Shelley Taylor?"

She grinned, though plaintively. "It'll come," she said. "When the Study's done."

That's the deal. Allegedly. Though lately I've come to doubt it. For now, I escape only on Thursdays. I cover for her. She becomes me.

"It went okay with Walter?" She shoveled a spoonful in the Monarch's mouth. "He didn't resent you?"

"Oh no no no," I said, waving this away. "I apologized. He forgave. The MRI went just fine."

"Well... now you know," she said, returning her gaze to the child. "Subjects don't want to have to tell their stories more than necessary."

"But Shelley—" I lifted my palms. "He offered it up to me! As I've told you—like, no big deal. I mean, if *you* shot me before we were married, I bet I'd tell that one too."

"It's a good story," she said, then glanced at me, smiling. "I'll grant you that."

"Great story," I said. "I'm not supposed to share it?"

She shrugged. "Just be careful over there," she said, and then, recalling something, pointed at me with the plastic spork. "And don't forget about Dominick." She half-nodded, sort of hedging. "I think he deserves an apology too." She turned back to Hank.

"You think?" I said, wincing.

"I do," she said, and looked up at me.

I'd been such the fuck-up at the Study lately—disastrously so. Before all the Walter business, I'd scheduled Dominick for an MRI that could have injured him further. If not killed him—though this remains, in my view, doubtful.

My fault, yes—undeniably—but he's not the only one who deserves an apology.

I watched my wife feed our son.

There's another story that's pretty awful, that I haven't shared and cannot share. She'd kill me. Kind of scares me a little.

I swung the door to the study shut. Back to the play. To—working title only—*Magnetic Resonance.*

For here I was thinking, against good sense, that as an added complication, Dr. Verde will have cheated on his wife. Or, no no—he can't recall if he has or not. If it actually happened.

And did it? Verde asks the audience, Act One, Scene Five-ish. Did it happen or did it not? We have all the instruments. The tools of verification are in widespread use. Camera phones and wiretap kits and everything, all things recorded. Did it happen if you have no footage? Not even a basic photo or low definition sound recording? Things begin to get hard to remember. Unrecorded reality starts to look a lot less real.

So Dr. Verde may or may not have had fleeting, unfulfilling sex with a night shift nurse. Nurse Tyne, we'll say. Margaret Tyne, a quiet, elusive beauty he seduced on a slow night in the dark of the medication closet. Verde had fantasized many times about just such an encounter with this very nurse, and—sleep deprived in his secret work—can't recall if he lived or dreamed it. Had he hoped it into memory, a false one? Or hoped it into happening, a reality unrecorded?

Then, in one of his patient's dreams that he captured and reconfigured—this Rubenesque redhead with a heart condition, quite handsome, nearing forty—she and the doctor sleep together. And in this patient's dream, the dreamer—this redhead—knows she is party to Verde's cheating. She even feels

107

guilty about it. Yet the sex itself is quite convincing, quite satisfying. On the video screen in his office, Verde watches the dream in wonder. He can't believe how smooth he is in bed. He's masterful. Turns out it's gratifying, even inspiring, to watch footage of yourself succeeding at fictional intercourse.

That is, until someone like Nurse Tyne walks in on you watching this dream, which she doesn't know is a dream and would never believe is a dream. She quietly opens the door to Verde's office and watches over his shoulder.

Verde doesn't notice. Then soon enough does. *"Margaret! What are—"*

There's a knock on my study's door.

Shelley peeks her head in, the Monarch in a snuglee strapped to her chest. I am sweating at the brow, wired and tight. Little Hank in the snuglee smiles at me, as if he somehow knew. She tells me they're going to the park. I nod rapidly and tell her I love her. I love her and Henry very, very much. She laughs at that, plops a kiss at my temple, and steps off peppily toward the front door, a trail of bright Canadian energy seeming to shimmer in her wake.

Oh it didn't really shimmer. Or even seem to. I was just nervous and enthused.

But I remained in this state, getting little sleep—quite little—something like half of what I'm used to. When I wasn't watching the baby—and even when I was—I took notes for *Magnetic Resonance*. Voluminous notes. Considerable research. Hadn't felt this driven in years.

I read Freud, Jung on dreams, Foucault on the birth of the clinic. Even read Dr. Joseph P. Hornak on the basics of Nuclear Magnetic Resonance. That's what an MRI is, after all. They've dropped the "nuclear" to skirt the issue, to avoid all the dark associations. Nagasaki, Chernobyl. Who wants that? Who wants the word *nuclear* slicing through them, drawing up their shadow like a mushroom cloud?

I planned to start actual composing any day. Very soon. My

project now called *Nuclear Magnetic*. Working title only. Had a nice ring.

But the following Thursday we were thrown a curve, me and my note-taking process. I was stepping at a rapid clip through the lobby of the spinal cord clinic, sleep-deprived and buzzed on lattes—two consumed in quick succession—when I passed none other than Dr. Joe Garcia, guiding his girth through space. Proudly, patiently. Shoulders back, face placid, he noticed me coming, then smiled slightly and up-nodded.

I nodded back, seeing here not Dr. Joe but rather my own Dr. Verde.

I ought to change that, I was thinking. Verde doesn't need the goatee and glasses. Change to mustache only. Or a shaved head. Perhaps acne scars or a prominent mole. And what, I abruptly asked myself, was Dr. Joe doing here anyway? Shouldn't he be at the MRI Center, ordering a scan of someone's dreams?

Fresh from the elevator, twentieth floor, I found another doctor waiting for me—smaller make, larger stature—at least professionally. Dr. Allan Meng, the spinal cord specialist. He was standing behind the front desk, examining some materials in a manila folder. Shelley's Study, I knew, was a mere side project to him, if not an irritant. That was my guess anyway. He was a star in his field, internationally recognized. Shelley was a mere PhD candidate, a sort of nutritional Epidemiologist—unless she was an epidemiological Nutritionist, I was never sure—making the fairly predictable argument that men in wheelchairs with SCIs, T-spine or higher tend to gain weight around the belly. And me? Merely the husband of the perky Canadian who ran the study he had no time for.

Yet still, he always held up. The Meng manner always won you. Made you feel welcome every time. Light, attentive, receptive, generous. Unimposing or imposed upon. The Meng manner. Every time.

"Mr. Phil," he said warmly, lifting his eyes from the paperwork. "Precisely the man I'm looking for."

"Oh?"

He had a slight, lean body, five foot five-ish. At rest you'd have to call the posture rigid, a brace seeming to prop the back. But in motion he was rubbery, agile, even fluid. *At the ready* was the body's message, crossed somehow with *relax, take it easy.*

He raised his brow. "I see you guys still use the BMI?"

I nodded. Body Mass Index I knew well. It was easy to calculate. Weight divided by Height squared equals maybe you should lose a couple pounds.

Meng ran his fingers through the coal black crewcut. He stood uncomfortably close to me. "BMI's essentially the standard, I know." He gently jotted his head to the side. "But I'm suspicious of it. So many variables get tossed from the boat. Bone mass, muscularity, frame size, etcetera. You realize there are alternatives that perform just as well?"

I stared back in silence, a clinical dummy. Dr. Meng smiled.

"Just mention it to Shelley," he said and patted my back.

I noticed then what he'd been looking at. Walter's MRI. Dominick's x-ray. Again, icy darts up the spine. Meng noticed my noticing.

"So... Walter tells me you really fished for his story."

"You mean... that his wife shot him?" I went a bit red here. "I'd hardly—"

"Before they were married."

"Yes. I know."

Meng touched at my shoulder with his immaculate palm. Something warm there, also something forceful.

"Phil," he said, catching my eye. "I'm not going to scold you. I bet Shelley already ripped you a new one in this regard."

"Yes, sir, she did," I said, stiffening a bit. "Still burns."

He laughed lightly. "My more pressing concern, Philip, involves um..." He looked down at the file and took out the x-ray. "Dominick. Dominick Lafuse. Remember this guy?"

I nodded. Now he had me.

"Clear as day," I said. "He used to live across from us before he went to Iraq."

"Oh? That I didn't know."

"Yeah, he's our uh... an ex-neighbor."

"You're friends?"

"I wouldn't say that."

"Enemies then?"

I looked back quizzically, shaking my head. "Not at all."

"I ask because—again, I imagine you've taken considerable heat over this at home."

"A rain of fire. Believe me."

"Ha. Well..." Again that sensitive force at my shoulder, the powerful palm of Dr. Meng. "You know how an MRI works?"

I nodded. A soldier now. "Nuclear Magnetic Resonance Imaging. Know it in and out."

Again, that laugh. Light. Encouraging. "So you know there are certain placements of metal where a given spine cannot bear its power?"

I turned to him. "Please, doc. Let me explain. I had a very rough week when that kid got scheduled. Very—"

"Don't explain. I'm not scolding you. You didn't *try* to do this, right?" I shook my head no. "Shelley says you didn't even know you scheduled him." Again, I shook my head no, a meek little puppy. If I whimpered a little and wagged my tongue, I wouldn't be surprised. Then—gently, abruptly—the Meng manner went into lockdown.

"We have to weigh the factors of the circumstance, right?" That easy, soothing voice, so not-accusing. "Calibrate the balance?" He weighed abstractions with cupped palms, as if they were balanced on a scale. "Knowledge versus negligence." One cupped hand rose, the other sank. "Intent versus inattention." One rose further, the other sank more. "Outright mendacity versus clueless malpractice."

"Oh my." I woke a little there.

Meng shrugged. "Which weighs more? What's the heavier force guiding any behavior?"

I thought about it but had no answer.

"In your case," he said, wincing a little, not liking to have to say it. "Negligence. Extreme inattention. Were you a doctor, you'd be sued."

I laughed, a nervous burst.

"Not funny," he said, lips pursed. The Meng manner had its moods.

I nodded, went sober. Absolutely. Got you.

"Dangerous," he furthered. "Very." He looked me in the eye. "That's all I'll say." Another pat on the back. "You're good people. Let's keep the eyes open, okay?"

Then he glanced at his watch, asked about the baby, and turned on his heel with a bright little jump, heading off somewhere he was needed.

Well, it's Dr. Meng I'm in debt to now. His gentle scolding changed everything. Everything. In the play, our doctor is no longer large and Latino but rather slight and Chinese, which I might change to sturdy and Korean. Dr. Kang, we'll say. And this Dr. Kang—the former Dr. Verde—has learned to measure the strangest things. An added discovery in the second act, with all the attendant dramatic complications.

Kang captures and measures abstract forces no one knew you could stable. He starts with dreams, those recordable, palpable *things* from Act One. Kang captures hopes. Kang captures fears. Kang captures passions, ideological aggressions. Kang captures futures and pasts.

But no, I realized. Stop. That's too much. Too weird. Way too out there. Strays too far from the first inspiration. Which, I had to ask, was... what again?

There's a knock on the study's door. I'm wide-eyed, tingling all over. Shelley enters with Hank in the snuglee. Before she can get a word out, I tell her I love her. I love you both so much, I say. She's taken aback, laughs.

"Go okay today?"

"Just fine," I say.

"How was Dominick?"

"Dominick?"

She tilted her head, puzzled. "He was coming by. For his check?"

"No, I... just talked for a while with Dr. Kang."

"Dr. Kang?"

"Meng. Dr. Meng. Sorry."

Confused, she looked at me then let it go. She looked at her watch.

"I'm surprised Dominick didn't show."

"Yeah well... I've got a big juicy apology waiting for him when he does."

She nodded and looked at me, half-grinning. "Right."

She informed me they were off for a walk, then stepped away and muttered to herself, quizzically, "Dr. *Kang*?"

When they left, I returned to my notes. The project I would now call, tentatively, *Body Mass Index.* Or no—maybe one of those cheeky titles that can't make up its mind? A wink of a title with its telltale or, signifying smarty pants complexity, like *Body Mass Index, or... the Nuclear Magnetic Shadow Machine!*

I forced a grin as I wrote this, then realized I was weary of it. Must start actual composing, I typed, then italicized. *Must start actual composing.* I walked to the far front end of our apartment and stepped out on the porch for air.

A crisp cool October day. Near perfect. Orange, damp, firmly set. A bit bracing but pleasing, focusing. Harvest seemed in the air. With my hands on the stone slab railing, I took in a breath, deep and grateful, then looked down and saw them there, together.

Shelley with the Monarch in a snuglee, standing in front of our building, talking to our neighbor from across the hall—oh shit. Melanie. The fetching yet ghostly Melanie Trident. I took a half-step back and watched them.

They were quite a sight, actually, these pillars of serious womanhood, my pair. Look at them there, chatting it up. Beaming, vital, crisp, cool. Shelley's robust Canadian health next to Melanie's hipster chick vigor—complexion so pale it seemed to glow. Nutritious reality, subversive fantasy.

Again came another. That icy stabbing. Then a flash.

My neighbor hovering above me, my back on her carpet.

She gently placing her body onto mine, this most recent neighbor sliding down *into* me—that's how it felt, her into me—briefly uniting us weeks before.

That happened. Not long. Just a few faint strokes.

Deciding against it, I'd lifted her up and off me. And she was light enough though denser than expected. The lean ethereal body—so alluring of line and curve—that in motion, while walking, seemed to hover or float but felt so substantial and warm up against you. Just that once. Just that.

Until it ... happened again. And had it? Again? Shit. Shit. No it hadn't. Not completely. But I keep forgetting or denying what had. That other time, a week or two later. Our second go across the hall—longer, lighter, maybe fuller, yet formally not in full. A slightly different shade of transgression. Also, in its way, a failure. Unless it was a success. Jesus. That also happened. But forget that, forget it, forget forget.

On the sidewalk, Shelley leaned over and hugged her. A friendly kiss. Melanie returned the favor, kissing Shelley's cheek, then the baby's. This word whipped to mind—a bit flamboyantly, I thought—*Judas.* But who did I mean?

After Shelley left and they waved goodbye, Melanie turned and looked up and saw me. Together, we let the moment hang. Neither said anything. I doubt she felt guilt exactly. I knew her coupling with Hugo was "open." All the same, she knew ours was closed.

Wasn't her fault, of course. Or not only. Obviously. Still, it was weird to see her down there. We'd avoided each other for weeks—at least I had—behind front doors only feet away.

She semi-smiled. I nodded back. Then I coughed, waved and stepped inside, perhaps a bit abruptly.

Back in the study, I opened my file, Notes for A Play, and made some quick additions. But as I looked again over my notes, fifty-seven pages, single-spaced, I had a horrible sinking feeling. Had to face this thing. My actual life. I might not ever begin composing. Had I killed the contest with preparation? Or did I need to atone before it began?

◈

Days later, a Saturday, Shelley off with the baby, I made my way to the corner store. It was late October but a gorgeous day. High of seventy, seventy-one. The air of false summer sneaking under the radar, trying to trick us the cold hadn't come. On the corner I saw two familiar figures, one standing, the other in his chair. Our neighbor Melanie held a can of La Croix, our ex-neighbor Dominick a burning cigarette. His thin earphones circled his neck. Melanie's satchel circled her torso.

They were discussing something, charming each other.

Melanie was talking—ebullient, breezy—and Dominick was nodding yes yes I agree. As I approached, each glanced over and nodded, though neither stopped conversing.

"Exactly," said Dominick, turning back to her. "Exactly. Music is changing so fast, who knows what we'll have ten years from now. We don't even know if hip-hop's the future of it. That could die too."

"Maybe," she said. "But I doubt it."

"Some whole new creature, right?" he said. He took a drag, grinned.

"Slouching toward Bethlehem?" she asked.

He shook his head no. "Fuck Bethlehem. Slouching towards the internet."

"Right. You're right."

Together, they laughed. I stood there waiting, watching them.

Now... Melanie is a music writer, that's what she does— but Dominick? I blushed at my surprise. The easy references, sophisticated claims. This twenty-three-year-old who'd once lived across from us, discussing the culture like a pro? And *with* the pro I'd—face it—slept with? At last, Melanie turned to me.

"Hello Philip," she said, at that moment, far too relaxed for my taste. "You know Dominick?"

"He knows me," said Dominick.

She looked at her watch and muttered oh my god. "Don't think I'm running away from you," she said, looking up. "I sincerely have to go. I have a uh..." She looked at her watch. "A phone interview. Like, in two minutes." We stared at each other. "But..." She shook her head, then leaned over and whispered in my ear, "It would have been nice, but I want no secrets. If Shelley were on board, I would be too. So would Hugo." She pulled back and said out loud, a bit shockingly, "But I don't think she's one of us."

She nodded ruefully, waved goodbye, and glided forth through the odd October warmth with that hovering thing she pulled off somehow.

We watched her leave. To my side, Dominick said, "She is fine."

"Yes. Yes, she is."

He chuckled. "I know you want that shit."

"Maybe I do." I nodded again, then held up my ring finger. "Can't."

Dominick shrugged. A slight tilt of the head, slight smile.

"Of course you *can*." He shrugged. "But you shouldn't. Or whatever. I wouldn't judge you. I think your wife's fine too, she is. But... for my tastes?"

We watched her hover off, blocks away now. Dominick went *wooo*, then tapped at his wheelchair with a biker-gloved palm.

"Just be glad you can't in the way you can't."

I looked down at an angle. Paralysis from the waist down. I suppose I hadn't quite acknowledged all that meant. And is that what it meant?

"If I could?" His eyes slid up to mine, locked in. "I'd take that shit home this very afternoon." He watched her go, shaking his head, as if recalling a future he'd never get to see.

I laughed. "You sound smitten."

He gave a "ha" and waited. "Like it matters." He coughed as we watched her turn the corner. "You smoke?" he asked.

"Sorry. Don't."

"I need some." He raised his brow, looked to the store. "You going in?"

I nodded. "I'll get 'em. What you smoke?"

But there in the store, I got that sinking feeling, tied to what came before it like attachable rope ladder, down to hell. Had to apologize on so many fronts. To start, right here, with Dominick. Though apologize seemed too light a word. So fraught with status and basic white guilt. Though—face it—he'd lost nearly all. Quite a bit at any rate. He'd been sent abroad to lose damn near all. Yet this was the first I'd witnessed any bitterness. He was chipper, plucky—remarkably so—in the face of having been floored by the war.

So maybe I didn't have it in me. Maybe I decided against it. An apology about an MRI appointment—what never happened—seemed insulting in the face of what had.

I bought him his Parliaments and we shared goodbyes. He rolled west, I south.

Later, Shelley and the baby and I picnicked in the park. Absolutely gorgeous day. The Monarch's starting to form words too. Language production! Today he said the word 'corndog'! Swear to god. I think he said 'corndog'. My one-year-old son!

Much later that night, deep deep into it after multiple glasses of pricey red wine and vigorous congress with my life-betrothed, I dreamt serenely, vividly, of an interwoven world, a sort of webbed orb you'd have to call a body—a planet or cell or cellular culture—capping this intricate film of a dream. A full-length movie far better than my play. Far, far superior. Some of the same characters, yes, but mostly just their inspirations.

Dr. Joe was there. Walter Jorgenson. Dr. Meng. Shelley. Dominick. Me. The Monarch. Melanie, of course. Plus a nurse from the clinic you haven't formally met, a Rubenesque redhead approaching forty who never fails to smile at me.

But now I sat awake, looking at my notes in the chair by the table in our bedroom. The black funnel nightlamp was on, angled down. I had my pen ready and was trying to remember it. Like, the first two and a half hours of it. But I could only remember the ending. And that was just the very *end*. It was so good. So much better than what I had.

I looked over at Shelley on the queen size, naked save for her red hood and cape. We role-played all the time now. Just for kicks. Wasn't my cup of tea at first, but recently I'd come to crave it. I watch her snore into the funnel of her hood. I fish for my dream.

Never been a screenwriter, but swear to god—it was great. So odd and intricate. I had to retrieve it.

I was clenching my eyes, trying to see it, what came before the dream ended, before we all were one and swam like a cell in the bloodstream of a giant. There were individuals, separate but together. There was intrigue, deceit, poetry, mystery.

I opened my eyes to see Shelley snoring. She was out cold and it wasn't coming.

The dream was nearly gone. I pressed pen to clipboard.

Must start actual composing, I wrote, then read, then underlined, <u>Must start actual composing</u>!

I heard something out in the living room proper. Faint, familiar, tantalizing. I stepped swiftly from our bedroom and walked the fifteen feet through the sort of second living room—past the Monarch's crib—and soon enough I was in the more dominant room, where I planted myself beneath the heating vent, not yet seasonally obligated.

The god Eros had occupied our vent before, but this was the first I'd heard the new neighbors. And now—yes—I recognized that. Or rather, her. Yes I did. I recalled that voice in that particular trance. Or something a whole lot like it. A throaty purring, slowly letting go.

I stood there and listened to Melanie, to Hugo—part turned-on, part-tainted, part-infected—knowing somehow, in that icky instant, that actual composing had already come.

THE FOLDS OF HISTORY

I showed one of those kids across the street my secret trick with a twenty. It was Adam's stunt actually. He taught me months before. Some kid at the copy shop had done it for him and I thought I'd pass on the favor. Crease the back of your bill into itself via this intricate, sinister fold, three panels inward-creased, and you'll see the frozen image of the towers collapsing, the billow of smoke, the familiar caving in, as if 9/11 had been there all along. It's a mere accident of the shadows and ink. I put no stock in it meaning-wise. But still, the kid was as amazed as I had been. Maybe even spooked a little.

Pretty cold out that day, colder than you'd guess for early November, and the little league gangbangers—at least on our street—seemed to have gone into hibernation. Then I saw this kid, about thirty feet off, interfacing with a guy I didn't recognize. There at the fore of the gangway, directly across from our place, exchanging exchangables, whatever they may be—this kid I half-knew and some blade-skinny black dude in a fur-ry-collared corduroy coat. Knotted brow, thick bottled glasses. How old is this guy? The kid, I knew, was no more than fourteen. Likely thirteen. This guy—I saw as we neared—was nearly thirty.

He trailed away with a furtive glance back as I moved with the stroller toward the kid. Sometimes I'd do this, stroll on the other side of the street. To see it from their side, their location, opposite our stone and brick second floor porch where I spent many evenings watching. This kid was a part of that scene. And something of an emerging kingpin, it seemed. Thirteen, fourteen, fairly hefty, with a premature poise that made him seem far older. Even thinner. In warmer seasons, clad nearly always in an oversized Bulls jersey that hung to his knees—Gordon's, I believe—here in a blue bubbled winter coat and incongruous NY Giants cap.

We approached. He up-nodded.

"Hey there," I said.

"Hey," he replied, then leaned down for a peek in the stroller. We'd met this way a few times before. We were barely acquaintances, but I had watched him for years. And he'd not watched, but noted me. Each of us regarded the other faintly, with predictable doses of neighborly suspicion. He leaned in and patted Henry on the knee.

"How you doing, little man?"

With some poise of his own, Henry looked up at him. He scrunched up his shoulders, as if to say "cold." The big kid laughed and held out his arms, one hand clutching a bill.

"I know," he said. "What happened out here?"

It slid from his fingers and hovered to the sidewalk, landing softly at my feet. He started to go but I'd already gone.

"I got it."

When I picked it up, we had a moment of weirdness. A very slight tension in the kid's face, the briefest suggestion of paling, perhaps the realization I'd guessed the bill's source—probably just a nickel bag of weed or whatever. And holding the twenty in that flash of oddness, trying to lighten things up, I surprised myself by saying, "You ever see the 9/11 thing?"

The kid halted. "What now?"

"Look," I said, and stepped back to fold the bill. "I can show you a trick that'll blow your mind."

It was an odd whim, my showing him this, though not entirely random. I'd been thinking a lot about Adam around then, and a few days before had remembered his trick. I'd even tried the fold already, to see if I recalled it. So it came quick—I was in practice—and again, there she was, the twin towers explosion, our overplayed history, so familiar, frozen there in his dirty money in a stunning bloom of green and black.

His eyes popped. For a second he was speechless.

"Nice, huh?" I handed back the bill.

He took it, grinning, then looked up with slight suspicion. "That's crazy."

"I know," I said. "I agree."

He shook his head. I nodded goodbye. Thought I'd just leave it at that.

"You have a good one," I said.

As we rolled off, Henry said softly, "bye bye."

The husky kid only muttered in reply, staring down at his still-folded twenty.

I strolled ahead into the clear sharp cold, passing what appeared to be another customer. A frizzed-out, aimless white dude, clearly jonesing. His torn-up Member's Only was too light, still Septembery, and he moved with a tight nervy paranoid hop. Business appeared to be booming over here, even in the premature winter.

But no need to harp on that, the illicit market or moods on my street. I tell you this, rather, because of what came later, and how it linked with the vanishing of Adam, who I'd sort of been panging for right around then. He was hardy conversation and liked his drink and I missed sharing both with him. Pretty badly, in fact. And a few days after this—a Wednesday, I believe—Adam in a way came back to me.

It was mid-afternoon, the Monarch napping, when the phone rang, breaking the silence. Caller ID coldly informed me that this was, in fact, the police. I held the receiver and stared at the tiny screen. CPD? Ring... Ring... Ring—

"Hello?"

"May I speak to, uh, Philip Palliard?"

"That's me."

"Hello Mr. Palliard. This is Detective Povich from Ward Thirteen. I'm calling in regards to a stolen Dodge Dart belonging to, uh... Adam Swivchek."

"Adam's Dart?" My heart ticked a half-beat faster.

"Yes, sir. We've retrieved the vehicle. Located it this morning on the far west side. The CD player's gone but it's otherwise intact, windshield wipers and all."

"Oh my god. That's... amazing."

The detective cleared his throat, steady, indifferent. "Amazing can happen, Philip, believe me. Seen it a bunch of times. This wasn't it. We weren't trying to find Swivchek's vehicle. The Dart, you could say, came to us."

"I see. And so um... how did it—"

"Our initial report shows you were in the vehicle when it was stolen? Driving it?"

I waited on that one. Did not expect it.

"Yes," I said. "Yes I was. Well, not precisely driving, but... Officer, that was August. While ago. I was borrowing his car and... well—"

"You got jacked in your own parking lot. I understand that. Listen." He waited, then took a bite of something and chewed on it quietly, methodically. He swallowed. "Your buddy Swivchek is nowhere to be found."

"I know, I know." I waited, breathing into the phone. "He's been gone a while. Since around then, actually. He, uh, disappeared."

"Disappeared?" said Povich, and took another bite. "In what way disappeared?"

"Well, he didn't—I mean... he moved out. Left willfully. Disappeared on his own, if that makes sense. Took his furniture and all his stuff but never even—"

"This happened just after the car was stolen?"

"About a week after."

The detective swallowed, then took another bite, chewed, ruminated.

"Listen, Philip," he said, with that seasoned indifference. "We're gonna need you to come down here."

"Oh?" The plastic phone seemed to lighten—even float—in the nook between my chin and shoulder. "Right now?"

"If you can."

A plaintive "Daaaaa-dy" rose from the crib near the front end of our apartment. Feather-phone at my shoulder, I gave Povich my affirmative, then hung up and walked in silence toward the child. They were having me in for questioning. How odd. But also—great! Adventure! Out of the house to Ward Thirteen!

"Daaaaa-da."

Might even prove redemptive. Official questions from the bona fide Law regarding the crime, that, for a while there, had gutted my mind, taken it captive.

"Daaaaa-da."

I lifted Henry up to my shoulder and walked back through the living room, where I saw, I swear, in the mirror there—what other word worked but—apparition. A flash. Half a second. The nervy wan face of the guy who'd mugged me in the parking lot that August. First my money, then the car. Toxic memory, local terror, staring out from the mirror.

Now I'm not really one for apparition-seeing. Just a split second. Half a half a second. Noticed the source right off. A trick of the afternoon light plus its shadow from a hooded sweatshirt in a dark corner, hanging where a column of sinister sunshine had stretched to fill its void—but still. It killed. Totally stilled me. Henry even turned to look.

Adam would be entertained, I know it. The cops calling, his car retrieved. Even my bush league hallucinations of persecution by pistol. He'd call the whole of it a gift, what the doctor ordered—adventure, adventure, adventure.

In the police station at Ward Thirteen, Henry on my lap, I

waited in a hard plastic chair. We sat, unattended, just off from their desks, as two detectives—one hefty and sloppily mustached, the other lean and pristinely shaven—did their best to ignore us. The institutional fluorescent lighting hummed above us. We sat in silence. So far, adventure was far from the picture.

Something came, though. It really did. Not quite adventure, just the slightest thrill, when this other one entered the office, some cop or detective with nothing to do. Medium beefy in a Black Hawks cap, the back half of a glorious mullet riding his neck like a built-in cape. Eyes excited, holding a bill—a twenty—he approached the younger more well-coiffed one.

"Here. You gotta see this," he said, and then started doing it. Adam's fold! Tiny daggers shot through my veins, a tingling from the outside in. My god. The 9/11 crease must be sweeping the nation. The mullet in the Hawks cap showed it to his cleaner-seeming colleague.

"Jesus Christ," said the latter, staring at the image webbed in the bill. "How'd you do that?"

"My kid showed me last night."

The clean one leaned across his desk. "Hey Marty, look at that."

The hefty detective with the droopy mustache examined it closely, chin up, mouth slightly agape.

"God," he said. "What *is* this shit? Like—" He waited a beat. "Origami of the Masons?"

Both his colleagues laughed, but especially the clean one. The cleaner and younger one busted a gut.

"Ha! Yes. Nice," he said, taking back the twenty. "That's good." He examined the bill. "Origami of the Masons." Then—weirdly, finally—he looked up at me as if he'd just noticed. "Can we help you?"

Wasn't much of anything, really. So they knew the secret fold. Just another network of need and neglect bubbling up its elusive signs, apparitions in other sorts of mirrors—U.S. currencies, private show and tells. But I couldn't help it—seemed foreboding somehow. I had fleeting notions of more cosmic-like forces, networks abroad, reminding me of god knew what.

That's when I started thinking Adam was in trouble.

The interrogation room, if that's what it was, didn't ease my fears. An airtight bleakly carpeted square with a blackened one-way window to the side. On the dingy yellow walls hung only a calendar, strangely still at July. A cheesy pin-up girl—fake-titted, blonde, bikini-clad, toothy—stared across the empty room. Her on one side, while on the other hung a small crucifix, bearing a tiny bronze crucified Christ. This speck of church they snuck in the state. As if sex and suffering were facing off. Having a staring contest. Perhaps even flirting.

My child was off to the side with big Povich, together there, with toys. Meanwhile, I sat in yet another plastic chair, sharper-feeling somehow, before a thin Formica table. The clean, young one, who'd since introduced himself as detective Kozlowe, kept asking me questions about the previous summer, specifically regarding getting jacked behind our building while sitting in Adam's idling Dodge Dart. Nothing too pushy. Just the basic what happeneds? Meanwhile, Povich played with my son to the side, digging in the Matchbox set I'd brought.

The interrogation itself was short-lived, essentially benevolent, just minutes, but I tell you—nearly soiled myself. Sleeves were rolled up on the long arm of the Law. With official-looking files, clipboards on tables. What was up? Was I a suspect?

Kozlowe started getting serious, bent over the table with his game face on. Just checking, I know now, that my story was legit, that Adam and I hadn't staged the Dart's theft to scam the insurance folk and split the booty. This is done a fair bit, Povich later explained, just after apologizing. Questions like theirs in situations like this were reflex, routine, and I shouldn't take offense. Besides, the situation had some shady complexities only attributable to chance, right?

Big Povich had been listening. And when he noticed new fervor in Kozlowe's voice, he lifted his gaze disapprovingly.

"That's enough, Jerry," he said and stood. "Here."

Povich handed my son to Kozlowe, who looked irritated, then pretty soon taken. He goo-gooed and bobbed, walked Hank around the room, grinning here, laughing there, then stopped at the calendar and gazed at the blonde. Povich unfolded a Reuben from its wrap. He took a bite, smiling, and gestured with the sandwich.

"Look at this guy," he said. "Real expert in child development."

I laughed. Thank god I'd brought Henry. Should you be interrogated, I'd suggest you take a baby. But then it got weird. Povich swallowed.

"You should know. When we uh..." He cleared away some sauce from the corner of his mouth. "When we found Swivchek's car, there was a body in it."

My eyes popped. "A body?"

"That's right." The detective took another bite.

"A uh... dead body?"

"That's how they usually come." Povich paused. "Shot twice at the base of the brain. Execution style."

"Oh my god, that's... it's not *Adam*?" My breath went tight. Povich coughed and looked down at the file.

"Is Adam a five-foot-nine Latino male with a shaved head and a lip beard?"

"Um... no. He is not."

"Then Adam doesn't have a bullet in his brain." A heavy pause. He'd noticed the lapse in his logic. "That is, as far as we know." He cleared his throat. "Not this bullet anyway."

I nodded, grateful, relief rising through me. Povich sat, looking down at the file, then took another bite of his Reuben.

I thought about it then, and started taking guesses, and shouldn't have, but did.

"You know, that sounds like—what'd you say? A Latino male with a shaved head?"

"Shaved head and a lip beard. Five-foot-nine."

"Jesus, that—" Not necessarily meaning to, I looked up at the tiny crucifix. "That sounds like the guy who mugged me."

"Oh?" Povich looked down at the file again, holding the Reuben at a strange remove.

"Wait." Kozlowe here, off to the side, smoothly shaven and ultra-alert, carrying my baffled son. "That description fits the perpetrator?"

Povich nodded, then took another bite. Specks of crumb hung in his mustache. "Apparently," he said, chewing. "But that description's not all that descriptive."

"Sure it is," said Kozlowe, alive to it, and handed Hank back to Povich. Kozlowe turned to me, game face back on. "Think you'd recognize this guy if we showed you a picture?"

"Jerry, come now."

Jerry unfolded his palms for Povich.

"What?" he said. "This is SOP. Or it oughta be. Let's do a photo array."

Povich sighed with my son on his knee. "I hate those. They're a bitch."

"Ah! Hardly. Takes twenty minutes tops." Kozlowe circled the table and patted my shoulder. "You got some time, right?"

A photo array lineup, Povich later explained, typically involves five photos of similar-seeming faces, one of course the presumed perpetrator. The problem here was Kozlowe only found two extra, one of whom had no lip beard. Essentially it was down to one extra face. And the other—with lip beard— had darker skin than I remembered. Thus down to one, and not so scientifically.

The remaining face—who really was the guy, they told me later, found dead in Adam's Dart—rang a bell, but only a faint one. He did look a fair bit like my summer's carjacker. Wiry and lean. The dull, desperate eyes. Same coloring. Same angle to the skull and temple. Young guy, just past twenty. But the photo—from a driver's license, Kozlowe'd explained—was smudged-seeming, a tiny bit off, sorta muddy. Plus the guy in the license seemed relaxed, at peace, which confused the memory of edgy, tense, murderous. My mind wasn't backing me up. When given a line-up, I had a habit, it seemed, of denying what was asked for.

"That the guy?" asked Kozlowe.

I held little Hank on my lap—fidgety, getting restless.

"I..." It just wasn't right. "I honestly couldn't say."

"But this guy resembles him?"

"Sure he does, but I just... "

"Couldn't be certain?" said Povich, standing to the side now, arms crossed and Reuben-free.

"No." I turned to him. "Not certain. Certainly not."

Povich nodded. "There you go, Jerry. Our shadow of a doubt. And quite a long one at that."

"You can't say *that*," said Kozlowe, irked at the misfire. "'Shadow of a doubt' is for juries. Juries deciding to convict or not. And I really don't... would you say your, uh, shadow of doubt was *long*?"

I shrugged, wincing. "Yeah. I guess I would."

Povich laughed loudly, then motioned to me. "Come on. Let's close down the show."

In his office, detective Povich loosened up. Here's where he apologized and explained the situation. Here's where he confessed that a photo line-up should technically present five photos, not three. He shrugged—yet unfazed—and opened his desk drawer, extracting a bite-size Snickers.

"My partner shouldn't have started all that," he said, tearing the wrapper. "Waste of time."

"Yeah." I shrugged. "Well, he thought he had his man."

"Ah—" Pooh-poohing the notion, taking a bite of the bite-size. "He thought he had an easy way to close the case." He chewed, shaking his head, gazing through the window in his door. "He's young. You know? A little lazy. Unique combination of lazy and overzealous. But all the same—that said—you're sure it's not him?"

He slid the photo from the manila folder and pushed the dead across his desk. Jesus. Just a kid.

"It wouldn't be conclusive. I'm sorry."

He grimaced. "Naw. Don't be sorry. It's a good thing." He took back the photo. "We're in Ward Thirteen, not Guantanamo Bay. Shadows of a doubt aren't welcome here."

"Good. Good. I'm glad for that."

"Anyway, it's highly unlikely," he said. "Someone steals a car, they don't drive it around. It's no trophy. You sell it for parts or..." He stopped himself, staring down at the photo. He popped in the last of the Snickers. "Look at this guy," he said, chewing. "Looks like a buddy of my kid's."

"Yeah, well... he's certainly young enough."

Povich nodded, swallowed. "A kid on the track team. Sprinter. Looks just like him." He looked up and caught my eye. "My kid's a shotputter."

"Oh yeah? Nice. What grade's he in?"

"She. Sorry—my daughter."

He turned the framed photo on his desk so I could see.

"Junior," he said. "Lane Tech."

Big girl here, nice smile. Steady, formidable, black shiny hair. Clearly they shared a gene pool. And she was cute in this eternal cherubic way that somehow unveiled the cuteness in her father, heretofore hidden by a Walrusy mustache and sandwiches and candy and gruffness.

"She's pretty," I said.

"Yeah?" He swiveled the picture back around. "She is, isn't she?" He thoughtfully rubbed at his mustache. "Such a good girl. Really is. Smart, funny. Top notch shotputter. She keeps working at it, she could be world class."

"Wow," I said, trying my best. "I bet that's exciting."

"Philip, it truly is." He looked over at Henry, napping in the corner. "You know, I felt your kid's grip. He's real strong for a one year old. He could shotput one day too." He cleared his throat and leaned back in his chair, hands clasped behind his head. "You should consider it. It's a challenging sport. Under-recognized."

I nodded, obligatory. "Yeah. We will. Definitely."

Povich grinned.

"Enough future family counseling," he said, leaning back further. "Who am I to say what your kid's called to be? His interests or whatever?" He leaned back down toward the desk. "What color is your parachute? My old man used to say pitch *black*. Funeral black with holes in the fabric. Ha!" He stared at his desk, at the manila folder. "Dead now. The old man."

"Oh. I'm... I'm sorry to—"

"I'm curious, Philip." He crinkled his eyes here. Let the interruption hang. "What about your buddy Swivchek?" He shrugged. "Where'd he go?"

This shift to Adam was abrupt. He had me. I shrugged in turn, shaking my head. "I wish I knew."

"Mexico?"

"I have no—" I stared at him. "What makes you say that?"

"You said something about Mexico to Jerry in the room back there."

"Oh." I remembered I had. "Yeah well, Adam's wife is from Mexico. She left him. Split town with their son for Michoacan. Right before his car got stolen."

"So I heard," he said. "Swivchek's a real swinger, huh? Got caught with some honey on the side?"

I felt myself go hot behind the ears. Had I said that much? I nodded reluctantly, bobbing my head side to side. "Yeah, he..."

"I tell you what I think," said Povich, lowering his voice, leaning into his desk. "And I speak to you absent of professional capacity. As a fellow human being. A curious human." He waited, maintaining eye contact. "My guess is Swivchek's gone for his son. He sounds arrogant, this one, a true asshole, but even guys like this feel the draw of their child. I mean, he was there as a dad, right?"

Again, my reluctant nod, a side-to-side hedging.

"He wasn't deadbeat?"

"No, no. Absolutely not."

Povich leaned back, shaking his head. "Deadbeat dads. They're the ones I can't fathom. Can't stand your spouse? Fine. So be it! Split up then. Work something out. But be there *for the kid*. That's the connection that cannot be cut, even if you try to sever it. Otherwise, they end up well—here, you know?" He tapped at the folder containing the dead. "Face down in a stolen car with their DNA on the dashboard."

I grimaced, nodding directly now, steadily. From the corner, Henry woke. He cried, calling daddy. As I rose and moved toward him, Povich grinned widely.

"Solid kid," he said. "Strong lungs." He nodded at Henry.

"Think about the shotput," he said as I sat again, the boy at my shoulder. "Or at least track and field." He pointed, grinning. "It'll keep that little tank off the streets."

Povich reached across his desk. We shook hands. They'd be holding the vehicle for forensic evidence. For both crimes, he told me—theft in August, murder in November. If Adam returned or made contact—whatever—I should have him call their offices immediately.

The mullet in the Hawks cap opened Povich's door. He smiled with mischief in his eyes.

"Marty," he said. "Come here. You gotta see this."

Povich sighed and stood. I followed to where I left the stroller. As we moved from his office, I noted the three of them there—Kozlowe seated, Povich and Officer Mullet standing behind him. Kozlowe was playing a video game on his computer, where crass icons of enemy combatants—hooded, arms outward, naked in a row—danced the CanCan for cartoon prison guards, who in turn took sniper shots at their periodically exposed gonads.

The cops looked gleeful, if guiltily so. Save for Povich—god bless him—who was still as stone, arms tightly crossed. Speechless. Perhaps appalled.

A few days later, the air had warmed up—unseasonably warm for November, in fact. That illusory Shangri La that can fall a few weeks before Thanksgiving. This was Saturday morning—Shelley and the baby off at the park, me taking my time in the bathroom, reading—when the buzzer rang.

When I finally got downstairs, there was a package waiting. A thin brown envelope. No return address, but I recognized the handwriting. Plus an inky stamp across the rumpled brown paper indicating origins south of the border.

I had the fleeting sense he was watching right then. Like Adam was near, but I couldn't see him. Hiding behind someone's curtains or blinds. Behind a tree, stop sign, car or van.

"Hey!" I asked the air, then shouted, "Adam!"

From across the street, the big kid looked over, curious. He was loitering at the fore of the gangway, wearing his knee-length Bulls jersey. This time, he had a partner with him, some skinny kid about his age with a buzz-cut and brightly hued Puerto Rican flag shirt. The big kid up-nodded. I up-nodded back, cracking open the package.

I tilted the envelope, reaching in, and found two photos. Polaroids. Adam had done this to me before. No explanations, just raw materials. Bits of him.

In this case, the Polaroids—nothing more. The first was a photo of Adam and his three-year-old on a streetcorner, eating chunks of mango. They both had ornery grins on, some joke they'd just exchanged, on a curb by a cobblestone street, the knobby legs of a donkey or goat off to the side in the background. So he *had* gone. For Jorge! This must be them right then. I flipped it over, saw Adam's loopy scrawl, confirming it.

Michoacan!

I slid this one behind the other he'd sent, which stopped me cold. I'd forgotten all about it. Pictured here were Adam and me, Shelley and Henry at the ballpark that past summer. Seated along the first base line, near shallow right field. Excellent seats—Adam's score. And I wondered who had taken this picture. No one else came with us. Adam left his family at home and invited ours instead—what we didn't know until we got there. We sat puzzled at first, looking around for Maribel and Jorge. Adam had some explanation, but still, it seemed bizarre. Chilled us a bit actually.

In the photo, Adam looks lit. We all do. Even Hank looks like he's had a few. Together there only four months before, a muggy, softly lit night in July. A different time entirely. The last hours of a silvery era. Before it cracked open like a shiny plastic egg to the toxic surprise inside. Hidden there all along, I guess. Collapse, car theft, failure of family. Everyone leaving. Adam pursuing. Unless he was back—right there, right then—playing grabass with a friend he'd left for dead. Watching from around a corner? Snickering?

I almost shouted his name again. Then someone spoke.

"Hey mister." It was the hefty kid from across the street, standing before me with his skinny pal. "Do that thing," he said. "With the money." He held out a twenty. "You know—9/11."

At first, I felt bad about it, twisting catastrophe into schoolboy show and tell, flipping it around like a paper football for the stoners in study hall, but then—I don't know—I just did it. The towers collapsed in his folded bill, this obvious icon of the end of an era—another, far darker—a split second stake in the fold of history. The first my generation—at least in America—had seen but never saw coming.

Well, I'll tell you, the kids were mesmerized. That look of wonder on their faces alone—that wow—it made my day. Someone at the Treasury ought to get on this. I put no stock in it, but many will. Word spreads too fast, or far, or whatever. They'll have to print new bills.

THE AX RISETH

As suggested by many, we planned a date. This thing where overly occupied couples formally schedule a date together. Quality time is the phrase you hear. And our first order of quality-time business was discussion of my new play—a second draft of the first act—*Do Your Part for the War on Terror*, which I'd given Shelley to read.

She sat across from me at the kitchen table, doing that thing where she makes me wait, where I've asked her what she thinks and she smiles or not and thinks about it, ponders it, the dead air rising and expanding around us. She was pensive like this a while, then, as if coming to, bit at a lip and said, "I don't know, Philip. I mean... with this one? I honestly don't know." She lightly wagged the manuscript at me, a weary gesture. "The point of the thing just seems too *easy*. At least what you've got here. I mean, the metaphor of it? If—" She waved a hand before her. "If that's even the right word. I'm..." She seemed to be pointedly avoiding my eyes, which was strange of her, not her at all. "I don't know. It just seems quite a *stretch*. The whole thing. The point, the conflict, the metaphor, whatever. And all of it in rather obviously self-serving ways."

"Self-serving?" I said, stung, brow up. "Really?"

She nodded firmly, twice. "Yes. Really." She looked off to the side, mouth hanging open, smiling slightly, as if amazed. "I mean, Philip, you're comparing—this is what you're doing, right?—you're comparing basic male domestic panic to the terror in the *war* on terror."

"No no no." I hunched up my shoulders. "That's not fair. That's simplistic. You're reducing it to something I never, ever intended—"

"It's a seriously twisted thing, Philip." She eyed me now, casting her whammy. "That comparison is vain. Totally narcissistic. But it's also like... in a political or social way—what's the word?" She reached for it. "Complacent?"

I shrugged. She shrugged back, though more tightly.

"It's totally complacent."

"Jesus," I said, punctured and deflating. "You don't have to be so forward about it. God."

"Don't be sensitive."

"I'll try."

She sighed with some impatience. "Philip, it's just... I can't tell what you're trying to *say*." Her lower jaw jut out to the side, a palsied, negative hunger. "I mean—" And again with that slightly amazed smile. "It's so obviously about *us*."

"Obviously?" I said. "You think it's obvious?"

"Philip." She stared at me, through me. "The protagonist is a stay-at-home father of Swiss-French descent whose Canadian wife runs a research study."

"Sure," I said with a quick tight shrug. "That doesn't make it us."

"Her study is at a clinic for spinal cord injuries."

"So?"

She shook her head, hunched up her shoulders. "And what's all this stuff about..." Her mouth hung open. "MRIs? And Magnetic Resonance? And dreams and dream machines and spying on people?" A baffled smile to herself. "Like somehow seeing inside people's *minds*."

"Really?" I said, surprised. "That didn't work for you?"

Weary, she sighed. "That's not what I mean." She flipped through the pages of the manuscript, looking for something specific. "There's that one scene where our protagonist, Murray—you, it's hard not to see it that way—where he contemplates an act of terrorism. We're not exactly sure why. Maybe he resents something about the smug comfort of the American way. Maybe he resents his role as the American house-husband. But, and here's the kicker, Murray chooses, as a healthy alternative to bombing a bank or a mall, instead, he sleeps around on his wife."

"Honey." I shook my head repeatedly. "That's not us. That's not *me*."

"You're sure?"

"Sure I'm sure."

Her mouth hung open. Still baffled. "And then... all that weird shit with the insurgency, with the coming revolt of the unemployed and homebound, with Murray—you—as the star soldier! And all that strange stuff with Bin Laden in league with the Gangster Disciples, Century 21 Realty allied with the Latin Kings? It's just..."

"You didn't like that? That's satire, Shelley."

She gave me a weary, withering look.

"Philip." She looked away. "Are you implying that being married to me and acting as the primary caretaker for your son..." She tapped at the manuscript, then turned to me. "This is, this being-hemmed-in feeling, this sort of domestic *sentence* you're serving, this is an equal terror to the terror of, say, the Taliban? Or Al Qaeda? Or even Guantanamo Bay?"

"No!" I said. "No no no. Honey, that's crazy. That's *insane*. You're missing the point, all these themes about—" I was pretty worked up. I counted them off on my fingers. "The presumed terror abroad and the obvious terror at home and poverty and gangbangers and gentrification and..." I was exasperated. I shook my head tightly. "Jesus, it's just... *way* more complicated than that."

"Complicated?" she echoed.

I nod-shrugged.

She took a sip of wine. "Or is complex a better word?"

"Yes," I said, though I didn't like her tone. "One of those."

"You," she said, crossing her arms. "You are complex."

"Oh?"

She nodded slowly, the bitterness in her eyes sliding toward sadness.

"Philip." She shook her head to herself. "*Why* would you give me this to read? With this character who seems so much like you? Who resents his life and bombs banks and cheats on his super-controlling wife?"

"I wanted feedback. Jesus."

She shook her head. "You are difficult to fathom."

"Shelley, please. What are you—"

"I know, Philip."

"You know?"

She nodded. Slowly, deliberately. "I know all about it. It's not a secret anymore."

There was a moment of confusion but I understood. She'd been leading up to it but I'd refused to hear. Melanie. She knew about Melanie and me. How we'd spent a little time together. I should have copped to the trouble right then, white flagged it and faced it head on, but something mulish in me wouldn't give.

"Shelley," I said. "Just tell me."

"Don't make me do this."

Without thinking, I lifted the package I'd brought—a gift regarding our in-house "date," this kinky outfit wrapped in plastic from our local Erotic Warehouse. I lifted it absentmindedly, gesturing, shrugging. "Shelley, I'm at a loss." I squeezed it like an accordion or squishy pillow. "Just tell me—"

"What's that?"

She stared. It was a sexy girl-devil outfit with a photo of a girl-devil model on the front. Horns and cape and suggestive toy trident; inferno-red fishnets, laced demon bodice, the whole of it encased in industrial-grade plastic, a fresh accessory meant to keep things sparking.

"Something we might try," I said, brow bobbing cornily, desperately. "You uh... you like?" I lifted it toward her.

"Oh my god," she said, fingers bridged at her brow.

The plastic-wrapped outfit hung between us. I lowered it. She said, "You are at a loss. You are functioning at a loss."

"Shelley..."

The phone, our landline, rang on the windowsill behind me.

"What exactly am I being accused of here?"

"Accused is the wrong word."

"Of ?"

"Philip. I *know*." She stared a the ringing phone, then raised her brow—like you getting that? I looked at phone and shook my head no. "Oh I will then." And she reached across me, lifting the receiver, aggressively grazing my shoulder on return. "Hello?" She glanced up at me, the bitterness, sadness afloat in her eyes. "Yes. He's right here." She passed the phone over.

"Hello."

"Hey, Philip. This is detective Povich. From Ward Thirteen?"

"Oh!" I glanced at Shelley who was holding the plastic-wrapped girl-devil outfit, staring at it plaintively. "Well, this is a surprise." Shelley looked up. I shrugged to her, then said to Povich, "What, um... what's up?"

I stood and stepped away from the table. Shelley sighed, shaking her head.

"We've made some progress regarding your buddy's Dodge Dart," said Povich into my ear. "The case just took on a different color."

"Okay." I paced toward the hall to the living room, glancing back to see Shelley waiting, fingers again at her brow. "Which color is that?" I moved down the hall.

Povich waited a moment. I kept moving toward the apartment's opposite end, out of the kitchen's hearing range.

"My colleague, detective Kozlowe, decided on a lark to search the Dart one more time," Povich said. "What he found in the backseat concerns us. A uh... a healthy little package of narcotics, Philip, hidden beneath the lining of the backseat cushion."

"Narcotics?" I said, half-whispering.

"Specifically cocaine."

I stopped at the far front end of the apartment, where the baby slept in the crib in the corner. I half-whispered, "Well that's..." Amazing how fast this took my attention. "What's that got to do with Adam?"

"It was Swivchek's vehicle, correct?"

"Well, yeah," I said, hushed yet clenched. "It was his before it got *stolen*. Before it was driven around the city for months. I don't mean to doubt your suspicions, detective, but that package could be anybody's."

"Sure," he said. "Good point. We thought of that. But my uh... my colleague Kozlowe has done some extracurricular research, Philip, and it's starting, I'm afraid, to bear some fruit."

I waited a second, taking that in. "Regarding the cocaine?" I said. "Or Adam?"

"Both."

"They've found a connection?"

"Not really," he said. "Not a major one anyway, though I must admit, Philip, it's begun to show some legs as potentially compelling." He waited, half-chuckled. "Some kid was dealing out of the Copy Boss. Swivchek's place. The shop on Division. Mostly pot, but a little coke too."

"I don't know anything about this."

"Didn't think you did, Philip. Didn't think you did. Just wanted to apprise you of the shift in this newly colorful situation. I doubt the case gets made or goes anywhere useful but—" He paused, then lowered his voice. "Between you and me? I think Detective Kozlowe watches too much TV. He just got the luxury cable package this fall." He sheeshed to himself. "But no matter now. He started playing detective in a stunningly thoughtful manner, and as I said, fruit was borne."

"Right," I said. "The fruit. You mentioned that."

"You need to let us know if Swivchek shows up in your life again. You knew that already, but I wanted to remind you."

"I understand."

"I knew you would, Philip. You have a good day."

The connection clicked off. At the front end of the apartment, I stood rock still, swallowed by the dial tone. Seemed so cruel. Why now? I tried one of those slow breathing exercises Shelley taught me from her yoga class, closing my eyes, imaging as instructed. The gentle lap of waves on white sandy beaches, the breeze and the quiet and the soft hum of nature. It was futile. I moved slowly to the kitchen, in no way soothed, off to Shelley's shock and awe and whatever else awaited me.

No telling what Adam would make of this one. And I'd lifted the concept straight from the guy. *Do Your Part for the War on Terror* was his slogan, *his* notion. A hatless and debauched Uncle Sam pointing at me from my own private poster, suggesting something off-center from the phrase, half-mocking or subverting it. The Terror at home. Terror already here, maybe, he'd say, from the very start—of our lives, our nation, our systems, institutions. And how would he name this one? This colorful situation?

My unhappy wife sat alone in the kitchen, looking up at me, depleted of her trademark grace. Her upbeat cheer and Ontario spunk had not come along this evening.

"Sorry," I said. "Had to take that."

She nodded, not so engaged. "Sounded serious."

"It might be."

"Do I sound serious? Does *this* sound serious?"

My mouth dropped. I nodded, conceding yes it did.

"Really now, Philip," she said. "The neighbor?" Again I nodded, searching for words. "Even on days when you had the baby?"

"Wait now, wait a minute," I said. "You make it sound like it was some sort of routine."

"It wasn't?"

"No." I jogged my head tightly side to side. "I mean... Yes and no, but now I'm not sure we're talking about the same thing. Actually, it's not a... well, it's..."

"A lie. That's what most call it. Something you're not precisely skilled at delivering." She moved past me toward the hallway, where she opened the closet and rooted around. She pulled out a relative obscurity—her long conservative gray felt coat, which she didn't often wear, reserved, as far as I could tell, for funerals and church in winter. Two places she wasn't often called. She buttoned it swiftly, looking down. "Contracts and honor, mister. Contracts and honor." She looked up. "It really does boil down to that now, doesn't it?"

At a loss, I said nothing.

"It took Hugo to open my eyes on that one."

"Hugo?" I stepped back, shaken awake. "*He* told you? Hugo's your source?"

She nodded slowly, then crossed her arms. "Hugo and Melanie have a very specific contract, Philip. As do we. Very specific." She gazed at me placidly, with half-pity eyes. "Open means open. Taken means taken. And I must agree with my good friend Hugo, who... well, he feels you've broken both codes of honor."

"Oh does he?" I said. She looked down, buttoning her coat. "Will he be challenging me to two duels?"

"Funny." Her fingers here at the final button, sealed now up to the neck. She looked up and took me in, then looked away. "Listen." Again, this avoiding of eyes. "While we're at it, it's only fair I tell you. I've been contacted by the search committee at MacGill."

"The visiting scholar thing?"

"I've made no decisions, but thought you should know."

"That's great, Shelley. I mean—well *is* it? Would we move up there or..."

Arms crossed, she stared at me. She shook her head and grinned, still amazed. "We?"

A chill ran through me.

"You need to take an extra long look at yourself," she said. "Talk to someone close about this. Open your address book and make contact with reality." She stood and moved from the table. "Give reality a call and see what it has to say."

She turned to leave.

"Okay, wait—honey!" And she was out the back door. "What about our *date*?" The door closed. "I already ordered food!" I was shouting hard at a thick wooden door. "Thai food!" She stomped down the staircase. "Cashew chicken!" But she was gone.

I looked down at the sexy girl-devil outfit, its pristine packaging, so cheesy and deliberately tantalizing. Playful surprises galore, I thought.

Something caught the corner of my eye. A picture on the fridge of Shelley and Hugo back in college, where they'd been close friends, even fooled around a little—just once, said Shelley, and I don't doubt her word. Should I? I never do. They were just friends now, buddies for years and years. I stared him down. Contracts and honor, huh Hugo? That's how you're gonna play?

I lifted the magnet and turned the photo on its face.

Back at the kitchen table, the tattered title page of my unfinished play stared up at me. I even included a graphic on the cover, just for kicks—a cool-eyed daddy with a baby in the Bjorn, though also with a glock in his grip, a bandolier of bullets across his chest, sniper's rifle across his back. *Do Your Part for the War on Terror.*

I turned the manuscript on its face.

I moved back through the hallway, back toward the crib in the corner of the living room. Earlier, the babysitter had canceled and we'd been forced to move the date in-house. Surprises galore indeed.

I watched the sleeping baby breathe, splayed out on his back in the crib.

Before my eyes, the child swiveled his head. Did he sense me? Smell me? He stretched out his little tugboat of a body, then wailed, damn near screaming, a wild wounded animal sound, as if terrified for the both of us.

The buzzer rang, and I was sure it was Shelley, returning, having forgotten her keys. Monarch in my arms, wailing away, I went downstairs to the building's front door. There, I found the delivery guy, a skinny Thai kid not yet eighteen, smiling broadly and holding our food. The baby cried harder, fiercer. But I had no money on me, I was trying to explain. My wife left abruptly and took her purse.

Well he couldn't understand me. There were language issues, sure, but the baby was a louder barrier by far. I could smell it. The Panang curry—my favorite—plus the tang of her cashew chicken. Yet I knew he'd walk off without leaving the bag. I had no money on me. Not a cent.

We stood in the cold on our building's front stoop, the Monarch wailing, this guy not understanding, me absorbing what I could of the maddening scent of the food I would not be tasting.

Perpetual Union

Shelley found the photo on the kitchen counter in the silence that fell just after. A loud and lasting fallout silence, considering what she's proposed. She lifted her chin like a haughty professor, eyeing the memory that had come in the mail. I stood in the doorway and felt it good.

Little Hank sat docile in the hallway behind us. He'd heard everything. The whole of it. Tones of bitterness, quivers of betrayal. Would the moment lodge inside him forever? A hidden infection in the folds of memory, later to impair his way of being?

Shelley would say that's neither here nor there. What counts most is this: that I've declared sovereignty and it's irreversible. My secret's out, so why bother?

Her gaze slid up from the photo.

"How sweet," she said, and laid the photo on the counter. "I remember that. June, right? Or July? Where'd you find this one?"

"Adam sent it. From Mexico."

"Mexico, eh?"

I nodded sort of timidly.

"So he's gone for his family then?"

"Looks like it." I stared back, trying to match her force.

"How noble," she said, eyeing me—and winning. Abruptly, she stepped at me. I moved aside. She swept to the doorway, then hallway, making a beeline to the baby. As she passed, she said, sort of under her breath. "You and your *pal*."

Behind me, she picked up Henry. I turned to watch.

She gathered her stuff. The door closed, a muted click. Gone.

I stood in the hallway a long minute, then turned to the kitchen and remembered the photo. I went and lifted it, held it at the white-framed corners.

All of us together at the ballpark only four months before. Fabulous seats on the first base side in the soothing of late July. Me and Shelley and the baby plus Adam, up in the stands next to shallow right field. Adam's score, these tickets.

I looked down at the image pressed between my fingers.

So much in this photo. Acres of territory stretching behind it. Histories. Connections. Heady Deceptions. But also that moment, that instant right then, a carefree vibe in the muggy evening air that remained unsullied until much later. Not, at least, until the seventh inning. Though that had nothing to do with us—Shelley and me, or even really Adam. It had everything to do, in fact, with *all* of us.

But perhaps that's hard to follow. Here's what I mean.

Adam, as I said, had these tickets to the game, which he'd win on occasion from an unnamed source—sometimes five, six tickets, usually nice ones—and had asked us if we'd like to come along. Bring the baby! We'll have a gas!

Well, Shelley and I just assumed. Neither of us even asked. Maribel and Jorge would be coming too. But when we reached our seats, we found him alone.

"Maribel and Jorge?" Shelley asked, after we'd sat and ordered beers.

"Oh... they're not here."

We both stared at him, stumped.

"Are they not coming?" asked Shelley.

"No, they're—" He took a meditative sip. "Jorge has music class. So does Maribel. At the Old Town School. 'The Mother and Child' or some shit."

We both knew right off that was a lie. Though later, discussing it, we couldn't pinpoint why. Maybe it was how he said it— the false casualness, not his style. But also, mostly, all the other things we'd guessed about the sun going down on his marriage.

So he left them behind. We were their replacements. In lieu of a happy family, he'd taken ours instead.

But the weirdness about this faded fast. We were helpless against what surrounded us. The green green grass and the crack of the bat and the cheers and the laughter and shouting. We forgot ourselves. Two beers in, waiting for another, and all of us were having a ball.

You can see this in the photo. Dreamy carelessness is in the air. Aimless and beautiful. We do not care. Since Adam sent me this image in the mail, I've examined it multiple times. Look at it enough and it leaves you curious. For example, who's taking this picture? That's one question. No one else was in our crew.

I've since remembered, though. Came to me recently. A few things have, in fact.

First, the woman who took our photo, as you may have guessed, was simply a random passerby. We were in the front row of our section, where people would freely stroll by, and Adam just asked.

"Excuse me," he said, hazy-eyed, playful, several in at this point. He held up the camera. "Would you?"

Nice woman, you could see this. Real nice lady—mid-fifties or so, all plump and rosy. Her amber hair a touch overdone. Cubs cap, Bermuda shorts, white canvas sneakers.

She took our picture, goo-gooed for the baby, and went on her merry way.

That's the first of what I recall. Just a flash. The second— and this part has lodged in me clearer—was the seventh inning stretch.

That's when the camera pans out from our lives, our little enclosures—our needs and betrayals and confusions of heart—and hovers behind us, floats above. The crowd, the mass before us now. Center stage, sauced and souffléd. Beery enthusiasm rising like batter.

First we all stand, relaxed, anticipating. Next, they introduce the soldiers. Random names from Iraq, Afghanistan. Ten to twelve of them standing in a uniformed arc behind home plate, four others about to sing from a smaller arc—this service quartet—in front of a microphone on the plate itself. The crowd erupts in generous applause. Lengthy and grateful. A bit proud of itself.

But thirdly—just after this, and pretty unexpectedly—they went ahead and read off a list of the dead. Dead in combat. Recent names, evidently.

Well, a heavy moment there, I can testify. A palpable bell-shaped something descended. These were the names of dead men. Quite recently killed men. And a moment later, I noticed the flags. Digital flags, undulating on a lengthy band of screen that circled the base of the park's second tier, that half-arc, once only concrete, now waving like digital bunting. This long thin screen pulsing red white and blue. Old Glory, pixilated. Flowing proudly. Gently.

Finally then, "America the Beautiful." This chorus of soldiers who had served together in the war, in the Green Zone or something like it—Green Zone Boys with golden voices—belted it out with soft aplomb.

Well, they sang it beautifully, I have to say. With, I suppose, that earned respect. Soft and funereal, aware of its weight. I have to say, we were rapt. Captured. Though a bell dropped that hard echoes other complications.

>*A-mer-i-ca A-mer-i-ca*
>*God shed his grace on thee*

The digital bunting with the flowing flags? The dead soldiers gone and the living ones singing? It was hard to know how to take it.

Which is when I looked or glanced to my left and saw her standing there—the woman who'd taken our picture. She had seats in the row just back of us, practically sat behind us, about six seats over toward home plate. And she was weeping. Just overcome. Not hysterical—quietly, a statue in tears, barely moving, whimpering intensely. At least as far as I could tell. From where I stood and stared.

The digital bunting undulated proudly. The chorus entered their rousing close. As she wept and wept and softly whimpered. I watched it. Don't think anyone noticed but me. Freaked me out, to be honest. Surprised me in a way I wasn't sure I liked. What? Her son died in Iraq? Or grandson? Just an unrelated breakdown? Simply a gush of federal love?

The song closed and again, we applauded. A glorious unified wave. Hoots, shouts, whistles, clapping, the buzz of it lasting even after we'd stopped.

Then the bell lifted as fast as it fell and we sat in the chatter and ordered beer.

Well, it didn't last long, I'll cop to that—probably only half an inning. But I had that weeping woman in my head and couldn't let her go for a while. And privately, at least for me, the evening took on a different pall.

I was reminded of this again—that night at the ballpark—when Victor came by about a week ago. He had Bulls tickets and hoped to cheer me up. The cheers and applause gone indoors now, reined and contained within four walls.

Victor didn't bring his family either. He'd never once considered it. He's an unmarried father with an easy ticket. Doesn't even live with her—or rather, them. A choice arrangement. I've thought this, I'll admit.

We coasted down Damen in his old school sedan, the mustard Volvo—rusted, lovable—he's had for just about forever. Stopped at a light, the engine chugging, he stared forward, shaking his head, that half-nervous inwardness that's always with him.

"This stuns me," he said. "She's leaving you?"

Reluctant, I nodded. "For a little while. It's not permanent. I mean, I hope not."

"But she wants separation?"

I took in a breath. "For now. Just for now."

He blew out a breath, his cheeks puffy, lifted his long rubbery neck and touched at the peppery stubble.

"Wow," he said. "Wow and wow again. I thought... I thought you two were rock steady. Forever rock steady. I'd have bet on it. This—seriously, Phil. This totally fucks up my worldview."

"Come on, man. It's not so catastrophic."

"Yes it is." He sounded certain.

I sighed.

He drove on snail-like toward the parking lot. His Travis Bickel-ish intensity was flaring up. He glanced in the rearview mirror.

"This has fucked me *up*, Phil," he said, and shot me a look. "I banked on you two." He shook his head, staring forward. "I reach over toward you guys in my mind sometimes to steady myself. That's no exaggeration."

"Ah, man... please. Don't say that. I... I'm sorry."

"No," he said. "I'm sorry. I'm really very sorry."

Victor hadn't looked like this since college, a desperate, lost look best left behind. The guy's known me sixteen, seventeen years. He's seen it all, every glorious peak, dismal valley, every tiny triumph or colossal loss. And vice versa. As I've seen his. He knew Shelley and me from the start.

"Can we shelve all that for now?" I say. "Please. Let's go watch these Bulls."

A wiry, tense nod to the side.

"That's fair," he said. "Agreed. Let's forget all that."

In the stands just before tip-off, Victor raised his beer.

"Here's to forgetting," he said.

"Absolutely," I replied. We touched cups. "Cheers to that."

But forgetting, I've found, can prove quite difficult when

surrounded by the mass, by the cheers and the chatter. Especially right there, right then, in the stadium.

For that night—and I have no idea if they do this all the time, but it wasn't at all like back in the day—that night, the game is nearly upstaged by the sideshow. A perpetual performance waiting in the wings. Every time out, every break, every unnatural pause for a TV commercial, they'd arranged an entertainment to keep you jazzed. Every extra second, I swear. Scantily clad cheerleaders dancing seductively. Actors in gigantic bull costumes—like actual bulls, horns and all—running with basketballs at trampolines, then launching to attempt a dunk. Toy machine guns shooting soft stuff into the stands. Lotteries with ticket numbers, half-court shooting contests, thirty-second rock bands, twenty-second songs. The game, I swear to you, seemed incidental to the spectacle.

All straight from the heart of P.T. Barnum, competing against itself. Like Barnum vs. Barnum. And the carnival strangeness kept escalating. What would they throw at us next? In the second half—no shit—they had a hypnotist. Not a very good one, I might add. If you've ever seen a convincing hypnotist, you'll know a sham in a second. And having rank exhibitionists who've been hand-picked from the stands dance the Twist and the funky chicken—this was not impressive. This was quite weak.

"My god, it's *obscene*," said Victor, almost whispering. "It's all so fucking decadent."

I agreed, though something other was coming. They threw in a surprise for virtue's sake. Just after the hypnotist, the next break in the game—I don't know why, but there were breaks galore—they gave their obligatory tribute to our fallen fighting men. Only this time, no names of the dead, but rather, surviving amputees.

They hobbled or rolled toward center court. About six or seven of them. Some with prosthetic legs, others with no legs. One with no arm. They announced their names, their tours of duty, and the crowd—halos on now—erupted passionately. A sustained wave of grateful proud noise. They hobbled off, wheeled off, limped—waving. It was hard not to feel it in the gut.

Then the music blasted and the Luv-a-Bulls shook some taut young ass. A fifteen second number before the game resumed. We forgot ourselves. Forgot lost limbs. Heinrich tosses to Gordon—and we're on.

Yet that's not the thing I'm left with most. What's truly lasted was the last of the acts. One final flash of carnival strangeness that reminded me of something I'd long forgotten.

For in this final, most key break in the game—a TV commercial, I believe—they actually almost trumped war and invested themselves in political bias. I mean, just the *balls* of it. The frank admission of our regional leaning. It was equally, I suppose, obscene. Though you really had to laugh.

Who knows who came up with it, but I was entertained. Seemed everyone was. This actor meant to be Abraham Lincoln—a pretty solid likeness, actually, down to the wart by the nose—started playing vigorous one-on-one hoops against other actors dressed as ex-presidents. He creams Washington. Embarrasses Reagan. Abominates Nixon. Destroys Clinton. And this all happened very fast. Like, five-to-ten second "games." Then, inevitably, came the final contest.

Lincoln vs. Bush. Our then-incumbent. Dubya. And no surprise here—Lincoln *kills* him. Dunks on Bush a couple times. Repeatedly, our Lincoln humiliates their Bush. And the crowd is going wild. Hooting, laughter. It was hard not to. The actors were both quite good.

On the way home, Victor mentioned aloud what I'd already thought much earlier. Or felt, I suppose. It involved no wording.

"You know that presidential bit?" he said. "The Lincoln-Bush thing?" Victor looked at me. Exhausted, it seemed. "You know what that reminded me of?"

Here I felt it—or thought it. The words.

"No," I said. "What?"

He stared ahead, driving. "Perpetual Union."

"I thought you might say that."

"So you did think of it."

"Just now," I said. "Just right now."

Early next morning I hunted it down, though knew it would cost—and likely severely—in sweat and raw agitation. The basement was my only chance. It was down there somewhere, in some box.

But standing at the entryway in the dank gray cool, I saw it almost instantly. Well, not *it*. Not precisely. A funnel of soft white morning light had fallen through the far basement window, landing in beatific creepy manner on the face of a life size blow-up doll. She had Betty Page sweetness to her come-hither mouth, plus a sheen of black hair, petroleum smooth— her plastic head lit by that cone of sunshine with a weird sort of holy symmetry. As if the light of the Lord were feeling horny.

This was an old joke gift—a wedding gift, actually—from this guy at Shelley's ex-office with limited social skills. And for a brief moment, the face seemed alive. But when I picked her up and held her before me, our pneumatic sweetheart's eyes were dead. Then I saw it, beneath her, in an open cardboard box— the fancy black font on a bound cover, half-lit by that horny sunbeam.

Perpetual Union

An original play by Philip Palliard and Bruce Habbit. On stage in this city a decade ago. '96. Part of '97. I don't know. I was a young dumb buck. Twenty-six, twenty-seven. That era of unmanageable, relentless depression. The age of endless good times.

Among the three I've written that got produced—the others one-acts with brief runs—*Perpetual Union* was the only halfway "success." Also my one collaboration. Ran, I believe, three solid months.

Here's where Shelley first saw me act, when she got intro-duced to the whole damn scene. The egos, the excess, the limited funds. Quiet jealousies, soaring joys, crossed principles, outsized personas. Drinking, drugging, sleeping around. We'd only been dating a couple of weeks. I wasn't even sure how much she liked me.

But there we all were, the entire cast of *Perpetual Union* in glorious period costuming. I can't recall how we afforded it. In memory, it seems so authentic and expensive. Black buckled shoes, white powdered wigs, fussy postures, dainty hands. Our silk stockings stretched to the knee. The women in bodices— powdered, perfumed. A bit over the top, but we liked it that way. And playing John Adams for a three month run was among the sweetest thrills of my life.

Until the closing weekend came. When from nowhere, I had to play Jefferson.

We'd lifted the notion from *The Federalist Papers*. "Perpetual Union," argued Madison, was what the colonies must see themselves committing to. If they hoped to birth the nation, no other words would do.

Nearly a century later, Lincoln would bet his ass on this abstraction, hitch his legacy to the very principle, his modus operandi as Commander in Chief, the only ever faced with real rebellion. The *Great* Rebellion. The South filing divorce papers, and Lincoln simply not having it.

But that's neither here nor there. Our play involved nothing Lincoln. Wrong era. This landed elsewhere. A boundary-pushing colonial sitcom featuring the Founding Fathers—that was the idea. Like, the steamy underside of the Continental Congress. Its hookers and whiskey and black leather masks. Its whippings and secret rages. Followed by mornings of reasoned debate, impassioned compromise. Sworn commitments to democratic principle morphing into all-night bacchanals. Adams smoking opium with imported French whores. Jefferson at it with his favorite slave. All that.

It was meant to scandalize. The Jefferson outrage with Sally Hemmings had come back to life only years before. Thus, the title's meaning was doubled: a critique of both the notion uniting the states and the cultural expectation of monogamy. And we let the thing get good and weird. Transgressive. Edgy.

Buzzwords we both adored.

Christ. I forget about Bruce. He was a different sort of friend than either Adam or Victor. A friend from back then, the bad old days, when I was headstrong and rising and easily swayed.

When Bruce and I collaborated, our company was in full flower—twelve official members, actually, each in his or her own way a sovereign state. All of us committed to original work—full-lengths, one-acts, sketch shows, musicals—and performing each without a director. That is, with *us* as director, but no one director. Our unified Wave, too often crashing.

So you claim that Ideal, call it the Reason, pretend to it, study it, and still never fails—here comes reality. It always arrives. Roles emerge fast. Always. The lawyers, bullies, the diplomats, counselors. And the core personality, without doubt, for our company—Theater Potemkin—was Bruce Habbit of Richmond, VA. Founding father along with two others. Most importantly this one guy Noel. Noel Roth. Big overtalkative New York Jew who came from money and power. A little older than us. At that point, probably thirty, thirty-one. Brilliant mind, that guy. Jesus—Noel! *He* was the talent there. Vital brainy Falstaff type. Overread. Underemployed. Smoked perhaps too much pot.

And then there was me. Emerging unknown wanna-be playwright with a sizable chip on his shoulder. I'd known Noel from this bar where I'd worked. He was my ticket in. So I was a bit of an outsider, a kind of Rhode Island, but we little guys will also have our say.

Then, during a belabored rehearsal of a scene near the end of the play, Bruce decided we needed more *edge*, that the whole thing was getting too cute. And he holds up a finger and says, "I know!" Nods, smiling, shadow in his eye. "A rape," he says. "This play needs a rape." And right then makes the change.

The authors of *The Federalist Papers*, while on smoke break between sessions of the Continental Congress, would witness a rape in an alley offstage, making pokerfaced comments as they watched indifferently, not intervening.

It'll be strange, he said. Perverse. Awful. But also—let's hope—hilarious.

The silent cast stared back at him.

Now rape is a difficult fit with funny. Very difficult to make that funny, rape. The sound of the word itself resists it. Murder has a better chance at laughs. But Bruce wanted it—insisted, in fact—and the scene went in despite our protest.

Most nights I played Adams; Bruce, Jefferson; the authors having cast themselves in essentially starring roles. But closing weekend, Bruce got sick—and violently so. Puked his guts out for days. Only I knew Jefferson's part down cold. Plus we had this kid from Columbia College—a lucky first—understudying the Adams role. Well, this kid, this Matt someone, ended up doing Adams quite well. Better than me. If not far better. He's a pro now. I've seen him on a Taco Bell commercial. He should have been Adams from the start.

Meanwhile, suddenly, I was Jefferson—the butt of the play, as well as its star. The play's success hinged on Jefferson. And Bruce was really quite good.

Let's set aside for now the fact that I was not. I was disappointing, I knew, but that's besides the point. Shelley had seen me already as Adams, then came again that final Friday and did not mince words, later, at the bar.

"Jefferson's not your natural role," she told me.

"Oh Jesus,'" I said. "'That bad?"

"Please. I just like you as Adams."

She nuzzled up against me with boozy warmth and stretched up to whisper in my ear, "I can't be your Sally tonight, but if you'd like, I'd be your Abigail."

I looked back at her, taken. I know that sounds corny but think of it, see it—this gorgeous capable Canadian nutritionist nuzzling up against me, offering herself. We slept together the first time that night. She kept me at bay for over a month. We had fun, I believe, though can't quite remember.

But that's not what I'm getting at. Shelve that for now. Reality came knocking in a louder way that Saturday night, closing night, when Shelley wasn't there.

I'd decided to take a smoke break. It was that simple, that stupid. It was the last night. I just didn't care. Plus Bruce wasn't there, so I went ahead and got cute about it.

Standing backstage in the dressing room, it came to me. To my left, Sally Hemmings was taking a nap, head cradled in crossed arms, her blue bonnet before the mirror. Why not? I thought. Just her and me back here.

I thought, I'm gonna go have a smoke. Fuck it. I'd been craving one the whole second act. This, back when I used to smoke. Assumed, at the time, I'd smoke forever. Couldn't imagine not smoking. A presumed—in its own right—perpetual union.

So I stepped past the sleeping Sally, opened the door, and walked through the weird musty back storage area—that long dark room—that came with the space we rented.

I stumbled a little in my black buckled shoes, then found the door knob in the fading dark, and opened the door, and I'm there.

Outside.

First, a soft gush of summer air. Then I took out my smokes from the side pocket of my embroidered vest and lit up and said to the world, "Ahhh."

So beautiful out here. That air. The sky inky black and on forever, above the bricks of building tops. Just having me a smoke on the closing night of a play I had co-composed. That audiences had paid to see! That a critic or two had actually liked, sort of even recommended. This, on the night after crossing into Canada, sleeping for the first time with my future wife—where I remember now, yes, it was charged and invigorating. Lovely!

So a bit smug here, I must admit. Lauded by critics. Recently laid. Having a Marlboro in the back alley. And relishing it, well aware of the irony.

For I'd re-enter the play in about ten minutes. Jefferson walking in from an "alley" off stage, stage right, to find the authors of *The Federalist Papers* having a smoke—and in the play amazed to see me coming.

I was smoking out there, in an actual alley.

An off-stage real-life simulation of a fake simulation of never-lived history.

I was way in my head, tripping on this notion, nicely buzzed from the unexpected smoke, when it sounded—startling me. A loud sharp discharge. Two of them—crack! crack! Then four teens, dark-skinned, black, Latino, I don't know—came bounding sort of *at* me from down the alley. Ten feet off, then rocketing past. Wild frenzied running away. Silence followed. Then a shriek.

Serious shriek too. Then again, silence. Another shriek. Then another.

I stood paralyzed, off twenty feet, dressed in immaculate period costuming. The sirens sounded and the cops came fast. Two of them were standing in the alley, one comforting a young black woman in a yellow tanktop and flip flops, the other kneeling down, examining something. Though I couldn't see what from where I stood.

I was terrified, yes, but a lot more curious, which outweighed the fear by far. I stepped gingerly toward the scene. Nearly tiptoed.

And on the few final steps I saw him. Splayed across the sidewalk like a poached fish. A big one. Old gray black dude dead on the pavement. His head was collapsed in the back like a melon, a stretch of blood oozing, blobbing out, staining the pavement.

Well, it froze me good. Bet it would you too. There he was, done forever. Old sort of grandpa black dude on the pavement. Jesus. What happened here?

Plus also that cop. That plump pink-faced boy in blue, speaking into his radio hitched to his shoulder like a pro. "Look. It's over," he said. "I'm confirming it." He listened, waited. The placid voice on the other end wanted to send an ambulance. "I'm telling you. No need to." He looked down at the body, then spat to the side. "Believe me. No hope here."

He glanced up then and saw me. He stared, sort of wince-smiled.

I up-nodded. "Hey."

He hunhed to himself, a halfway chuckle. And I'd like to think I represented hope to him. Perhaps I was proof it still lived in the world. A Founding Father standing behind him, done up in eighteenth-century regalia. Bet for a second he thought he saw a ghost.

Then the cop stood and, again, looked down at him, this old guy. Sixty, sixty-five. Old black man in a shock white button-down short sleeve, his black-framed glasses sunk to his nose, his skull divesting itself of life in a strangely shaped oblong puddle. Looked like a liquid cactus. A purple three-fingered hand.

A minute—maybe only thirty seconds later—I stood there in the wings of the well-lit stage. Noel had called from the open back door, our Benjamin Franklin looking testy and amazed.

"Phil!" he shouted. "Come *on*!"

Under a minute, and I stood there in the dark, stage right by the fake velvet curtains. That old dead guy, the horrible pattern of blood, stuck in my head, potted there. As I waited, sweating, for my horrible cue, a line from Madison or perhaps John Jay. After they'd observed a rape in progress and commented on it, not intervening.

HAMILTON: James, look [staring off-stage, to "alley"] Is that a... rape?

MADISON: I... [raising reading glasses to the bridge of the nose] I believe it is. Yes yes... he's raping her. With a uh, a kind of quiet vigor.
[a muffled scream is heard offstage]

ADAMS [from behind, no one saw him coming]: Oh come, boys. You can't be serious. [they turn and notice it's Adams.] You call that a *rape*?

And me, I'm standing in the dark dark wings, the image

from the alley still hanging before me. I'm paralyzed. And here comes my cue.

HAMILTON: Wait—is that?... oh my stars... *Thomas*?"

The joke is that they realize it's Jefferson. He's the one they've been watching in the alley. It often got a laugh when Jefferson appeared. Sometimes only silence. He'd been sent up throughout as a playboy lech, a dainty aristocratic horndog. And this line was my cue to enter from the "alley," to stroll in with haughty nonchalance and announce my "commitment to personal liberty." But I didn't go. I spaced it, or my body refused. I was sweating, pale as ice. Crippled to immobile, there in the wings.

Yes it was weird. Yes it ruined the play. Then that kid Marcus, who was standing next to me, gripped at my arm in the dark. Marcus played Jupiter, Jefferson's loyal, dandified slave, and would enter the stage behind me. Hey, he whispered. You're on. But I didn't move. The house went silent and confused.

Only that violent push from Noel, standing behind me, sent me out there. I stumbled, then fell, my wig askew. That got a laugh, but still, I was lost. We improvised through it—or rather, they did—desperately, awkwardly. It killed the play. Me, the deer. That crowd, the headlights. Man, it was painful. Exposed. Exposed.

That's how I felt a decade later, I got this same sensation watching Shelley put the baby in a cab—red white and blue, an American United—after a struggle with inserting his seat. And she looked up, not seeing me—or choosing not to see—as I stood, helpless, on our second floor porch. She got in and closed the door, not waving.

That week, she'd arranged it with stunning speed, her single purpose since our encounter in the kitchen. The moving van was packed and would meet them in Montreal. They'd take off from Midway in an hour or two.

I was paralyzed here, just as then. I wanted to run down and stop her, grab her lapel, and say, like Lincoln to the rebel South—no. We *can't* break up. It's illogical and doesn't make sense. We are *one*.

I stood immobile and watched them go. The cab rolled off to the corner.

When would I absorb it? She'd taken Henry and left me. And appeared to actually mean it this time. And she *never* means it. Not the hard stuff. Almost never.

The taxi stopped at the stop sign, then turned, going north. I watched as it gradually hovered off, the fading blue stars on the taxi's back bunting slowly leaving view.

AFTER WINTER COMES SPRING

Beth Briefly Visits

Her coming was a sudden, stark surprise. She had called to announce it just the night before and like that—an airplane, a snap of the fingers—my sister was on my sofa, holding a tall glass of pricey red wine, fresh from Midway and the cab ride in, to discuss what ailed me and the trouble attached.

She'd planned a layover—one night only—before her connecting flight the next day. She would miss the opening blow of the conference, but really felt she ought to see me. Nearly two months of separation from wife and child was, she thought, a brutal sentence. She worried I would grow too lonely on my own. Lonesome or lost, likely depressed, prone to self-loathing or acts of self-ruin. Symptoms of what we're susceptible to, she said. It's *in* us, Philip. A genetic trait. The Beast. What nearly killed dad. Maybe even half-killed mom.

Thin crystals of snow still stuck to her brow, her hair and shoulders, vague confetti evaporating fast. "You really must keep an eye on yourself," she said, brow raised, standing to pour a glass for me. "This is the sort of life scenario when The Beast will invade without asking. When you're vulnerable, it pounces." She kicked off her shoes and reclined again on the sofa in her skirt and nylons and soft pearly sweater. "Especially in the dead of winter."

She looked out the window at the benevolent snowdrop, brief, wimpy and soon to end, leaving only the cold.

"This is when it visits," she told me, gently swirling her glass. "Nights like this? When you're alone?" She caught my eye. "Watch yourself, Philip. I mean it."

She calls it The Beast like it's a living thing. And it kind of is. We used to make that argument. Like an actual organism living inside you. We would talk about it, name it, back in the day, when she was just finishing college and I moved out here to be an artist of the stage, or tried to be. Then, she would visit in the heart of summer, in July, for the festivals and balmy weather. Clearly those were easier days, far warmer, yet that's when we'd named it—if not gotten off on it. The Beast. The Bigfoot in our DNA.

Beth kicked back on the sofa, glass held at a slight remove.

"It's hard for me to fathom, Philip," she said and looked around the place. "Now that I'm here, it's just..." She shook her head slowly. "They've left you."

I nodded tightly. "They have."

"They've left the *country*."

I nodded.

Beth shook her head slowly, then stopped. "You think Shelley had this planned for a while?"

I shrugged.

"Even before the uh... incident?"

Slightly wincing, I shrugged again. "I think that's possible but I don't know. She went up there last summer to visit her sister. On a lark, she applied for a fellowship at MacGill but no one thought she'd get it."

"Yet she did."

Again, I nodded, taut and nervy, sensing fresh beadlets of sweat on my brow. Beth took a sip and stared at the ceiling, all cool and breezy, in command, though hardly yet begun. She took in a breath.

"So," she said. "Let's review. The hard facts. You slept with your neighbor." She looked over. "And just once? Really?"

"Beth it was . . . well, okay, you could argue twice. Sort of. But not really. Not really even *once*."

"Excuse me?"

"Once and a half then," I said, exasperated. "Something like that. Doing the math gets difficult. And the first time hardly counts."

"It all counts."

"No no, Beth, that was like... nothing."

She stared back, doubting me. My mind stammered.

"We'd just started," I said. "Like, three faint strokes. That's it. Then I stopped. I resisted."

"Three faint *strokes*?" She grimaced. "You didn't tell it like that to Shelley?"

"Well, no."

"Honey, it was nothing, really. I put it in her for like, five, six seconds. That's it!"

"Alright."

"Three faint strokes, Shelley! Three *faint strokes*!"

I gritted my teeth and gave her a look. She shook her head, grinning, with slight touch of pity.

"What happened there? You, um," she whispered. "You came?"

"No." I hung my head, praying the questions wouldn't last all night. And a dark regret rose up through me as I told it. "I... well, I saw Henry on her futon, where I laid him down to sleep and I... just couldn't."

"Jesus. You had the baby with you?"

I nodded, the shame shooting up through my veins.

Beth looked aghast. "You didn't tell me *that*."

"How could I? It's... sensitive."

"It's awful is what it was. Goddamn, Philip. What—were you high?"

I waited—the answer hurt—and said, "A little, yeah."

"While you were watching the baby?!"

"It never happened before, Beth. Never will again. A

167

onetime thing! I've explained that to Shelley. Over and over I've explained it."

Beth took a sip. Went contemplative. Meditated on it a second. She looked over at me. "But it happened for real later on?" she said. "Correct? With your neighbor?"

I dropped my eyes. "Sort of," I said, pretty weakly. "But not really. I mean . . . we went longer. Also a bit lighter. Just once." I sighed. "Plus the other time."

"Jesus, Philip. And you're calling the whole of it once and a *half.*" She shook her head, part amused, slightly disturbed. "I hadn't heard about the first time."

"Well... there you go. Now you have."

She turned and propped herself up on an elbow, wine glass dangling in the other hand. She pursed her lips, keeping her cool.

"I'm trying to understand it, Philip," she said. "I really am. I don't think Shelley ever will but... you're done with it, right? The sleeping around?"

"I'd hardly call it sleeping around."

"You're so sensitive. God. Well... what shall we call it?"

"Let's change the subject," I said and took a long bracing swallow. "How about that? You're here to cheer me up, not practice your cross-examinations."

"Ha." She thought about that. "Practicing. That's funny. Very." She shook her head to herself. "I hate the fucking law, Philip," she said. "I sincerely despise the practice of law. Why'd I ever wanna be a lawyer? And this kind of lawyer to boot?"

"Because you're great at it."

"Hardly." She poured another glass of the high-end Shiraz she'd brought with her from Philadelphia. "Let's get drunk then," she said. "Let's put on some music and tell it like it is." She nodded to the side, just as I do. "Except for your thing. We'll leave that aside." She looked over, raised her brow. "For now."

"Thank you."

She held up her glass. I followed suit. "Cheers," she said. "To things getting better."

And this warmed me a bit but I knew it wouldn't last. For things getting better is the tallest of orders, while things swept aside have an uncanny talent for sneaking back into your path. Several times that evening alone, swept-asides would return to undress me. The timing was awful a few times over. If Beth hadn't come that particular night, it's likely I never would have faced the extra trouble. Which began in subtler, pettier doses when she noticed that long lost photo on the shelf

"Is this him?" She lifted it. "That's him, right?"

She'd seen it there, lying on a row of books. I had returned from a short visit to the john and she was holding it in her hand.

"That guy Adam?"

This was the good vibes photo from the Adam package. Me, Shelley, Adam and Maribel, out on their porch several summers before. A lost idyll. Totally lost. That was the feeling of the thing. Probably left it on the shelf inadvertently some time back in September. But I didn't much want to talk about it now. Whatever it represented.

"That is a *really* nice picture." Beth looked up. "You and Shelley look radiant together. And..." She looked down. "This is his wife? Adam's?"

"That's her."

"Who left him? Correct?"

"She did."

"Fled to Mexico with their only child due to his excess philandering?"

I halted, wincing. "Did I tell you *that*?"

"You did." She smiled through her eyes, thinking it out. "You've talked about him since—and more than once—but I also remember meeting him, having a beer down at the corner. Remember that? Maybe two, three years ago?"

"Oh." I searched for it. "Right. Forgot that." I shook my head, all disbelief. "You met him."

She had come to visit a few years before, though I couldn't quite remember why. Maybe just for fun—or so it seemed— the public defender on a Midwest bender, some flavor of vacation at the dawn of spring. This was back before we'd produced our Monarch. Me, Shelley, Beth, Adam plus Victor and others at the corner bar. We tied it on pretty good. Beth bit her lip, remembering.

"He was a character," she said, half-grinning at the thought of him. "He had his allure. Wit and vitality. Sex appeal. But half insane—that was clear too. Like... all about *him*." She looked up to me. "Devoted narcissist. Purebred solipsist. Fancied himself magnetic. And he was, kinda. He really was. But not as much as he imagined." She crinkled her nose. "Not nearly."

"Maybe so," I said, and shrugged. "But whatever—he's no longer with us. I know I told you that much. He's gone now."

"Not entirely."

"Oh?" I said. "Meaning?"

Beth waited coolly, took a sip of wine. "I think you kind of want to *be* him."

My head cocked back. "I do?"

"I think you wish you were this Adam guy."

I winced—and fiercely. "Where do you get that?"

She smiled, shrugged, extra composed. "I don't know. Just a guess."

"Well, you guessed wrong," I said. "Sorry."

She nodded, then dropped the subject just as fast, satisfied with having taken the shot. She lifted her chin with ornery eye. I could see she meant to bring me trouble. A challenge at least. Jar me to reality. And she wanted to help, her motive was sincere, but she also just wanted to *know*. Get right down to the root of it. Find the source of my wayward ways.

A moment later, from nowhere, she suggested the corner bar.

"Let's go for one," she said. "I feel like walking."

We closed up shop, gathered our coats and soon enough we were in the hallway. As I locked the door behind me, she touched at my arm. She stared at the door across the hall, then whispered intensely. "So they live right there?"

I whispered back, "Afraid so."

She gripped at my arm. We stared at their door.

"It amazes me, Philip," she said in a louder whisper. "You must know that. I mean, Hugo? Shelley's Hugo? Right across from you? And so... inextricably involved in all this?"

I nodded solemnly. The questions, it seemed, would not be stopped. I steered her down the stairs. She stayed close.

"So..." Her breath was warm in my ear. "Hugo's a swinger too, huh?" She sheeshed. "Obviously." Her whisper grew louder. "God, Philip. Who knew? Shelley's best friend turns out to be a card-carrying—?"

"They aren't *best* friends." I stopped on the stairs. I shook my head, annoyed. "They're college friends. Merely old friends, and... those guys aren't necessarily quote-unquote swingers." I waited, searched for the words. "Not formally. Their relationship is just—you know—open."

"There's a difference?"

I shrugged, not sure myself.

Outside, Beth stopped to light a smoke. She took a long drag, exhaled, and stared off pensively into the distance. The air and sky were cold, clear, the snowdrop recently passed.

"It's because they're writers, right?" she said. "Is that it?"

"Excuse me?"

"Hugo's a writer as well, correct?"

I shrugged. "Tries to be. Aspiring novelist. Mostly a bartender. But he's published a little."

"A lot like *you*," she said, as if exposing the unexpected secret. "Is that part of all this?"

I winced. "I don't follow."

"They're working writers. Like you used to be—or rather, should be?"

"Naw. Well maybe, but... I do still try to write here and there."

"Do you?" Her eyes sparked. "You *should*. That's what you need. Not the free-wheeling fuckfest across the hall."

"I know." I looked away. "At the moment, it's difficult. Believe me. I've got the job at the warehouse now. I'm alone and not so inspired."

We started off toward the corner bar. She leaned in toward me.

"Do it," she said. And this is Beth too. The encourager. The uninvited life coach. She walked by my side, smoking. "Both your plays were terrific, I thought."

"There were three."

"Make it four!" She took a long drag and exhaled. "Philip, *write*." She nodded to herself. She'd found her answer. "That'll keep The Beast at bay."

I'm the one who first named it The Beast. Beth was visiting way back some summer, maybe a junior in college, and going through real psychological trouble. I was twenty-four and unsuccessfully striving, working in a bar and a bookstore and depressed. And we were at my place, likely high, watching for whatever reason, cartoons, when an old-school Bugs Bunny came on we knew well, involving the head-humped, near-faceless beast Mel Blanc nicknamed Gossamer. Those Gossamer episodes can get scary, actually. The Beast chases the snarky bunny down long dark tunnels and halls. The Beast makes no sound. He is mute. He is desperate and strange and fearsome.

We decided to see it that way. Our conditions. The Beast—near faceless, hairy, mute—equaled depression or coming psychosis. Something like that, if not even heavier. Like the weapons-grade blues, a hairy Superfunk, chasing you down a long dark hall.

Beth said managing oppressive moods, especially depression, is the ultimate mark of adulthood. The faster you can control it, get past it, the more adult you are.

But I don't know. I've come to question that assumption. Maybe it's not about getting "past" or "over" it. Maybe that's nothing more than weapons-grade denial. Maybe it's all about embracing it, diving deep down *into* it, allowing it to take the wheel, so to speak. This was, in fact, a special project of mine. I'd been trying to muster up the courage to allow it.

Beth and I walked in silence toward the bar.

Just then, about thirty feet off, someone was leaving the tavern, stepping down the small set of concrete steps. Oh my. It was him. Hugo. That unmistakable easy confidence. Ruggedly handsome in knit cap and warm woolen coat. Hands in the pockets like he does it. Loosely, coolly prepared.

It had been a while since we'd crossed paths—easily over a month—and I very much liked it that way. Bet he did too. My old friend Hugo, the swinger who'd gone snitch. Apparently Melanie told him about the first time, that "half" time, and he'd waved it off without much fanfare, but later, when confronted with the second transgression, longer but lighter, he simply couldn't accept it. Neither could I, for that matter.

Hugo approached through the February half-freeze, the after-storm air having warmed a bit. He smiled broadly, looking mostly at Beth, who smiled back, wryly amused.

"Hello Hugo," she said.

"Such a surprise," he said, hands still in pockets. "I remember you well."

"And I you." She gave him a coy look. "We talked for a while at the wedding. The reception, anyway."

He glanced at me, a pinpoint dart, then turned warmly back to Beth. "Yes. The wedding." He cleared his throat. "The exchange of vows." He elongated the last word to be sure we caught his meaning. He smiled without malice, looking only at my sister. "And how have you been? Um ...*Beth*, no?"

"That's right," she said. "Good memory. And I'm doing quite well thank you." She slid her arm under mine. "Just visiting my bro."

"I see that." He nodded to himself serenely, still looking only at Beth. He had an aura or vibe like a phantom force field. He could dial the intensity up or down as he pleased. Square jawed, taut muscled, sexy, collected. Clearly hard to resist. "You look good, Beth," he said. "You've changed."

Beth went ha, chin rising. "I've lost a few pounds," she said. "You met a larger version. That was mega-Beth. This is me."

"Oh not just that," he said, wincing. "You're in *charge* now. This is clear." He pointed at her heart, then gently tapped there.

"You got stronger here too."

Beth grinned skeptically. "I don't know about that," she said, half rolling her eyes. "That's debatable."

"No it's not," he said. "No debating *that*." He started to walk off from us. "So nice to see you, Beth." He lifted a black-gloved hand and waved. "We'll see you later at the bar."

Beth froze a little. "Okay."

"Mel and I are coming down later."

"Oh good," she said, as Hugo shipped off toward our building.

We watched him go, saying nothing. Then Beth said: "How'd he know we were going to the bar?"

I shrugged, watching him go. "It's the kind of thing he knows."

"He really works it, doesn't he?" She laughed lightly to herself. "You know ... I think he'd like to fuck me."

"Probably."

"I don't remember him coming on so strong at the wedding."

"He came on to you at the wedding?"

"Don't act so surprised."

I shook my head and started walking the other way. She leaned into me as she followed.

"He's obviously not so fond of *you*. He could barely even look at you."

"I noticed."

Beth walked along, pleasantly amazed, her head on my shoulder.

"It's all so complicated, Philip. The guy rats on you for messing around with his girlfriend, who can usually sleep with whoever she pleases. And he does this not for love of the girlfriend, but for the love of Shelley. The *best* friend. He's concerned for *her*."

"They aren't best friends!"

"Old friends then," she said, and again laughed lightly.

We walked along. Beth lifted her head to look at me.

"What a rare web you're tangled in, Philip. You're the housefly who can't get unstuck."

"Thank you. Thanks for noticing."

I kept my eyes on the bar ahead and walked on. My sister was starting to push it.

Inside, after we settled at our table, I told Beth the tale of the second Incident. The afternoon Shelley took the Monarch to a playdate, leaving me home alone. It was announced as an especially *long* playdate at someone's house, including dinner, as much a playdate for toddlers as girlfriend get-together for a couple of closeknit moms. They'd be gone for hours. And returning home from the store with beer, I ran into Melanie and we had a long chat, our first since the original Incident. Hugo was out of town, she informed me right off. And of course we decided to have a drink together.

I knew what might happen, I told Beth, even what probably *would* happen, despite Melanie and I deliberately agreeing beforehand that it shouldn't. Not again. Yet it did—and only a week or so after the first. All the same, I'd observed some limits. That is, we did plenty—I win no awards for purity—but when it came to the actual act, I balked. Somehow that was too much.

Beth chuckled, again amused. "You're mister halfway, aren't you? With all your special *rules*. You get all Bill Clinton about it."

"I do a little." I chuckled, maybe nervously. "I suppose, yeah."

She took a sip from her pint, then touched or patted my hand on the table.

"You're a glorious mess is what you are." She was smiling in a mixed way I'd seen before: half pity, half adoration. "Yet you seem so composed."

I nodded, smiling. "Glorious mess huh? You really think that?"

"I kinda do." She took a sip of beer and thought on it. "But that's just you. And I kinda love it."

"Oh?" We were having some fun here. "Do you?"

"In a way, I do. Absolutely. Don't you?"

For a while then, the night grew rosy. We exchanged mock insults, told inappropriate jokes. The night started easing freely along in the comfy to cozy corner bar. Our honey-hued pints of ale before us, the candle flickering, conversation aflow. We drank and talked, the essential chatter. Work, sex, parents, death. Old friends, future plans. And as we talked, Beth impressed me as terribly attractive—more than I could ever remember. Her sandy brown hair hung loosely above her shoulders in a pristine bob. Really quite fetching. And her puggish nose—much like mine, which before this I hadn't thought an asset—was working for her now, ever since she'd lost all that weight. The warm, infectious smile and emerald eyes, neither of which I possess, adding up to someone quite different. Little sister fifty pounds lighter. In a single year! And with a new kind of confidence—warmer, more at ease. She grew agitated only when she remembered her purpose—raise my spirits, show concern.

She recalled this about an hour later. Again, she remembered her mission. She asked what friends I still saw consistently.

"Victor?" she asked. "He still around?"

I winced briefly. "I've been avoiding him."

"Do not avoid contact with your friends, Philip. Isolation only feeds The Beast."

I shrugged. "I'm just taking a break from the guy."

"Victor's *great*."

I sighed. "He is, but lately—"

"I don't *care*," she said, with a tight shake of the head. "You need to keep your friends. Forget the Adams and easy neighbors. Genuine friendship is what saves your ass."

In retrospect, it's almost like she'd summoned up the trouble by invoking Adam's name. In another blithe turn toward warmth, Beth recalled a story from childhood, the time she made a list of her friends as opposed to mine and hung it up on the bedroom wall—she had twice as many as me easily, a sort of primitive pencil-and-paper Facebook meant to make her brother jealous. Right after she told this story, and we laughed it out, I felt—or rather, we felt—a presence to our side. We both looked.

He was standing next to our table, potted there firmly—who knew how long he'd been waiting—staring at me with a quiet half-smile. Big guy, real hefty boy, holding one of those super-tall pint glasses, half-filled with a foamy Weiss. Unwashed mop of raven black hair, darkly peppered speckles of stubble, army green parka still on, unzipped, worn jeans, formidable belly, with this smug joke written on his mouth I instantly wanted to wipe away. He was lifting his chin, nodding hey at me.

"Hey," I said, and then remembered who it was. Ah! I saw him clearly now. He'd gained a few pounds since our last encounter. This kid worked at Adam's shop—relative kid, twenty three or four. Worked at the Copy Boss down on Division. We'd met briefly a few times before, once at this very bar.

"You're Philip, right?" he said. "Philip Palliard?"

I was pretty surprised he knew my name. "That's me," I said, cocking back my head a bit. "And you're, uh, you work for Adam, right?"

"I did," he said, nodding slightly. "Not anymore."

"Okay." I nodded to myself—hadn't much thought about it. "Is that still... they're still open? His shops?"

"He sold 'em," he said. "About a month ago. Phoned in the news from abroad."

"Really? Now... this is interesting." I turned to my sister. "Beth, this is... what was your name again?"

"We need to talk." His voice was blunt, not pleased. I was surprised at the swift change in tone—as, it appeared, was Beth.

"About?"

"In private," he said and wagged a finger in the space between us. "Just us."

"Okay... this about Adam?"

"No no." He sniffed and downed a swig of beer. He pointed. "It's about you."

I stared at him, wondering if he was putting me on.

"Right now," he said. Evidently he was not.

"Go on," said Beth. "I'll be fine."

"Give me a minute," I told the guy, who nodded and started to turn.

"I'm right back there," he said and pointed back toward the pool tables. "Come pay a visit. Won't take long."

We watched him go. Beth laugh-winced. "Now who's this guy?"

"I barely know him," I said. "I have no idea, actually."

"He looks a little unhinged, Phil," she said, brow up, doubting me. "You be careful."

I stood. "I'll be fine. Sure you're okay here?"

"I'm a big girl," she said. "But you know, don't be long."

As I made my way through the crowd—the bar had filled considerably since our arrival—I looked back at Beth, who was watching me go. She waved. I waved back and moved on. She must be judging me. Wonder how all of this looks to her. That was my worry more than anything. The summons from the hefty Copy Boss kid just seemed too weird to be trouble. I still thought it might be a joke from Adam. Something he'd set up to razz me. Hell, he might even be in the bar somewhere.

But when I sat at his table, our hefty dirtbag in the army green parka gave me a look that chilled me. Whatever this was, it was serious. He handed his pool cue to his partner—fatty but muscular black dude, older, bigger, in an LA Raiders cap—then leaned forward a little in his seat. He glanced slightly to the side, then took me in.

"What's all this fucking shit you told the cops?"

"The cops?"

"The detectives," he said. "Whoever."

I raised up my arms, speechless. My mind was spinning dry.

"Why would you say that?" he asked, eyes fierce. "Why would you so openly *lie*? About me? You don't even *know* me."

"Hold on. Hold on." I was patting the air. He settled back in his chair, shaking his head. I waited a moment, hoping he'd cool. "I *don't* know you," I said. "And I have no idea what we're discussing."

He stared at me with doubtful eyes.

"I don't!" I said again.

He stared some more, then took in a breath through his nose.

"Jerry Kozlowe? Detective Jerry Kozlowe? That ring a bell? Because Detective Kozlowe says you said some things about me. He says *you* told him I was dealing out of the shop."

I was stunned by the revelation, how I actually had a face now to pin to this whole fiasco. And evidently that shiny white detective—who I didn't much like—had been pimping out my mouth as a source of accusation. Using my actual full name. Wow.

First, fear. Then a gust of courage.

"Well, were you?" I said, but backpedaled fast. "I mean, I heard about this thing but swear to god, I never... " I raised my hand oath-fashion. "Swear to god."

He stared at me more, then shook his head and lowered his voice. "I dealt a little dope from the shop. I'll admit that—not to the cops, but I'll say it here. Pot. Only pot. Just weed. And not even that much of it. No *coke*. No cocaine. I'm not a gang-banger, you *fuck*."

I was shaking my head, agitated, insistent. "I said nothing. Swear to god."

"You better swear to god, motherfucker. Keep that up." He was simmering now, heat rising. "Why would *he* say that you said it? What? Kozlowe's lying?"

I nodded, again insistently. "Yes! Yeah. He's lied to you."

He was set firmly in the worn wooden chair, eyeing me coolly. "I don't believe you," he said and stood. "Doesn't add up." He took the pool cue from his partner. He stepped toward the pool table, still turned to me. "Don't you go anywhere." And then leaned over and lined up his shot.

His friend in the Raiders cap, in the sleek black form-fitting sweater—muscular and silent and semi-hefty—stood feet from me, near the wall, sometimes looking over, always slightly smiling. He was hovering near to keep me in my seat. A guard of sorts. My own private watch.

Well, I felt a good wash of it then. That creepy crazy closed-in feeling. The Beast will make appearances here as well. It will collude with the threat of violence. Flip open switches, start fires. Internal flames of fear, panic, self-disdain, flashing around the mind, the viscera. Dark demon vibes. Voices and shit. Almost that. Nearly that.

But I calmed down a bit in the aftermath, for my hefty friend in the unzipped parka was making quite a run at the table. Must have dropped five or six in a row. When he finished, he went and stood off to the side, barely glancing my way, perhaps testing to see if I'd leave. Five to ten minutes passed like this, when I remembered Beth, alone back there. I stood, swiveled, went tippy-toe, looking over the crowd for my sister. I found her fast, at the table where I'd left her, in the far front corner, only joined now by two fresh arrivals. Hugo and Melanie had come to the bar and were sitting with her, talking. Which was nice of them. It brought a very brief relief. I felt warmth and longing for all three of them, despite any previous differences.

When I turned back around and sat in my chair, the Copy Boss kid stood before me, holding his pool cue, chalking it.

"Still there?" he said. "Your girlfriend?"

"That's my sister, actually."

His eyes went wide. "You're fucking your sister?"

I gave him a look, meant to be withering. Smiling, he handed the cue to his friend, then came and stood next to me. Him, standing. Me, sitting. "Listen, Philip..." His voice was hushed. He hovered next to me. "Nothing came of this, Philip Palliard. Nothing's going to come of this. Looks like I'll go forward with nothing on me. Because they *have* nothing on me. Although, in a way, in another way, they do." He shook his head. "I've been marked by this, man. I don't want you to forget it."

"Honestly. I said nothing to anyone about you."

"We're done though. We're clean! For real. I don't give a fuck. I just needed you to know. Alright? Do *not* forget though. And... well, this is Carlos." He swiveled and turned to his friend behind him, no longer smiling. "He'd like a word with you."

The Raiders cap guy handed the cue back to his partner.

I shook my head to myself, half-laughing, not quite buying it still. In my nervousness, I glanced to my left, and there found Beth, standing in line for the ladies' room, a mere ten feet away. She rigidly tilted her head to the side, curious, smile-wincing. I shrugged and made a face to imply *don't worry. This is nothing.* And now this Carlos was sitting across from me, looking sturdy and super-collected. He was eyeing me solemnly. He waited, then said, "Miles told me what you did."

"I didn't do what he's saying." I waited. "I swear."

"Doesn't matter," he said. "That's the story he got and you're in it. Can't control that either way." He leaned in toward me. "Whatever you said, don't say it again. Even if you never said it. This time, the only time, you have found yourself lucky." I felt Beth's eyes behind me. Then Carlos leaned in closer, getting up in my space a little. I edged back. "You listening?" he said. I didn't move. "Wake *up.*" He gave me a tart little tap-slap on the cheek, open-handed, on the word up.

"Hey!" I said. Near us, someone gasped. A tight moment of staring contest, then he did it again. "Wake *up!*" But this time a—sharply—full-on Crack!

My head swung. "Hey!"

Everyone turned—or continued—to stare.

I stood, as did Carlos.

It was still tight air and I was scared. The sting of his palm sang on my cheek. Just as quickly, Beth intervened.

"Enough!" she said. "You're grown men. Whatever this is!"

Carlos unfurled his hands, mock-innocently, half-smiling.

"You will not *strike* him again."

"That's right!" I said. Again the unfolding of hands, the smugness.

"What's up here? Everyone okay?" This, the voice of one the bartenders, a pug little brute with a boxer's nose who wouldn't stand any guff. Several near still stood at their tables.

"We're good," said Carlos.

"It's cool," I said.

Beth sheeshed at us and walked off.

I nodded at the bartender, then Carlos, shooting for menacing—likely showing scared—and followed her through the crowd. Many watched us go. Then, fast enough, the chatter started up again.

Beth was gathering her coat at the front table. Hugo and Melanie were quizzing her, justifiably curious.

"Ask him," she said, as I approached. "He'd know."

"Beth," I said. "Please. Listen."

"Can we go?"

Hugo and Melanie were confused. Clearly they wanted to know what happened. My newfound nemesis and his girlfriend, my transgression, simply wanted the story. To help if help was needed. Then Beth shot me a look.

"Okay, then," I said and we gave our goodbyes, raising further looks of concern.

Soon coats were on and we were heading home, out in the clear cold air.

Beth walked in silence, more worried than ever. "Jesus, Philip. That's the sort of guy I represent. I mean, maybe this guy could afford a lawyer, but really." She stopped walking, as did I. "What *is* this? What's he want with you? Either of those guys? This some Adam thing? Some *drug* thing you're involved with?"

"No!"

"Philip, you are not built for that world." She walked on. "You are not *equipped.*"

I tried to explain back at my place, but I had exhausted her generosity toward unanswered questions. And she understood more clearly as we swiftly polished off the wine—Adam's stolen Dart, the drugs they found, the detective fabricating, all this she got—but still she thought I was hiding some secret, some awful unknowable from which I held out.

Meanwhile, I asked the same of the sky above. Some awful unknowable seemed to have my number. It must—the voices whispered. Payment for debts on one account had been written to another ledger—what I'd never seen or known or suspected. Plus, I couldn't shake the notion that Adam was involved. In an oblique way of course, he was. He hadn't gone entirely. Not by a long shot.

It marked me too. For a while there, I felt that unexpected sting on the cheek. I looked over my shoulder as I walked the streets, feeling vaguely hunted.

The following morning, Beth left early. I would punch in at the warehouse just before she boarded for Seattle. We stood on the curb in the chilled morning air, waiting for the cab. She grinned wearily, staring in the distance. She was leaving more concerned than she came. She'd told me as much over coffee. You need a project, she'd said, some commitment—civic, artistic, whatever. Something to fill this void. To fend off whatever curse has come for you—she didn't say this, but I think that's what she meant.

Outside on the curb, I wrapped my arm around her, pressed her to my side.

"How'd it ever turn out like this?" I was grinning, shaking my head. "Remember how it was growing up? *I* was the achiever and you were the wild one. You're the one who worried dad."

She shrugged. "I know."

"How'd you end up the success and I end up the fuck-up?"

"Shush. You're no fuck-up. You're... confused. Or something. I don't know."

I unwrapped my arm from her. The taxi was approaching. Bluntly, it came.

Well, I nearly cried standing next to the cab.

"You should write," she said through the half-open window. "Try, at least. Why not?"

"I will. I promise."

"Good. Do." Then final goodbyes and up slid the window. The cab zoomed off and she was gone.

Everyone was leaving, even my neighbors across the hall. In a week, they'd disappear for Colombia, six solid weeks to visit Hugo's family and bathe in the southern sun. I'd be on my own in a thousand little ways. I had to find a way to deal.

So I took Beth's advice and tried to write. The very night of the day she left after a bleak Friday warehouse shift. The writing was crappy, but at first, that's how it goes. I would have acres of crap to plow through, in fact. I couldn't be sure it was worth it.

What I tried to write was an absurdist one-act, featuring our friend The Beast. With an actual on-stage character dressed as Mel Blanc's Gossamer—hairy, head-humped, near-faceless, mute. Sort of Harvey-ish, but everyone sees him. Only the protagonist, the one being haunted and chased, thinks he's invisible.

It was crap. Trust me. I fell asleep at my desk, then woke with a start hours later after a troubling and poisonous dream. Beth and I were riding in a car on a dark highway at night, a mysterious figure tailing us—this black car behind us. But we didn't care. We talked, reminisced, sang old songs. Until a silence fell abruptly. I looked over and Beth had disappeared. Meanwhile, in the rearview—the figure in the black car behind. A faceless blackness following me. A figure with a black sheet draped over the head, like a body-length burqa that covered the face. Fearsome and mute. Driving blind. Clearly after—clearly gonna *get me.*

When I woke with a start, I looked around the room, unsure where or when I was. I ran to the guest room, looking for Beth—had to tell her the dream!—but when I got there, the bed was empty, just the smoothed-over sheets and still dead air. She was gone, I recalled. Wouldn't see her for a while. I muttered to myself, "Damn."

Sleep was not likely, I knew. Not for some time.

On the sofa, I stared at the silent TV, at the big blank screen before me.

Philip Lends a Hand

Each rotation was reflected in the shiny red Formica. The wheels spun round and round and round—the actual wheels plus their distorted shadows—as Adam and I chatted it up last summer. Probably out in the back hallway there. Maybe in this very kitchen. I sat and listened, mouth a bit slack.

Adam had recorded me without my knowing, and it seemed a deeper, more intimate transgression than the ways he'd cheated me before. And it wasn't such a bad performance. I'd held my own. Though mostly it's Adam you hear. In a way, I was listening a second time over. Like listening to myself listen. Then, from nowhere, comes my agitated voice, sounding tenser, squirrelier than I thought I deserved. Jesus, Adam, what *is* this?

Both sets of wheels spun round and round.

I'd found the tapes that morning in a shadowy pile in the back end of basement storage. Just nosing around for the extra set of windshield wipers. And our pile of extra crap was butting up against Adam's, the considerable mound he hadn't taken, or forgotten, when he fled our lives six months before. I felt around in the dank cold dark, rooting for the stupid windshield wipers, but finding instead a pile of cassette tapes, the hard plastic feeling of that.

I lifted it out to daylight. A tattered old shoebox—running shoes, New Balance—brimming with old school coal black cassettes, each with a purple striped stick-on label. Most were mixed tapes or tapes of old albums, recorded from the vinyl ages ago. Six or seven lying near the top, however, contained what had come to chill me. Voices conversing, among them my own.

There was a tape of Adam's wife. A tape of our friend Victor. Two tapes devoted to someone named Grace, likely the mistress he'd cheated with for years. Plus a few with quirky cryptic labels that sounded like album titles, such as *Ontological Infomercial* or *Chillin' with the Big Black Birds*, the sole tapes, I would discover later, that contained his voice alone. Mine was right near the top of the pile, titled simply, directly, like a benevolent children's book, *Philip Lends a Hand*.

I tried to remember when Adam recorded me or invited me to do so, but no memory ever arrived. So he had a whiff of Nixon in him. A low-rent, bush league fuckup's Nixon with no real crime to conceal. No big league crimes anyway. No public ones. No—this was just some hobby. Some creepy need or way of capturing, and at no point letting the other know.

Actually, with Nixon, I believe they knew. Didn't they? At least the inner circle? Kissinger? Haldeman? Erlichman? Dean? Adam would know who among them knew. That's the sort of thing he knew.

Philip Lends a Hand was a hodgepodge of random conversation from the past year, most of which I could pin in some small way, at least to the given season. Some were just snippets, three-to-five minutes. Others far longer. Fifteen, twenty. I have no idea how he did this or edited it down to what remains, if that's what he did. I never saw a recorder—ever—but then again, I wasn't looking for one.

The instrument I found in the shoebox—what I had before me here—was unusually thin, slightly thicker than a pop tart, with flat round buttons, essentially soundless. You could keep it in the waistband of your shorts if you wished. Even tape it to your chest like a wire. Exceptionally light and thin, yet for old school cassette tapes, not micros. Tapes. They settled into the thing snug to form, as if sliding into a second skin. From 1992 or so—the old school future.

I listened, fast-forwarded, part amazed, touch amused. Some of the talk was tiresome, indulgent. Some of it fairly entertaining. Then I found this, about two-thirds toward the end of Side B, and it gave me sharp pause.

The funhouse reflection spun on Formica. The sound of silence, frizzy nothing, then you hear Adam lifting his whiskey, sipping, setting it down with a soft glassy clink.

ADAM: But I understand it. I do. Absolutely. I get the impulse to wiretap. I mean... without asking if you *can*? I understand that completely. Only... I don't want to spy on my enemies with impunity. Fuck that. I want to spy on my *friends*. [PHILIP laughs lightly.] Or—okay—my acquaintances. My acquaintances too. Even the ones I dislike. Perhaps especially them. But still—I don't know—my friends. My friends and neighbors. They'd come first.

PHILIP: [Clearing throat.] Well I am, in fact, both your friend *and* neighbor. You, uh... ever think about spying on me?

ADAM: [Giggles wickedly.] How do you know I haven't already?

PHILIP: [A pause.] I guess I don't.

ADAM: [Laughter, some edge here.] No sir. No you do *not*.

He had Nixon in him, clearly. Why was I surprised?
Flat distorted wheels spun on the smooth red surface of the table.

ADAM: We all have it, Phil. It's not like it's unusual. The desire to see inside other people's lives? To spy? Come on, wouldn't you do it if you could?

PHILIP: [pause] I'm not sure what you mean.

ADAM: [exasperated] Get invisible! Like, full-on disappear! Get cloaked in air like a fantastic Phil and sneak over to my place and *watch* me. See how I act with Maribel. See how I roll with the boy. Or—no. See me alone. How I am *alone*. That'd get your rock off for sure. Watching me talk to myself? Or drinking alone while the family sleeps? Muttering, staring into space. Or even—the inevitable—whacking off. Watching me polish it. Christ! Can you imagine?

PHILIP: [brief nervous giggle] Not until now. Until you just said it, I couldn't have—or wouldn't have—imagined it. But thanks all the same. Thanks for shoving that in there.

ADAM: [laughs, lifts glass, slurps, then gently returns it to surface] Fair enough. That's unnecessary. I went blue too quickly, but I bet you would too. If you had those powers? [pause] I *know* you would.

PHILIP: Well, you would. That's clear.

ADAM: [half-chuckle, half-scoff] Please, Philip. Drop the sanctimony. My god. [little pause, rustling, reaching over, etcetera.] You're the most dedicated voyeur I know.

PHILIP: What?
[the click of a lighter and ADAM inhales audibly, exhales]

ADAM: Nothing to be ashamed of. Mark me, sir. It's *built in*. You're just curious. We've evolved this way. The more enclosed we become, the more we want to see inside the secret enclosures of others. [inhales cigarette, exhales, waits] And sometimes—maybe most of the time—we like the secret power that gives us.

Now... those *in* power, those who hold *real* power—our President, say, and his commissioned crew of voyeurs—those guys take it to the limit. They do it with the desire to *control*. Purely. They've got the tools and technology, the power of access, to essentially *become* invisible. To actually kind of do that.

PHILIP: Okay, sure, I agree, but seriously. What's that got to do with *me*?

ADAM: [sheeshing] Come on, we were just discussing this. [takes a drag] The dead kid, Philip. Your ghost across the street. The one you've been taking bets on? Correct me if I'm wrong but I believe he's disappointed you by showing up so defiantly alive.

PHILIP: [mulling this over, set back] Well... you might be on to something there.

ADAM: See? I *am*. I don't mean to play gotcha, but... well, I got you. Exhibit A—The neighbor you spied on, who you quickly grew to wish had died.

PHILIP: Aaah. I didn't *wish* for it.

ADAM: For a while there, you tried to make him your whole story.

PHILIP: [defensive] My *whole story*? Jesus, Adam. Barely any of it.

ADAM: All due respect, Philip, all due respect, but you tried to hitch a ride on that kid. On his literally broken *back*. You probably call it social conscience, the loyal itch of liberal sympathy, but you and I know it's the voyeur in you, the little peeper, that's who—

I clicked off the recorder. He'd grown tiresome and pushy,

even at a six-month distance. It had been a while since I'd thought of the dead kid—Dominick, the dead kid who'd shown up living—and I resented the reminder if for any reason because what Adam had to say was fairly spot on.

I'd forgotten we called him the dead kid. For a while there, he really was Exhibit A. He would take me abroad by not existing. He would plug me into the grief of millions in the actual on-my-street way. That hadn't happened, of course. Reports of his death were just grand exaggerations. But if I'd had the power to get invisible, I could have walked across the street and figured it out, planted myself as the so-to-speak camera. Get the real reality the camera can't.

Clearly, it boils to knowing and consent. Like naked vs. nude. Sudden shame vs. clueless beauty. Angrier now, I pressed fast forward—nude on tape, naked as I listen. What else you got, Adam? What else you got for me? I hit stop, then play. Where I land, we're both laughing. Sharing some joke. Adam inhales, exhales.

ADAM: The dead kid's not even the *half* of it, Phil.

PHILIP: Man... will you please stop calling him 'the dead kid'?

ADAM: Why? [pause, bewildered] That's what we call him.

PHILIP: He has a name now, okay? Dominick. He is quite alive.

ADAM: [pause] Okay. Okay. Dominick then. Dominick the dead kid who came back to life. Ra-ra. Shish-boom-ba. We're all very happy for him, and especially for *you*. Philip's secret phantom appears in the flesh.

PHILIP: He's not mine. Come on. Now why—

ADAM: Albeit with a bullet in his spine. Correct?

PHILIP: [pause] Yes. Bullet in the spine. It's not going anywhere.

ADAM: [sheeshing] Jesus. And *why*? He put his literal back-bone on the line for what? Some abstraction, some principle he barely understands? Democracy's advance in the Middle East? Is that it? Or is it he protected us from terror?

PHILIP: [waits a beat] I believe he did it for the college tuition.

ADAM: Tuition! Nice. Exactly what you hoped to *hear*. Plumb in line with the plans you drew up. Nice find, Philip. Applause, applause.

PHILIP: I had no plan for this. And I don't like your tone.

ADAM: But what about you, Phil? What about *your* condition? I mean... aren't you paralyzed too? At least partially? And in fact by way of the backbone?

PHILIP: [sharp pause] You're pushing it, Adam.

ADAM: Don't misread me. Do *not* misread me, sir. I've got it too. In the same place. That blow to the backbone? Can you feel that? [long pause, lowers voice] Comes by way of the lives we lead. We could have used a little war but no one ever asked us to, never gave us a reason—not outside the little life wars *everyone* fights. We got no abstraction, no shimmering principle. Just predictable middle-class safety. Half-baked achievement and the gloss of security. Goo-goo for baby, kisses for wife, beers on Friday, the Times on Sunday. Isn't it pretty and thoughtless and *nice*?

PHILIP: Oh stop. That's not you.

ADAM: [tone shifting] Feels like it is. More and more it really does.

PHILIP: Nah, man. You crave war. You go seeking it all the time. And in your brash little way, you sort of make it happen.

ADAM: [pause, liking this] You think so?

PHILIP: Your grad student, for starters. What about her? That's like... your covert war. Or one of them. Undeclared without notifying Congress.

ADAM: [scoffing] Oh that's only what everyone everywhere wants. You too. It's not unusual. The difference is I actually *act* on it. That's no golden greater principle. That's just scoring a companion outside the one we've been told we're allowed, which—okay, I got you, I hear you, yes—that's fighting for one kind of freedom, right? [pause, thinking it over] But I wouldn't suit up with a combat helmet and a rifle to protect it. It's only a little appetite, brother. A side dish of secret freedom. Exactly what *you* want but can't find the—

PHILIP: Don't assume what I want.

ADAM: [sheeshing] Oh you want it. There's nothing wrong with wanting it. Everybody wants it. You're a good boy. I understand.

PHILIP: You think so, huh?

ADAM: [heartless chuckle] I know it's not on the map you drew up. Not yet at least, but it may well arrive. And when it does, sir, what you'll discover is this: the fucking itself is overrated. It's the freedom, not the fucking—that's the heart of the prize. The freedom and the fresh attention—

I clicked it off. Here he'd struck sharply—a knife to the head, landing with a *thwock* as if against a tree. The fact of my present existence, my relatively recent, so-called freedom. The little war I hadn't planned to declare.

I pocketed the recorder and moved toward the far front living room. There, I found Henry's overly large, picket fence-ish crib, empty as a desert. Barren over three months now. I gripped at the padded adjustable bar and stared at the pastel sheets, the puffy pillows, the stuffed pink pig with the sinister smile. The stuffed animal that creeped me out most. Is that why she left it here? Behind me, the queen size in our bedroom loomed loudly, the smoothed-over perfection of the tucked-in sheets. Shelley would be amazed at the steady upkeep. Months of it, all on me.

The hazy muted light of March shot through the half-up blinds. Nothing stirred.

This didn't feel much like freedom. Early on it had, but no longer.

I went for a walk to the corner store, trying to forget what was missing, the skinny recorder with the soundless buttons riding in the pocket of my jeans.

Down at the store, I surprised myself with an impulse I'd never guess I'd follow. Just standing in line with some chips and salsa while the cashier was talking to the customer before me, something about the Latin Apostles going to war with another gang. The skinny recorder was there in my pocket, so easy and soundless, and I thought why not? It erased a few minutes from *Philip Lends a Hand*, but whatever. I'd heard all I wanted.

The next morning, I tried it again at a diner, catching the conversation in the booth behind me. Then at the warehouse that afternoon as my co-workers talked some serious trash about the top brass assholes downtown. None of this was riveting or all that revealing. I taped over what I'd recorded more than once. Still, I couldn't seem to help myself. It seemed harmless and not quite Adam's disease if I limited the practice to strangers and work folk. Besides, I was capturing nearly nothing. Just unexceptional quotidian talk, the kind we produce more than not.

◈

Two days later, however, I caught something cold. Buying a six pack at the corner store, I pressed record through the pocket of my jacket, hoping to ask the cashier some more about the gang war down the way. I set a five on the counter and waited for change, preparing my question, when I noticed who was wheeling by outside. I stepped from the counter and toward the door, ignoring the cashier's offer of change.

He passed like an especially mischievous ghost. A kind of streaker.

That uniquely tattered knapsack across the wheelchair's back? Those particular biker gloves? That profile, so unmistakable—fatter features on a once-lean frame. I stood on the corner and watched him wheel off. I picked up the pace, but he was motoring swiftly. I started a run. That's *him*. That's the dead kid! Hey! Hey, the dead kid! Wait up!

He turned west two corners up ahead, toward my place, which was toward his mother's place and once his own. I scurried fast, circling the block the other way around so I might bump into him. I ran hard, a full sprint, six pack cradled in my arm like a football.

You can hear me breathing hard on the tape. Here and there, I muttered inaudibly. Sounds desperate, actually. Amazingly, I arrived without blowing a vessel. And I hadn't a clue what to say when we met but meeting right then seemed imperative. I down-shifted some when he came into view, sort of briskly race-walking toward him. He must have thought I'd lost my mind.

PHILIP: [approaching, feigning surprise] Hey! [catching breath] Hello there. [catching breath] Thought that might be you.

DOMINICK: [chuckling] What the fuck? Is someone *after* you?

PHILIP: Oh. No. No no. [catching breath] Just... getting some exercise.

DOMINICK: Always take a six pack with you when you jog?

PHILIP: I try to, yes. Helps to have something to work for.

DOMINICK: Damn. [laughs.] You're fucked up.

PHILIP: Yes. I am. I really am. That's observant of you. [pause] But seriously, it's been a while. So. Wow. You look good.

DOMINICK: Please. I look like shit.

PHILIP: Nah. You look *great*. You look vital. How's... how's college?

DOMINICK:[long pause, amused, maybe suspicious] You're the guy from the Study, right? You work for your wife?

PHILIP: I used to, yes. That's right.

DOMINICK: And you used to live across the street from me.

PHILIP: Still do. I mean, still across from your mother. You moved.

DOMINICK: I did. [odd pause, slight laughter] That's very observant of *you*. Listen, jack. You need something from me?

PHILIP: I do kind of. I do. It's just... like, really good to see you. Life is... life is good? I didn't catch where you're going.

DOMINICK: Going?

PHILIP: Where's college?

DOMINICK: [laughs tightly] What do you know about me and *college*? How do you even know I'm going?

PHILIP: Well I guess I don't. I thought you told me—

DOMINICK: What I've got is college and something more. Starts in the fall.

PHILIP: Okay um... college and something more *where*?

DOMINICK: [chuckles] Afghanistan.

PHILIP: [laughter] Excuse me?

DOMINICK: Kabul. American University of Kabul. A special program for the injured vet. But covert. Hush-hush. If you told a single soul, I'd have to kill you.

PHILIP: [light laugh] Understood. Mum's the word. So... you'll be a freshman in Kabul? Really?

DOMINICK: You study one semester in Kabul. The next semester, you fight.

PHILIP: Fight?... Fight how?

DOMINICK: [pause] You think I'm too weak to pull a trigger?

PHILIP: No no I... never said you were any—

I clicked off the recorder. On second listen, I knew he'd been playing me. But my, with what speed! He had a whole scenario mapped out here. Seemed he hatched it on the spot. Unless of course he wasn't lying. Either way, it was pretty elaborate, mostly concerning this hush-hush program for vets with spinal cord injuries, involving but not limited to college attendance in Afghanistan, study of the Koran, the engineering of hospitals and dams, and covert combat work as first-floor snipers.

But that was only the first part. Our encounter took a darker spin after I offered him a beer. He rolled up to his place and I sat on his stoop. The interview in proper began. And I went a bit faux Charlie Rose here. It gets embarrassing in places.

Alone in my kitchen, I fast-forwarded the tape. Let it go for a while. I took a meditative swig from the current can. Pressed play.

DOMINICK: [laughs] First you ask me about women? Then you ask me about *God*? And now you want me to define 'freedom'?

PHILIP: Not a strict definition. Just, you know, off the top of your head.

DOMINICK: That's some personal shit, man.

PHILIP: Is it having no responsibilities to anyone but yourself? Is that it? Is that what it boils down to?

DOMINICK: Fuck no. [dismissive laugh] Freedom has to be more than *that*. Last I checked, freedom was... not being enslaved.

PHILIP: Ha! Okay. [pause] That sounds right. Yes. That's more direct.

DOMINICK: But it's mostly in your mind, okay? Unless you're in prison. Or kidnapped or whatever. It's a state of *mind*. That's all. I discovered that shit in Iraq.

PHILIP: I bet. Do tell. This uh. . . this is what you were talking about earlier, yes? The dark thoughts you had there?

DOMINICK: Man... that's some personal shit. I've been trying to relay that to you. These are highly personal, private matters. Between me and God.

PHILIP: I thought you said God wasn't paying attention.

DOMINICK: No. No. What I said was God is *asleep.* And out cold. Snoring very very hard.

PHILIP: Yes, right. I remember. [chuckles.] Fat, lazy. Passed out like a drunk.

DOMINICK: [pause] Did I say 'lazy'? Man, I meant *depressed.* Like... hospitalized with it.

PHILIP: So he's an overworked, clinically depressed drunk the size of the universe who—

DOMINICK: I don't even know you, okay? Why so curious?

PHILIP: Well... why shouldn't I be? We're having a beer on the stoop. Man to man. We're talking. And we haven't in a while.

DOMINICK: You keep saying that like we used to be *tight.* Like we gave a shit about each other. [pause, sip] I don't even know you, man!

PHILIP [exasperated] But I do know you.

DOMINICK: No. Not really. I did some tests for your wife's study, but that's it. We've talked a couple times since then but—

PHILIP: No—I knew you. I knew you before that. Before I even knew your name. You were my neighbor. I saw you here. I *watched* you.

DOMINICK: [Little chuckle.] You 'watched' me? [pause] How'd you watch me?

PHILIP: From my porch, while you hung out right here, when you lived right *here.* I live right over there. [pause] And then you were gone. And—well, I shouldn't say this, but—for a good long while I... thought you were dead.

DOMINICK: [pause, taken aback] Now that's fucked up.

PHILIP: But it's not! Because you're *not*! And who knew how close you'd come? Twice, you've escaped it. Twice you almost—

DOMINICK: How twice?

PHILIP: Well, first is obvious, your uh—

DOMINICK: The bullet I took. Yeah. What else?

PHILIP: Well, you were just talking about it. Just right now. You uh... you said you had some pretty bad thoughts while you were in Iraq. Pretty dark thoughts. You were considering... I believe you implied you were thinking about, well ... ending it all. Like—

DOMINICK: Hey! I never said *that*!

PHILIP: [tense pause] I believe you implied it pretty strongly.

DOMINICK: That's not your business, motherfucker.

PHILIP: Sorry. I'm sorry. I thought you were opening up that way.

DOMINICK: [lowers voice.] You know what? I'm done with your questions. You don't tell a soul I said that, okay? That's misrepresentation. You heard wrong.

PHILIP: Okay. Absolutely. I must have.

DOMINICK: Yes. Yes you *did*. [pause] Ma! Hey Ma! Let's go! [silence.] Excuse me. I have a date with my mom.

He hadn't mentioned that he was waiting for his mother. We must have been sitting there over half an hour. She was certainly ready to go. Evidently, she'd been upstairs waiting all along. She appeared at the door minutes later in a gray cloth topcoat buttoned to the neck. I hadn't seen or noticed her in a while, but everything about her seemed the same: the tall red hair, beanpole leanness, lively eyes and taut proud bearing. She nodded at me, perhaps confused—she hardly knew me either—and spoke to her son in Spanish. Dominick shrugged, responded sharply and handed me his empty can. I said goodbye and he nodded, more to himself than to me. They rolled off the way he'd come, mother and child, quiet as a funeral.

A few days later, I came home exhausted from the warehouse and saw the recorder on the kitchen counter. I had no plans to listen any further. Still felt cheap from the other day. I also had a pretty strong feeling that this would be the last Dominick spoke to me. The tape recorder had colluded with this closure—I disliked like it all the more for having been there. I ate my takeout burrito in silence, the skinny recorder before me, not moving.

I had this feeling before, however—that I'd never speak to someone again—and fifteen minutes later, my meal almost done, the landline rang to unravel all that.

Seeing his name on the caller ID, that alone was stunning. I hadn't spoken with the guy since August.

"Adam!"

"Hey there, brother," he said, and chuckled. "Guess who's on his way?"

He was calling from a hotel in northern Texas, taking it good and slow. He'd arrive on our street in a couple of days. My low-rent Nixon was coming home. For a little while at least. Driving a U-Haul up from Michoacan to retrieve all he had left behind, including the pile of crap in the basement that had spilled so inconveniently into ours.

We yakked and laughed, told the stories we could. Filled in some gaps, connected dots, but we couldn't get to everything, if nearly anything. He seemed fairly surprised, even disappointed, to hear that Shelley and I had split, even if only a "trial" separation. I was in turn surprised to hear that he and Maribel were doing the reverse—giving it another go. I couldn't help but think that was wishful thinking but I guess you never know.

I never got around to telling him I'd found that box of tapes. Didn't seem right to challenge him so soon. Prodigal neighbors who are practically ghosts deserve a welcome home.

Later, I went down to the basement and put the shoebox back where I'd found it. He can do with the rest of the tapes what he wishes. Maybe I'd tell him, maybe not, but I'd had enough of the Nixon in me. I hiked the stairs, then the creaky black ladder that led to the building's roof.

Up there, on the roof of our building, you can clearly see the skyline. And airplanes and steeples and lights for miles. The night air hung on the edge of warmth—cool but not cold. Spring was on its way. I savored this a little but didn't wait long. Sometimes we are called to act.

I stood at the rear corner of the building and cocked back my arm and *whizzed* it, just hurled it—that flat little pop tart recorder with my secret cassette inside. It went head over heels, over the rooftops, into the cool night air. I watched it spin and swivel and arc until it caught the edge of an old brick building and smashed with a crack into smithereens.

A Friend of the Professor

But I wasn't entirely done with Adam's tapes. I couldn't get one of them out of my head, especially after he said he was coming. Next morning, I found myself back in the basement, rooting it out of the box. Of the two containing only his voice— the monologues—*Chillin with the Big Black Birds* is by far the more compelling. *Ontological Infomercial* has its moments too, but that's just more of what you'd expect. The Adamisms of an Adamist, peddling his party lines. Philosophies, rants, negative prayers. I'd heard it before, sir, all of it. Could we pretty please hear a new tune?

With *Big Black Birds*, it seemed to come. A secret cassette of another order. If only I'd treated it with more care. This went inward in a way the others hadn't. Captured a vulnerability I rarely heard from the guy. Contained perhaps the frank confession of his struggle with psychosis. Of some kind—who knows? I won't name it because I can't. Just as I'm at a loss to name my own. Let's leave that guess to the professionals.

Chillin' with the Big Black Birds unveiled Adam a second time over, half-finished what little I knew. The curtain rose a bit, if only halfway, and I felt I had to hear it again—and beyond what I'd caught the first time. But I'd thrown away his hand-held recorder in a fit of moral certainty, and our cassette deck at home had been dead for years. When I finally rooted out our old school recorder—a plastic brick with those big flat buttons—it played the thing for maybe two minutes, then ate the cassette in a dizzying whir, leaving a tangle of chocolate-hued tape bursting beneath it like raw intestine.

It was gone, done. This sincerely depressed me. I recalled a great deal of what I heard, but what struck me after the second attempt were those first strange minutes—before the tape got eaten—a nakedness I hadn't caught the first time. This low-voiced and intense muttering, mostly incomprehensible. Adam seemed to have caught himself off-guard. He had captured the sound of himself, talking to himself—like, unwittingly, unself-consciously, which is the only way, really, to go about it.

"Aw shit—you're *on*?" he asked the recorder, suddenly realizing. A stunned pause, then laughter. "How'd you do that?" You can hear him lifting the recorder, examining it. "You're ahead of me, aren't you, you little prick? Well alright then... let's unload."

The tape got eaten seconds later. I was left only, for the most part, with the sound of that eerie muttering, its shifts in tone and volume or intensity, sometimes wild, sometimes whimsical, though never clear enough to make out. Sounded crazy of course, but why should it? Talking to oneself is underrated. Too swiftly seen as a sign of mental illness or the coming of the Great Unhinged. But if no one's around? I say get it in while you can.

Hearing that muttery unguarded self-talk quickly recalled this one time I caught Adam, or rather watched him, talking to himself intensely in his car. This happened a few years before, when I was heading back from dumping trash in the alley to enter the building's back door. That's when I caught him. Or rather, let's de-emphasize the "catching." He was merely in the act of that chatty release, and I happened to see him and remain unseen.

It stopped me in my tracks though. Captured me the moment I saw him in his car, talking like that—in involved conversation or heated monologue, hands sometimes gesturing. Can't say how I knew it wasn't a phone call—his cell on speakerphone, say. Probably just the look of him, that fixed agitation in the eyes and mouth. Really getting into it. Like I do, as I've said. I just hope no one ever sees me like I saw him.

I was still smoking then—this was pre-Monarch—and I swear I took one out and lit it. Like, staying a while. Enjoying the show.

Then Adam looked up. Almost right when I thought it. Our eyes met, and he waited—stunned-seeming—then soon enough he smiled. He knew what I'd been up to. He saw me smoking there, watching the show, and knew he couldn't erase what I'd seen. He laughed, then waved me over. I approached the Dart apprehensively.

"I didn't see you there, you bastard," he said as I moved toward the car.

I stood by his open window.

"Sorry to interrupt," I said. He waved that away, grinning.

"You scared me, sir," he said. His eyes were slightly red-rimmed, maybe sleep deprivation or smalltime drugs, if not the onset of tears—though I doubted it. "For a second there, I thought you were a ghost," he said. "Like in Dickens."

"What? Ghost of Christmas past?"

"Present. And this is Easter. Or almost Easter."

"The ghost of Easter present then. The ghost of almost Easter present."

"There we go," he said, grinning, and cocked his head toward the passenger seat. "Join me, ghost. I feel like talking."

I got in and we sat in the late April evening—cool but not cold, out in the parking lot behind our building. Adam lifted a flask, drank, passed it over.

He went into an involved critique of his day, of "the way we live now." It was madness, he said. Discussing here specifically Crate and Barrel—where Maribel had dragged him and dropped a grand on the card—as well as other stores of their froufy ilk, jam-packed, as he put it, with "pretty pink unnecessaries." Only not just pink, but cream, beige, sea foam, mauve. Those places crippled him, he told me. It wasn't just a macho aversion. They were filled with "bourgeois poison gas."

I liked these arch assessments, even though I knew they were nothing but whimsy, mere delay. He was warming me up like an opening band, prepping the house for the headliner. He went from the side effects of "bourgeois poison gas" to the actual benefits of "emotional air-conditioning" to—and I knew all along he'd end up here—"the baby, the baby, the boy, the son! All baby, all the time!"

Then he went silent. He bluntly let the quiet fall and I made no effort to break it. He lit a Winston and dangled his arm out the open window. He watched the smoke curl and rise. After a moment, he turned and took me in. He was sincere here. He'd gotten off stage.

"You got family, Phil?"

"Like... what? A mother and father?"

"Yeah—and siblings. Whatever. That all intact?"

"Intact I don't know about. Partly, I guess. I've got a sister. She's a lawyer in Philly. Dad teaches high school in northeast PA. Had a little heart attack about a month ago but he's doing okay now. And Mom's... well, she's no longer with us. She's been gone a long while."

Adam dropped to a whisper "No shit?" He stared at the steering wheel. "How?"

This was maybe the only time in the career of our friendship we discussed this sort of thing. In the Dart in our back lot a few springs before, I told Adam the tale of my dearly departed. I was nine when she left us, I told him. My sister Beth was seven. Mother died in a car crash driving home on the turnpike from summer stock in Jersey. Fell asleep at the wheel, they say. Closed casket. Never saw her again.

Adam clucked his tongue neutrally. "I know that wound, sir," he said. "Too well." He looked over. "Mine died too, you know?"

"Is that right?"

He nodded solemnly. We'd found the link between us we'd never speak of again. The dead moms. We haven't touched on them since. Though perhaps that's part of what tied us together—early on, at least. Without our much knowing it.

Well, Adam dove into it then—or started to. He told me his story of family, where he'd meant to land all along. The details were fast and sometimes hard to follow, though, as you'll see, he had barely begun. He grew up an only child in a medium safe suburb of Baltimore. His parents divorced when he was six or seven, custody handed mostly to the mother—an ex-high school teacher, then book or magazine editor, something like that, plus part-time lefty activist. The father, an only child of Russian immigrants, was a well-minted suburban cop with a deep thirst for wine and women. Their marriage, Adam told me, had been an odd match, likely cursed from the start, though he'd been too young to see it that way.

Long to short, the father got busted, axed from the Law, some inside job involving kickbacks or bribes—wasn't clear, Adam kept it murky. This happened just a year or so before his mother died. She was taken by some high-speed cancer when Adam was twelve or thirteen—this "caustic clairvoyant Hungarian beauty," who pushed and prodded him to study and achieve, who called him "my little professor." And though the father had always been a bit of lush, when he lost her, on top of the job—or in fact, the career—it "frankly got a little nasty."

Then, suddenly, in the car there, Adam amended himself. He hated all that self-pitying born-a-victim shit. At least in his circumstance, he'd had it pretty good. He considered it a self-involved cliché to have this sort of issue with one's father— or if given, mother—but he'd been thinking about the old man a lot lately. His father had died the year before, almost to the day. Lung cancer, big smoker, only in his mid-sixties. Ran a small security guard company in Hyattsville. He and Adam hadn't spoken in decades.

Taken aback, I told him sorry to hear that.

"Sorry?" He winced. "Don't be sorry. Christ. It's just what *is*." He took a healthy kick from the flask, then pointed at me with its mouth. "I am far, far more than what I appear to be," he said. "I just am." He took another swig and stared out the front windshield.

"Now get out, ghost," he said. "Go haunt someone else."

I wasn't sure if he meant it. He stared ahead, then said quietly, "Please."

I opened my door, nodding. "I got you."

We left it at that. I closed the door, then moved toward the building's back door. Either the rest of the story unnerved him or—and this seems more likely—he'd recognized the weight of his candor and didn't care to waste any more on me. He had never—until now, via *Big Black Birds*—really finished the tale.

But it wasn't really finished. Not decisively. And now we would never hear the whole thing. The tape's gone—metallic spaghetti. And what was revealed in the half I heard, I only half remember. Stories of escape and misguided purpose, of faking signatures on financial aid forms, of earning a fat and unlikely bundle from some unnamed enterprise, possibly criminal.

On the tape, there were delicious extras he hadn't included that night in the car. The life insurance windfall his mother left him, for example. This helped as much as anything with the murky "investments" that made him his miracle nut. A very young man too. Only in his twenties. Returns from these investments are, I gather, what funded the first Copy Boss as well as his attempt at grad school.

The nature and source of this money remained elusive, that and his eventual failure at school. Both seemed shadowy. And you had to wonder—what? Stolen goods? Drugs? Something even darker? Suffice it to say, he'd made "a real nice tray of cake." Set him up for some time. Gave that kick-start to the Copy Bosses while in dogged pursuit of the doctorate he would fail to earn—what would come to devour much of the funds.

He even mentions "The Ravings of Safety," his one published essay. It would have been chapter one of his dissertation, he says, but was probably the piece they hated most. Although please understand, he added defiantly, that A. Swivchek hated *them*. Their self-importance and above-it demeanors. Fakes presiding over "fiefdoms of air!" He'd cited *many* sources, framed an airtight argument. Unconventional, maybe. A bit off-the-grid, maybe. But... well, he went on like that, his bitterness rising up from the tape like the heat from a compact blast furnace.

It had the feel of a final testament, the rant of a suicidal despot or fringe cult leader. Yet it also seemed somehow open and true. You had to wonder what else was revealed.

Perhaps there was a chance the tape could be saved, the recorder repaired. Again, I took the machine out for a look. The gnarled tape was bunched up in a wildflower or weed-ish way. One giant plastic button was still pressed down—PLAY.

I opened the laptop, went online and searched for an easier answer.

Soon—that very evening, in fact—I found myself driving south on Western, the Civic's engine humming, no music on, our ancient tape recorder on the passenger seat, *Big Black Birds* twisted up in its mouth like, as I've said, raw intestine, also called guts.

I'd pored over Craig's List, seeking some obscure service that might save us. Something like, "vintage tape recorder repair." Including perhaps the "salvaging of gnarled tape."

I found the very service with astonishing speed. It was number two on my internal search. I dialed the number provided.

His actual name was Craig. That was part of the joke—that this was his list. He was the actual and original Craig. And one of Craig's specialties, apparently, was repair of any given machine, vintage or otherwise, including a long list of the items he saw most, closing with this clever threesome, "turntables, tape recorders and Atari sets".

Craig and I had this joke on the phone. I asked if it helped with business, his being named Craig. He answered—best choice he ever made. That is, putting this fact in the ad. His given name really was Craig.

Nice, I answered. I never doubted it was. So... when should we do this?

I drove in silence toward the address he'd given, what seemed further west than necessary. Which is to say a rougher hood than expected. I glanced over at the eaten tape. Was this worth it? I could ask Adam for the story when he returned. But no. I wanted *this* version, the unguarded version. And Craig of Craig's List believed he could salvage the tape. Though we'd have to see, he added. Depends how far gone it is.

I glided slowly past the front of the building, a tall redbrick monolith that seemed perhaps a rehabbed housing project, what Craig had called his condo. Out front, a sizable crew—ten, fifteen people—were having some sort of party. Music blared, bombastic and violent. In bulky jackets and baseball caps, they drank beers and talked, laughed, passed joints; here and there a joyous head bobbed along to the music. I thought I caught a glimpse of someone I knew but couldn't quite pin it. Some face.

After I called Craig on my cell, he opened the big iron gate by remote, and I steered the Civic down the given incline to the parking garage beneath the building. It felt weird and slightly scary—the original Craig of Craig's List lives *here*? But it had to be a condo, no? The projects don't have parking garages. Or I was pretty sure they didn't.

I parked, clubbed the car, then walked at a steady clip toward the elevators. I took the rickety heavy-seeming ride up to Craig's place.

On floor five, the doors slid open. A figure stood at the far end of the hall—must be Craig. He waved. I waved back and moved toward him. The mustard carpet, a foam or rubber, creaked a little with each step. There was party in the air up here as well. Muted music behind closed doors. Somewhere, if faintly, serious thumping. I passed an open door, where a gorgeous young girl in an unseasonable tanktop gave me a smile that was part wince. You in the right place? her eyes seemed to ask. Unless I only asked myself.

After a long silent walk, I reached him, the original Craig of Craig's List—a stocky little black dude in Coke-bottle glasses, moth-eaten sweater, with tight demeanor and fucked up teeth. He lifted the tape recorder and winced.

I can fix this, he said, tapping at the machine. This? He touched at the gnarled tape. This is gone for good. Sorry. I hope I haven't misled you.

I went "oh," thinking he had—and almost said as much—when two people passed us in the hall, one of them sort of swiping or grazing me. Swiveled a bit by the contact, I looked over my shoulder.

That's when I saw him looking back at me. He had a sparkle or dagger in his eye, as if the contact was intended. Oh my. It was *him*, the muscular guy from the bar, that Carlos dude who'd slapped me—and hard—leaving a monthlong sting on my cheek.

The big guy gave me a half-friendly up-nod as he and his girlfriend entered an apartment. Or not exactly half friendly. More like a third. Though it's possible friendly wasn't even a part of it.

I decided it was time to go. Didn't like the vibe. Nor the recent company

I left it all with the original Craig from Craig's List, the tape recorder and of course the tape, that last unguarded trace of Adam. We said our cramped farewells and I headed back toward the elevator.

I approached the door Carlos had entered, which was still open. As I passed, he was there, standing by the doorway with his girlfriend. Others in their party mingled in the room behind them. Our gazes met. He smiled through his eyes, over the girlfriend's shoulder. A mischievous I see you man. I picked up the pace a touch.

At the end of the hall, I pressed the down button fast. The little disc lit up but I was forced to wait. And wait. And wait. And wait. And wait. No more than a minute or three but it felt a lot like forever. I stood alone in the brightly lit hallway, absorbing the muted thump. Competing stereos behind closed doors. Distant voices, wisps of laughter. Mostly just the silence in the hall.

Behind me then, footsteps approached. The creekity creek of the foam carpet. It was him, I knew at once. When he came and stood by my side, I waited to turn and confirm it. Hey, I said, tight at the neck. He nodded back, grinning; delighted. Something mean in his eyes maybe, though also something playful. He was loving, you could tell, the chance of this. A second later, the elevator opened, as if we were the show it had all along been waiting for.

We got in and the rickety metal box sank slowly toward the parking garage. I settled in and stared ahead, while my hefty friend stared only at me, his back against the elevator wall.

"You remember?" he said.

"Yes. We met," I replied, staring ahead. "In the bar."

"I remember," he said, with a knowing smile.

He went silent and swiveled to look up at the numbers. The elevator took its time. Through gelatin silence, the lights shifted.

Two... One... P... *Ting!*

The doors opened. I hesitated.

He gestured dramatically with the arc of an arm, meaning of course after you.

I walked forward toward the car, sweating at the base of my neck, a pinpoint of heated alarm. My steps clip-clopped, echoing through the cavernous garage. His did the same behind me. Clip clop on garage concrete.

When I reached the Civic, I turned to the car and fumbled for my keys, my heart thumping. Behind me, the clip clop stopped. He stood ten feet away on the unparked pavement, perpendicular to me and the Civic. In crisp black topcoat and Sox cap, he was bright eyed but not quite smiling. No one was near.

"Listen, I'm..." I looked down, couldn't find the right key. "Please. I don't know what you think I have, but I assure you—"

I looked up. "I have nothing."

"Now that's a lie."

"Swear to god," I said, lifting my hands, keys dangling. "Nothing. Honestly."

"You got detective friends."

I waited, struck, then said, "I have no friends who are detectives, I assure you."

"And an unreliable *mouth*."

I bit my lip. Best to let that one go.

He spat to the side. "Look, I've got no beef with you. Or I didn't, but now I'm not so sure. That one night was only business. I was helping out a friend with a problem."

"There's no problem!" It burst from me nervously.

He cocked his head back, surprised at that, and furrowed his considerable brow. "Maybe we do have a problem." He stared at the concrete and thought about it, then looked up abruptly. "I just might have to fuck you up."

An icy whir sang through me. "Really?"

He nodded woefully like he wished he didn't have to.

"Why?" I asked.

Deadpan, he shrugged. "It seems like the right thing to do." And he took a step forward. My hands slid back against the wall. I moaned, pretty much involuntarily.

"But... I've done nothing to you. Have I?" My back was literally against the wall.

Carlos said, "I don't think so. But you tell me." He spat to the side, then knitted his brow. "I mean why are you even *here*?"

"To fix my tape recorder!" I held my hands up. "Only that!"

"Your tape recorder?" I nodded. He scowled. "Who you gonna tape record?"

"No one," I said, then muttered, "That's Adam. I'm just... listening in."

Carlos lifted his chin and leaned back. He nodded to himself, as if he just now understood. "That's right. You're a friend of the Professor."

"Excuse me?"

"You're Adam's friend."

I loosened a little. "Yes," I replied. "I sure am."

"You two are tight, yes?"

I nodded.

"Real tight," he emphasized.

"Exactly," I said, deciding this was the better answer. "Almost like brothers."

He stared back, still reluctant. "Well, it can't be all bad. I trust the Professor. I used to anyways." Still staring into me, he aimed his arm behind him and clicked his keychain beeper thing. A sleek black Benz beeped on, lights flashing, several cars south on the other side. "Good night then," he said. "Um... it's Philip, yeah?"

I nodded.

He nodded back.

"Stay alert, Philip. I mean that. I do suggest you stay alert."

He moved toward his car, deadpan, then was gone. I stood by my door and watched him off. He honked a farewell. Wow. Look at that. Adam had functioned as the stamp on my passport—friend of the Professor. I wasn't sure how I felt about that. In my quest to hear Adam's secret story, I'd bumped into a present from his past—or a part of it at any rate. That was the feeling. And no telling how lucky I'd been. Or if lucky was even the right word. It seemed likely Carlos had only been toying with me.

I got in the Civic and drove up the incline into the pale fluorescent night, passing the parties I hadn't been invited to, trying my damnedest to stay alert.

U-Haul at the Diner

Adam's vintage Mexican U-Haul was a rare and gorgeous creature. A silvery-orange sort of spaceship U-Haul. Gently curved where you expected corners, wind-resistant and faintly egg-ish, like a "future" U-Haul from the U-Haul museum, a future—in Adam's words—already past.

We ate patty melts and fries and stared at the thing, parked directly across from our booth. He'd discussed the future at length in this way, earlier, back at the bar. He felt for the first time he'd been living *in* one: a time and place he hadn't seen coming. Michoacan. The future. His ass-backwards brave new world. If not, he said, a brave new grave—there, he chuckled.

He chewed, ruminated, stared at the U-Haul, lashed back a strand of his failed combover, lifted his patty melt and bit in. No. His decision was final. He wasn't going back to that. Fuck that. Don't even question it.

I stared at him staring at the U-Haul.

"On the phone, you sounded so committed," I said. "Like *devoted*."

"Last week's a long time ago," he said, grinning slyly. "And don't look so glum. My choice is a joyous one."

I shook my head slowly. "I don't know, man. How long were you down there? Was it long enough to even know?"

"This last time? A full month." He shrugged. "I went for two weeks before that in November." He looked up. "I sent you a postcard. Get that?"

"The snapshot of you and Jorge?"

"Is that not a beautiful picture?"

"It is." I nodded. "It really gave me hope for you."

"Ah," he said, waving this away. "Forget about hope for me. Focus on hope for *you*."

I sighed, nodded, bit, chewed. "All this talk about staying split after all that talk about reuniting. I can't quite fathom it. I mean... what about Jorge?"

"I'll visit—and frequently. I'll call, send money." He gestured with his sandwich, a holding-forth gesture, a defensiveness present in the bracing of the shoulders. "Look, it's not abandonment. He's got the influence of manhood in *spades* down there. More uncles and cousins than anyone needs. Uncle Reynaldo?" He shrugged, resigned to it. "Already more the father figure. Jorge *loves* him. He expresses this openly. Meanwhile, the kid's awfully iffy on me." He shook his head, looking weary. "I fuck him up, Philip. I know it."

"He's four."

"He'll be stronger without me. I fuck him up. Trust me."

A cop cruiser drifted by the diner. It slowed near the U-Haul, stopped, had a look, then floated off into the black of morning.

"But Maribel wants you down there?" I said. "Right? That's her desire?"

Adam nodded. "You don't think Shelley wants you up in Montreal?"

"She doesn't," I said and faced it square. "Not yet anyways."

"Christ. That's a crime." Adam chuckled unfeelingly. He shook his head in wonder, looking down at his ketchup-and-cheese-strewn plate. "You're such a better person than I am. I mean... in that way. In the settle-for-the-middle way. You're humble, generous, essentially benevolent, though... let's face it, that shit gets you nowhere."

"Nice. Thank you."

"I'm kidding. I'm half kidding."

I nodded, smiled, thought about it, forgot it, then took a quick scan of the diner.

Not yet six in the morning and the place was filling up. Day laborers, uniforms, ne'er-do-wells, suits. And I saw, just then—or felt—a pair of eyes. Watching me, then sliding away. Elusive eyes from the far back end, though I couldn't make out whose.

Adam lifted some fries and pointed.

"They left us, Philip. *They* left *us*. Nowhere is it written that we have to follow. We will contribute—certainly. We'll send money—absolutely. But no law says we have to trail behind." He gestured with his sandwich, almost sort of snarling. "Like two shamed strays desperate for a master. Fuck that. I won't have it."

Again, the elusive pair of eyes. I felt them, saw them, knew they were there. I looked over Adam's shoulder at the backs of heads, baseball caps, random faces, cigarettes, coffee cups, forkfuls of egg. We'd been out too long. I was losing it.

Adam shook his head no. "There are other sorts of values," he said. "If we must, let's distill it to that. What it means to *have* a value. To hold or hold *to* a value. Because the culture tells you theirs must be yours; that you have no choice but the choices offered and then they offer them up in stark biblical black and white."

I nodded, agreed—sort of, maybe not—essentially tuning out. And then again that pair of eyes. I felt, or saw, someone watching me. Who was that back there? I searched and sought and came up empty.

"You there?" Adam's fingers snapped at my face.

"Right here."

"And whaddya think?"

"Think?"

"You should come."

"Come?"

He pointed at the U-Haul. "Along."

"But... you don't even know where you're *going.*"

"Sure I do." He lowered his voice, looked over his shoulder, then back at me, grinning wickedly. "The future."

"And where's that?" I said. "I mean... specifically?"

He shrugged. "Maybe Portland. Maybe Alaska. Maybe some unseen Shangri La yet to be announced." He ate the last of his patty melt and said softly, coaxingly, "You should come, brother."

Another cop cruiser rolled gently by the diner. It slowed, stopped, just near the U-Haul, had a brief look and motored on. We watched this then laughed.

"Everybody loves your U-Haul," I said.

"Especially cops," he said. "Cops are gaga about it."

"Well," I said, and let the moment hang a bit. "That makes sense in a way. You *are* a wanted man."

"Oh good Jesus. We're gonna run through that again?"

"It's the facts, Adam. I can't imagine why you'd take them so lightly. Your Dart was—"

"I know. I know. They *found* it. They kept it. You said."

"Yeah well, they didn't just find *it.*"

Adam sighed. "There was a body in it. I understand." He traced a fry in ketchup, grin-wincing. "And a stash of cocaine hidden in the backseat of the vehicle. I know. I heard you." He shook his head to himself, more tightly here, then stared down at the ruby red Formica. A slow-rising grin, a real shit-eater, slid up his sharp lean mug. "I have to say, I love that you met Miles. Or I should say that Miles met you. That's just too beautiful. Or no—Carlos! Shit!" He laughed with a gleeful burst. "Big Carlos! *He's* the one who left the mark."

I stared back. "Adam. He struck me."

"I know. You said." He grinned wickedly, gleefully. "You got bitch slapped in front of your little sister at your favorite corner bar. Forgive me if I don't consider that traumatic."

I grimaced at the dismissal. "He showed up again, Adam. Just recently. It truly freaked me out."

"In the parking garage?"

"Correct. Where I'd taken my, um, my machine to get—"

"Fixed by the original Craig of Craig's List. Yes. We've been through this."

I nodded, dissatisfied. I bit into a single lengthy fry. "Well, it was fucked up."

"Most things are. Be happy you caught him in a warm mood."

I hadn't told Adam why the tape recorder needed fixing. He had no idea I'd found his secret box of tapes nor that I'd heard the fruits of his subterfuge. I'd gotten sneaky about it myself. I was trying to milk him for info.

"Seriously," I said, truly perplexed. "Who *is* that guy to you?"

Adam shrugged. "Well, Miles used to work for me. Basically ran the shop on Division. Great kid, actually. He sold a little pot outta the store but I didn't care. That's the spirit of the entrepreneur."

"And this Carlos? He's a friend of the fat one's?"

"Nah." He winced, had a sip of coffee. "A friend of *mine*. Old friend. I introduced them. It made sense to."

I shrugged. "So who is he? To you?"

Adam warned me, through a deadpan gaze, to back off.

"Just someone I used to know," he said, and looked down at his plate, then up at me. "Different time. Different planet. I ran with a hard crowd there a while. I was someone else." He hunched up his shoulders and held them there, meeting my eyes. "I was someone else!"

I looked down at my plate of half-eaten eggs. I knew he'd give nothing more. At least not to me. This was simply how he'd fill in the blanks—the same stale answer to cover the lot. He'd been someone else, in a different era and ecosystem, some long-forsaken grisly business he'd rather not discuss. We would delve no further there. This night was sold to the future.

"Have a little faith, Phil," he said. "Shit. It's like..." He stared out the window at the U-Haul, then glanced back at me. "Almost like you suspect *me* of foul play."

"Oh please. I suspect you of nothing."

"When they found the Dart, it was what? November?" He bunched up his shoulders. "I was down in Michoacan, okay? Failing a crash course in family values."

"I know I know. No one's accusing you."

Another cop car passed. Then another. Each stopping for a look at the U-Haul.

I said. "What's up all with the cops?"

"There's a—" Adam took a bite, chewed. "There's a station right near here." He jogged a thumb over his shoulder. "Right back there."

I looked sideways out the window down the street, couldn't see it, and then, once again, felt the eyes—what is you want, pair of eyes back there?

Adam stood, excusing himself.

"I'm going to let you pass on this one," he said, grinning aggressively. "But don't suspect me, sir. Of anything. In fact, instead, *come* with me." He lifted out his hands, meaning—come now, it's obvious. "You got nothing going on here, Phil. Nothing." He shrugged. "Why not get out on the highway and breathe a little fresh air?"

I nodded. Yes. Perhaps I should.

He lifted a discarded *Sun Times* from the empty table next to us, then crinkled his nose. "I may be a little while."

I watched him go. Adam Swivchek. Off to the restroom with reading material. What a piece of work. You'd think after disappearing for eight solid months he would apologize for never having said goodbye, or ever mentioning that he meant to leave. But whatever. That's just him. Swivchek, face it, was a confirmed sneak, the kind of guy who chronically cheats on his wife, who philosophizes one way and lives another. The sort of undercover creep who secretly cassette-tapes conversations and saves them in a shoebox in the basement. A shoebox his neighbor might easily find!

I eyed his satchel in the corner of the booth. Was he recording me that very minute? Might be.

I looked out at the silvery U-Haul. Skip town with this prick? What was I thinking?

Another cop car coasted by slow. Jesus, so many *cops*. I craned my neck to see where we were. A station right near here, huh?

And way down the street, I saw—like a crack of plastic orange lightning—the Popeyes. I stopped chewing like someone in the movies stops chewing. I lowered my patty melt into its drippings, the cheddar and onions that had slid to the plate. Oh my. We're here. We're near it. The mustard brick station I knew so well.

It shot to mind that odd afternoon—early November, four months before—when I bought a three piece value meal and sat across from the Ward 13 station, where, for an hour or two, I'd been interrogated. Or rather, simply questioned—good-naturedly and without much pressure—though it left me feeling nervous and abused.

The detectives said let us know. If Swivchek shows up in town again, give us a holler. That'd help out a lot.

After, I sat in that crappy Popeye's with the baby asleep in the stroller. I ate rapidly, famished, really dug in, counting the ways I might be cursed—unless I was lucky. Jesus. So that's the Popeye's just south of the station. And I *hate* Popeye's. Hunger has sometimes forced me to its trough, but it always makes me feel like hell. If pleasing on the taste buds, hell in the belly. Like a parasite begging to be freed. A palpable knowledge in body and soul that the attempt at nourishment has not succeeded.

I eyed the hallway to the restrooms, then Adam's satchel. This guy. Everything he touches turns to cloaks and daggers. I reached across the booth and grabbed it, rooting for the tape recorder I suspected was spinning there. I searched thoroughly but couldn't find one, coming up instead with a ream of bound pages. A draft, perhaps, of his book, the one he claimed to be working on. Or a chapter maybe, titled, with bitter certainty: *Don't Call it War it if Can't Be Won.*

I scanned the page, then started right in.

Don't Call it War if it Can't Be Won

My neighbor has came to whisper a horror, another, the worst yet: two severed heads impaled on fence posts outside his uncle's car lot, one head belonging to the local police. He said they looked like *colmenas*—hives. Only insects live inside them now. The devils have come, he tells me. They said this little town could not be touched but no mas! He gripped at my arm. We been touched.

This act wears the signature of *La Familia*. Beware The Family, he tells me. But I already knew this—and absent the capital F. Beware the family and ties of blood. Beware all vows sworn at sacred altars. What an overrated under-funded sanctimonious institution—mafioso or no. Big Family, little family, same trip, same destination. Maribel thinks we want to be one again. But I see her seeing through me. My heart is hard and black and sticky and wants what it wants, to eat itself. So don't tell me I need to choose my battles. Don't call it war if it can't—

"Any good?"

I looked up. "Excuse me?"

"Your story there."

It took a second but arrived sharply. Scissors of recognition sliced through me. That uniquely large head—considerable, formidable—the Walrusy mustache, the broad chunky frame.

"It's not bad," I said and laughed weakly. "How you been?"

My detective from back in November—one of two who'd questioned me.

"I thought that was you," he said. "Philip, right?"

His were the eyes that watched me. My god.

"Yes. Good memory. Nice to see you, detective... I'm sorry—"

"Povich. Detective Povich. Call me Marty." He held out his hand. His grip was firm, the palm fleshy and calloused. He released my hand and extracted a bite-size Milky Way from the side pocket of his undersized suitjacket. "You work around here?" He popped in the bite-size and chewed.

"No," I said. "No work today. Just uh... out with a friend.

221

We're um... neither of us has work today."

Povich nodded. "Celebrating?"

"I guess you could say that."

"Up all night?"

"Pretty much. Yeah."

He chuckled lightly. "You smell it."

I stared back, set dumb by the bluntness. That's the Povich way, I was recalling.

"Really?" I said.

"I don't mean that you literally smell."

"Oh. You mean I look it?"

He jogged his head side to the side.

"No. I mean you smell it." He reached in his pocket for another. I winced.

"Just not literally?"

"That's correct." He unwrapped a bite-size Snickers. He chewed, ruminated, serious-seeming. "You don't feel right about it." He stared into space. "Being out all night, probably drinking. Maybe other nefarious activities—I don't know." He looked at me. "It's the unease I smell. Very similar, I should say, to the smell of *lying*. Or more generally, shame. In extreme cases—and I may be a lunatic for saying so but—extreme cases? It really does give off a scent. Faint, but it's there."

"But... not here?"

He chuckled. "Relax. You smell like a friggin' tulip."

I smiled at him.

He smiled back. "Albeit a tulip that's been drinking."

I chuckled at that, then stole a glance at the slim hallway leading to the bathrooms in back. Adam would emerge any moment.

Povich said, "How's the kid?"

I turned to him. "He's great. Wonderful."

"Don't have him today, huh?" He licked at a finger.

I met his eyes, stealing a peripheral at the hallway in back. "I don't. It's... " I sat up in my seat a bit abruptly. "I don't at all anymore. That's changed. A lot. Our arrangement is... well, it's not really—"

"Not really my business. I read you." He nodded, slow, inquisitive. "Correct me if I'm out of line here, Philip, but... do I catch a note of defeat in your voice?"

"Well... *no*. I think you're wrong there."

"I can be," he said, tonguing his gums. "But not all that often." A mischievous smile rose beneath the mustache, which seemed bushier, bolder than four months before. "Enough with the third string psychoanalysis," he said. "Who the fuck am I? Dr. Drew? It's that I remember your kid, I guess. He was strong. A little force. And his eyes were so alive." Povich pointed at his own eyes with two fingers. "Real sharp, real electric. A potent light there, Philip. Cadillac wattage. Which is rare. My daughter has that too."

"Right, right. I remember her," I said. "Or you know—her picture on your desk. Track team, right?"

"Shotput, yes. Thank you for remembering." He reached in his pocket, took out another, then leaned down and lowered his voice. "Olympics, Philip." His brow rose. He tore the wrapper. "No shit. They're talking Olympics. My little girl! Her coach thinks, if not Beijing, definitely London. Well, the trials. He means the trials. She'll have to make the team. But... we all do, right? Trials first, games later."

I nodded nervously. "Couldn't be more true." I stole a glance at the hallway in back. Take your time, Adam. Take your time.

Povich nodded slowly, deep in thought.

"I'll leave you be, Philip," he said. "And I *am* out of line, I know that. It's disgusting. Side effect of the goddamn job. I won't judge you—how could I? What do I know?—but I see you sitting there, shot sideways to Zion on a weekday morning, and please allow me to suggest... whatever happened between you and your wife, it's not worth destroying yourself over. Don't wave any white flags yet." He knocked twice on the ruby red table. "Keep the chin up, buddy." He raised his brow. "You get no younger."

"You're right there."

"No judgment from me, Philip. None."

He patted me on the back—a hardy double-pat—and looked out the window meditatively. Then the thing caught his eye.

"What is that?"

"I know. Weird, huh?"

Povich half-grimaced, half-grinned.

"What kind of art deco turd is *that*?"

I chuckled. He shrugged to himself.

"Is that like a U-Haul dinosaur egg? It hatches and a truck is born?"

I grinned, nodded.

He nodded, grinned. Then Povich looked down to me and said, "*You're* not moving?"

I gazed at the U-Haul. "Thinking about it," I said, and realized it was possible, then quickly tensed at the thought and muttered, "Just might have to."

"Huh." Povich snorted. "You're weirder than I remember." He sniffed at me, at the air above me, goofing around—and soon to leave, you could tell. "There *is* just the slightest scent there."

"Oh?" I chuckled nervously. "Literal? Actual?"

"You need to decide that for yourself." Povich stepped away and pointed at me. "Though I do suggest you bathe."

I eyed the hall to the bathroom—still no Adam—then swiveled to watch big Povich go, that barge-like force for the door.

The klanky set of bells on the exit door rang.

I stared at my plate, then glanced again to the hall by the bathroom—you lucky bastard. I sighed, relieved.

The klanky set of bells on the entry door rang.

In a flash, Povich stood before me again, just slightly out of breath.

"I meant to ask you, Philip. You uh... ever hear from your buddy? Uh, whatshisname?"

I glanced over his shoulder toward the hallway in back—experience argued Adam would be in there a while. "It's crazy," I said. "But no. Haven't heard a word."

And right then—defying experience—Adam appeared at

the lip of the hallway fresh from the men's room and moving our way.

"I see." Povich nodded. "Just thought I'd ask."

Adam hesitated, stopped, patting at his pockets. He dug in them, searching.

"Yours was a real unique case," said Povich.

"I know."

"Do you?" His brow was raised.

"I mean—I imagine! I don't know."

Adam turned back toward the bathroom, hunting for whatever he'd lost.

"You okay?" Povich asked. "You look pale."

"No, no. I'm good. Just feel a little—you know—off."

"The cuisine here is solid," he said. "But wouldn't surprise me if you caught a bum egg."

"I'm fine. My eggs were beautiful. Immaculate eggs. It's just..." I let out a long tight breath. "Long night," I grinned guiltily. "Much too much. You know?"

"I been there, mister. Not in a while, but I been there."

Adam appeared behind him again, grinning at the hallway's mouth. He was moving toward us, dangling the keys to the U-Haul like a long-dead rat he'd found. He grinned, shaking his head, approaching. I nearly shot up and stood—had to stop this—but Povich patted my shoulder—leaving, already in motion.

"You keep us posted about your friend."

I settled back in my seat. "Yes! Absolutely!"

I nodded tightly and turned to watch him go.

When I swiveled back, Adam was standing by the booth. "Who's that?"

The klanky set of bells on the exit door rang.

"Someone I'm glad you missed. I wasn't... I didn't know how to signal you."

"Signal me?"

When I glanced out the window moments later, Povich was passing on the sidewalk. He gave me a farewell up-nod with the faintest little doubletake, a glint or pressure in the eyes—

though he didn't seem to notice Adam. Or not much. I don't think he even knew what Adam looked like.

Then, about ten feet later, Povich slowed his pace, stopped a second, and took a moment to think it through. I held my breath, staring through the window at the broad back on the sidewalk.

"Philip?" said Adam. "You there?"

The detective stepped forward then, moving on toward the station, seeming to slouch slightly inward. I exhaled. Holy shit. Whatever had occurred to him hadn't registered as worth his time.

That very evening we were riding in the U-Haul, heading west, making our way out of city limits. And Adam thought we should read it as a sign, a glorious karmic reprieve. Povich at the diner! It was entirely unclear what it would have led to, but we'd definitely have had to stay an extra day. Perhaps a week. Or weeks. Months. Years.

I smoothed my hand across the dashboard, its immaculate old new school.

We left that future behind, he kept saying. We chose another. This one right here.

The interior of the silver and orange Mexican U-Haul was consistent, I saw, with what the outside had to say. The dashboard in particular seemed before its time, though not before ours, which it was well behind. It was padded bright orange via hard smooth foam that was somehow very Space Odyssey. There were shiny silver levers and knobs and controls, each striped creamsicle orange and white. The vinyl-encased seat cushions were remarkably comfy, pliable yet firm, and especially generous while the carriage was in motion. It felt, as Adam put it, "like you were riding on a carousel in France."

He was right too. It was gorgeous for napping. I fell asleep just outside Oak Park.

When I woke with a start, we were riding up an exit ramp

to a shiny highway McDonald's somewhere. "How about it?" said Adam. "Up for a dose of the Great Satan?"

But over my Big Mac value meal, I couldn't get the dream out of my head. All I could remember was the part before I woke—me and Povich in the stands at the Olympics, watching the women's shotput. I'd brought the baby in the carrier seat, and we were having a ball. Povich was like, "Look at that. That's my daughter, Philip. That's my kid. Look at her go!" He glanced down in the carrier seat. "Where's yours?" When I looked, the baby was gone. Henry had disappeared. I ran and searched through the stadium, the locker rooms, the alien streets, but nothing, nothing.

I shot up, awake, to see the golden arches.

"Up for a dose of the Great Satan?"

Sometimes Adam has an awful way with words. And it wasn't just the lingering dream, or the fast-rising indigestion. The force of this was something other. It was why, in the parking lot after we'd eaten, I opened the passenger door to the U-Haul and took out my shoulder bag and knapsack. I said to Adam no thank you. Goodbye, friend. I'm sorry, but I'm simply not *up* for this. And I knew where I was going. Not west but east. I started right off toward the highway.

"What the hell?" Adam stood by his U-Haul in the lot. "You're not serious?"

Earlier, admittedly, I'd been a willing accomplice. We joked around, found the old camaraderie. We smoked, hung out and got on famously. But now Povich had sounded that siren in my dreams, and I was focused and sober and drawn back east. It's like someone flipped on my GPS. I knew where I was going.

"Phil!" I was ten feet off now. I turned, stopped. Adam's arms were out, that rigid gesture of disbelief. "Seriously?"

I nodded nervously, also sort of smiling. "I want to be with my son, Adam. I have to be with Henry. With Shelley too, if she'll have me. That's the only place I want to be."

"No it's not."

"It is," I said. "It just is. Probably destined to fail, but... I don't care."

Adam grimace-laughed. "What? You've decided this just *now*?"

I nodded side to side. "Sorta. Yeah."

He shook his head pleadingly. "Come *on*. We're on our way to Alaska! You and me, man. Have we not made plans?"

"Did we decide on Alaska?"

"You know—wherever!"

I laughed, then lifted my arm in salutation. "Sorry, buddy. I'm out!" And I shipped off toward the highway.

Adam waited by the U-Haul, maybe stunned. "*Really*?"

I nodded, not looking back.

"Fuckin' A," he said, to himself as much as me, then waited, gathering steam. "You're an automaton, you know that?" His voice was tense and deeply peeved. "A preprogrammed robot!"

"Maybe I am!" I shouted over my shoulder. "Maybe so!"

"It's a fool's devotion, sir. It will eat you *up*!" He was fuming, beside himself.

I lifted up my arms as answer, sort of waving goodbye from behind. Looked a little, I bet, like the flapping of wings. I walked onward, forward, determined not to look.

"Go on!" he shouted. "Eat that poison, you whore for *comfort*!"

I kept walking, not looking back.

"Run that treadmill like a rodent!"

I nodded for him—yes yes, I agree—then pointed back the way we'd come.

See that? That's it. That's it right there. The future. That's the actual future.

I crossed the highway, sprinting, panting, not looking back, plunging straight into it as best I knew how.

Port Hope

Twilight was sinking faster than expected and the border could not be far. The billboards looked cleaner, kinder somehow. Lights in towns seemed to gently throb. As if that bright Canadian energy had burst from its container and leaked across the line.

Felt so good I had to watch myself. Twice, I'd veered into another lane—mindless, oblivious. They'd honk; I'd wave sorry so sorry. Eventually they'd pass, likely suspecting I'd been drinking.

Enthusiasm was distracting or blinding me. The enthusiasm did it, not me. Couldn't quite believe I was on my way. A mere half hour from crossing!

I drove on in airhead comfort, the American sun sinking fast.

Then I saw the first of the signs, which woke me some. The sign read:

DO NOT PICK UP HITCHHIKERS
THUMB CORRECTIONAL FACILITY IS NEAR

Thumb Correctional Facility. No shit. That's its name. And they have these signs on the highway for miles, warning us all—DO NOT PICK UP HITCHHIKERS. Made me laugh of course, though I also had to question the command and its tone. It was almost like a challenge or dare. Seemed so absurd, as if the roadside were overrun with upright thumbs, borne by men in bright orange jumpsuits, sawed-off chains still clamped to their ankles and hoping we wouldn't notice.

Well, I found no hitchhikers not to pick up but kept on the lookout for a while. I loved that a lonely someone might still be out there, trying. Days before, I'd almost done the same. I hadn't raised a thumb on the roadside, no, but all the same, I'd bummed a ride. From this aging trucker at a truck stop in Iowa who was heading straight for the city. If he hadn't been so kindly, collected, old and fatty, I'm not sure I'd have taken the ride. Seemed too at peace to be a killer or kook. Only wanted some company.

But I didn't tell Shelley about it. I knew she'd only question my sanity. Though I'd done it for her—her and Henry—to get to them both as quickly as feasible.

In the beverage holder by my side, my cell vibrated. I looked at the name and number on its face. Ah-ha. Here we go. I flipped it open. "Hey."

"Hello, Philip. So... where are you?"

Shelley's precise Ontario accent, up there in Montreal.

"Real close to the border," I said. "The place we've crossed before."

"Okay. Just be safe. I worry for you. This whole thing unnerves me a great deal."

"I'm being totally safe."

"Good. Please continue to be."

"How's Henry?"

"Sleeping. He misses you."

"I miss him. So much, Shelley. So, so much."

She waited. One of her signature pauses.

"I shouldn't say this but... I guess I'm a little excited too.

About you coming."

"I'm so glad to hear you say that. That's beautiful."

She cleared her throat. "Listen. Philip. I'll admit I'm excited but I'm frankly also a bit *disturbed*. I mean, I think it's misguided. Honestly. I still think we should wait on even a visit. You're being rash about this, in my opinion. That said, well, I can't help it. You're an impulsive prick but I miss you."

"I miss *you*."

"God knows I could use a hand with Henry."

"Rachel's not helping anymore?"

"I think she feels I've taken advantage. It'll be nice to have your help for a while."

"Ah, yes. The Monarch needs his top valet. He recalls my quality of service."

"That may be." She waited, then said to herself, "The Monarch. God." She huffed, near chuckled. "Haven't heard that one in a while."

"See? You like. You secretly like it when I call him that."

"No. Still hate it," she said. "Don't you dare bring it back."

"I'll try not to," I said, and she laughed politely.

"How long are you planning to stay?"

"How long?" I said. "I thought that was clear. I'm staying."

An odd, abrupt pause. "You mean... for good?"

"Shelley. I'm *staying*."

"You've brought all your stuff?"

"It's in storage. I'll have it sent later. Or go back and get it. I don't know."

I could practically hear her biting her lip, shaking her head. "This is not wise, Philip. I still need room. I'm not ready for you to *stay*. Not in that way."

"Wait. Honey, can't you see? I have to. If I—"

"I'm sorry, Philip," she broke in. "I'm not comfortable with honey. Not yet."

I paused, set back. "I can't call you honey?"

"Or sweetie or baby or any of that."

"Wow," I said. "You're serious."

She held off a moment, then said, "You think your actions

have no repercussions? Think you can pull your funny guy passive act and win me back like *that*?"

It was an unexpected show of force and halted me a few long seconds. "Funny guy passive act?" I said. "That's a first."

The cell started to fizz in and out of connection.

"I don't like this plan, Phil," she said. "I'd have appreciated your being a bit more *forthcoming*. I mean, we've separated. How do you know I haven't, well..."

"What? Started seeing other people?"

"Or whatever. Even more casual than that."

"Jesus. What's that mean?" She gave no reply. "*More* casual? What is...?"

Again, the cell went loopy, fizzy, in and out.

"Honey, I'm losing the connection!"

"Please," she said. "I'm just not comfortable with honey yet."

I sighed. "Okay okay! You're not honey!"

She laughed, semi-exasperated. "Philip, come *on*. You get it, right? You *get* that? It's different now. Our reality together. We can't pretend—" And click. The connection was gone. I stared at the dead black eye of the cell, then remembered I was driving when a truck honked behind me.

I drove on in silence. Heavier, foggier. I'd *like* a drink, I was thinking. Must the facts always come so cold? I watched the passing trees in the blue-green darkness-to-be. Little white ranch houses. Industrial plants. Billboards. Tim Hortons. NHL promotions. Everything warming, more accepting, quieter. Soon came the signs for the border.

You could see the lights for the crossing way up ahead. No flags yet visible, but I sensed them there. On both sides. Giant flags. Huge, significant statements.

Again, the enthusiasm started to rise.

The border agent was a breezy blonde Adonis who affably asked me why I was there. I informed him, he seemed convinced, and after close examination of my passport—plus the official rote inquiries—he let me pass. Which surprised me.

Just seemed too smooth and congenial and not how my luck had lately rolled.

I passed on to the other side.

About twenty minutes later, on a darkening patch of northern highway, my headlights brought someone into stunning view. Thumb upright on the roadside, he held a sign for Port Hope. A white shock coursed through me. I slowed.

Lean tall guy, kindly-seeming—but in a few swift seconds, how could you know?

Yet I had already slowed. Without stopping to inform me, my foot slid from gas to brake. Why not? That sign—really, you *have* to! I knew Port Hope. Shelley and I'd once stopped there on a lark on the way back from Montreal. It seemed a propitious and glorious sign to see those words flash from the highway. It was just some lonely Canuck seeking transport. And I thought I ought to return that lonely trucker in Iowa's selfless favor to the world. Plus, I liked defying the earlier order. Somehow that seemed just.

I waited. The engine idled. Behind me, he approached, first walking swiftly, then a light jog. This faceless darkness trotted toward me in the rearview, expecting to ride by my side, the same who'd been standing there with a sign out on the pitch black road.

He came closer, closer, then my foot moved again.

I'm not proud of it exactly, but I left him in the dust. He must have thought I was a world-class asshole. All the same, in retrospect, I sincerely feel reason had prevailed. He stopped and stood on the roadside behind me, this barely perceivable shadow in the rearview, lifting out his hands like what the hell?

Can't tonight, friend. Sorry.

Thereafter, I went in and out of that glorious feeling—the same from earlier—like a radio signal or wave I'd pass through, then just as soon leave behind.

Eventually, I saw signs for Port Hope, where we'd once stopped to visit just because of its name. Quaint little hamlet. Did the trick. I honked when I passed it. Port Hope! I still felt a little bad for that roadside guy, but not terribly. He'd find a way home. Or whatever that town was to him—though you had to wonder why he flew by night. My fleeing at roadside seemed right for a trip like this. Just me on my own. I would pick no one, nothing else, up.

I rolled down the window and let in some air, the damp Canadian April evening gone brisker, bolder, more of a challenge. Quebec was coming, my test was near, and the air was giving me notice.

I reached over for a CD, and laughed when I saw what I'd chosen. Mutilation. The CD I'd purchased online after recommendation from the dead kid. This seemed right too. I slid it in and skipped ahead to song five. Why hadn't I done as much before? Nothing like music in a moving car. It is intimate and practically in you.

I can't be stopped and I won't be stifled

I sang along, the window down, in love with the briskness, with the song and the singer, heading north for Montreal.

ACKNOWLEDGEMENTS

Big thanks to all who helped encourage this project to completion. Christopher Grimes, Chris Fink, Chris Messenger—all the Chrises. Luis Urrea. Of course Eugene Wildman. Your notes were invaluable. Plus the other outside eyes who had a look: Mike Hannan, Brian Warling, Molly McNett, Garrett Brown, and above all, Jane Kennison, who put up with me and graciously supported this project, despite my moods and both our insane schedules, from start to finish. Thanks finally and most gratefully to the people at Cairn Press, especially Joshua Cochran, the editor whose keen insight—and faithful investment—this book so needed. Cheers to all.

CPSIA information can be obtained at www.ICGtesting.com
Printed in the USA
LVOW05s1103220614

391137LV00007B/599/P